中英雙語典藏版

二十世紀百大小說之一
世界被讀最多的美國小說

野性的呼喚
The Call of the Wild

世界著名動物小說家

傑克·倫敦

(Jack London)——著

吳凱雯——譯　楊宛靜——繪

晨星出版

導讀

面對危險與未知，成為真正的自己

　　傑克‧倫敦是位一生充滿冒險的作家。

　　他貧寒的家境以及所處的時代，讓他擁有十分特殊的生命經驗。比如成為「蠔賊王子」、遠赴日本捕海豹、失業後流浪全美國、投身阿拉斯加淘金熱行列等，他的身份從盜賊、水手、流浪漢、賭徒到最後成為一名作家，那些位於社會底層的種種挑戰與磨練，最終都成為他筆下角色與故事的靈魂。

　　《野性的呼喚》是傑克‧倫敦的巔峰之作，是以一隻名為巴克的狗為主角的動物冒險小說。後來這部作品被譽為「世界被讀最多的美國小說」，自一九零三年出版至今仍受到讀者的歡迎，在美國亞馬遜網站上幾乎是最多讀者推薦的一本書。

　　為什麼《野性的呼喚》足成經典又如此受歡迎呢？讓我們從故事內容說起。

　　主角巴克本來是一隻生活在美國南方莊園裡的大型犬，因為園丁的貪婪被販賣到北極當雪橇犬，生活突然產生大幅轉變。本來養尊處優的他，在新主人身上及新狗群中學會了「棍棒與利齒法則」，是他在北方學會的第一個生存之道；在當雪橇犬的過程裡，他捨棄過去在南方的優雅，學會搶奪、弱肉強食的規則，成功在雪橇犬的隊伍中為自己爭下一席之地。當他適應了北極、適應了競爭，也在過程裡逐漸喚醒了心中的野性。

　　不過他在北方大地的挑戰與冒險並沒有止步於此。

相較於溫暖的南方，北方帶給巴克許多未知與危險。我們可以從故事中巴克一次次面對挑戰的過程裡，發現他總勇於面對未知、快速適應新環境，他調整自身去面對未知，在過程中找到自己、找到立足空間的能力與靈魂，也許正是傑克·倫敦此生面對無數挑戰與未知時的真實寫照。

　　《野性的呼喚》的故事便是讓我們知曉，就算所處的環境並非自我能決定，只要鼓起勇氣冒險、面對挑戰，我們最終仍能決定自己是什麼樣的角色。

　　除了冒險與挑戰，傑克·倫敦在《野性的呼喚》中也有許多對人性的描寫，從貪婪、愚蠢、懦弱到敦厚、真摯、勇敢，他運用巴克的雙眼與經歷帶我們從側面看見了人的多重面貌，以及在險惡的環境中每一種人的不同結局。這部小說除了巴克的北地冒險故事外，更傳達了傑克·倫敦對於現實人性的觀察以及對文明社會的反思。

　　我們所處的時代與傑克·倫敦已有大幅不同，文明進程亦抵達不同階段。也許我們無法經歷與他一樣的實地冒險，但在這步調緊湊、變化頻仍的當代，我們也有許多屬於我們的未知與挑戰必須面對。

　　故事中的巴克突破了多重挑戰、見證許多人性，最終傾聽內在與自然的呼喚，找回了自己與屬於他的真正自由；那我們是不是也能夠鼓起勇氣、面對未知，在屬於我們的世界中逐步成長，成為「想要的自己」呢？

延伸閱讀
不願浪費一生的作家

　　傑克·倫敦（Jack London），本名約翰·格利費斯·倫敦（John Griffith London），一八七六年一月十二日出生於加州舊金山，為二十世紀美國文學史上一位重要的現實主義作家，然而享年僅僅四十歲，於一九一六年十一月二十二日病逝於加州。

　　傑克·倫敦一生短暫，卻擁有著異常豐富的人生體驗。他的母親芙蘿拉·威爾曼（Flora Wellman）出生於富有人家，但在年輕時即離家出走，與家裡斷絕關係，且與一名星象學家威廉·錢尼（William Chaney）未婚生下傑克·倫敦，隨即在他八個月大的時候，嫁給了喪偶帶子的退伍軍人約翰·倫敦（John London）。與傑克·倫敦毫無血緣關係的姊姊愛麗莎·倫敦·雪帕（Eliza London-Shepard），反而代

▲ 親生父親

▲ 母親

▲ 養父

▲ 8 歲時的傑克‧倫敦（1886 年）

理了母職負責照顧年幼的他，在傑克‧倫敦的一生中，扮演了極爲重要的角色。他們一家在搬家無數次後，終於定居於加州西部奧克蘭市，這也是傑克‧倫敦讀完小學的地方，但在完成小學學業後，家裡的經濟狀況讓傑克‧倫敦必須暫停上學，挑起養家糊口的責任，到處做苦力、打零工。他甚至在認識了一群專搶牡蠣的蠔賊後，加入他們的行列，短短的半年內，他驍勇善戰的大膽行爲，爲他自己贏得了「蠔賊王子」的封號，這時他才十五歲。隔年，他又變成了海上的巡邏員，靠著他優異的駕船技術，追捕偷蝦的中國人和偷鮭魚的希臘人；之後，他又成爲獵海豹船的一名水手，甚至遠航到日本去捕海豹。這些經歷讓他熟悉了水手、漁人、賭徒、航海家等等的生活方式，也體驗到傳奇般的冒險生涯，都是成為他日後創作來源的寶貴經驗與題材，例如著名的《海狼》（The Sea-Wolf）等等。

在歷經海上探險之後，傑克‧倫敦回到了陸上，於黃麻廠和發電廠工作之餘，也開始根據自己的經歷來寫作。在一九八四那年，美國發生嚴重的經濟危機，失業的工人紛紛前往華盛頓向政府要求就業的機會，傑克‧倫敦也在行列之中，但隨即離開了請願的隊伍，開始了流浪的生涯，到處餐風露宿，甚至曾被警察以無業遊民

▲ 怪獸號（Snark），傑克‧倫敦自己設計的大型雙桅帆船

的罪名，責罰三十天的拘役，這也讓他體驗到苦役犯種種不為人知的內幕。這次的流浪，讓他的足跡遍及全美國，他到過加州、紐約、波士頓後回到西海岸。這當中所經歷的日子，讓他的思想產生很大的變化，開始尋求人生的意義與答案所在。他認為必要的條件就是得受教育，因而一邊工作一邊讀書，終於在十九歲時，考進了加州大學，享受著學校裡藏書豐富的圖書館資源，大量地閱讀書籍，嘗試各種文學創作，不斷地寫作。但在一年多之後，他又因經濟問題離開了學校，投身到阿拉斯加淘金熱的行列中，在殘酷的大自然裡，深深地體會到、觀察到最真實的人類生活與自我。他總是不放棄任何可以讀書的機會，大量地閱讀世界名著與大師名作，像是愛倫‧坡、狄更斯、惠特曼等人，同時也對史賓塞、達爾文、馬克思、尼采等人的思想極富

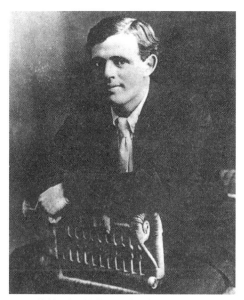

▲ 執筆《野性的呼喚》時的傑克‧倫敦

興趣，這些都影響了他的創作過程。

　　後來，傑克‧倫敦因身體狀況欠佳，回到了奧克蘭，將他在庫倫戴克的生活體驗寫成小說，終於如願出版作品，也結了婚，在短短的三年之間，就出版了《狼之子》（The Son of the Wolf）等三部短篇小說集。一九○二年，他在偶然的情形下，於倫敦的東區貧民窟住上一段時間，在深入觀察之後，寫了《深淵下的人們》（The People of the Abyss）一書。而回到了美國，他相繼發表了著名的《野性的呼喚》（The Call of the Wild），以及《白牙》（White Fang）兩部描寫動物的小說。之後他積極參與了政治黨派的活動，再婚後陸續發表了《鐵蹄》（The Iron Heel）和《馬丁‧伊登》（Martin Eden）等書。一九一六年，他因長期的腎臟疾病而死於腎衰竭，享年僅有四十歲。

《野性的呼喚》與《白牙》這兩部以狗爲主角的作品，可說是傑克‧倫敦所有作品中最具有代表性的佳作，在本書《野性的呼喚》中，他栩栩如生地描繪了寒酷的北極世界，更令人懾服地以著動物的角度，呈現出弱肉強食的世界，彷彿將殘酷的北方舞台眞實地帶到了讀者的眼前，無一不讓人感到驚心動魄。書中描述一隻叫巴克的家犬，在一片淘金熱中，被人偷走賣到阿拉斯加當成雪橇犬，從文明的社會中，突地跳入了最原始、最蠻荒的地帶，使他不得不拋開過往的文明洗禮，屈服於棍棒與利齒法則。一個紅衣男人對他施以第一次的棍打，他學會了不與手中握有武器的人交戰；而第一次看到自己的夥伴，在一瞬間被一群凶狠的愛斯基摩犬咬得皮開肉綻、死在一片血泊之中，更是讓他久久無法忘懷，深刻地體會到在這個殘酷的世界裡，絕對不能倒下，否則就是死路一條。

　　而在這種原始的生活裡，巴克逐漸拋開了過往文明的枷鎖，體內那股自古遺傳下來的野性，也漸漸復甦，開始懂得欺騙、偷竊，有著強烈的慾望想要支配一切。而他潛藏的能力爆發之後，竟然以一隻家犬的身分，贏得了雪橇犬隊的領袖地位，令人刮目相看。原本以爲巴克已然變得冷酷無情，他卻在遇到救命恩人約翰‧松頓之後，對他付出了全心全意的感情，可說是無條件、也毫不保留地奉獻出自己。這段人狗之間的感情，在小說中被描寫得十分感人，而約翰‧松頓最後罹難時，巴克甚至憤怒到失去理性，這是他認爲在這原始蠻荒的世界裡，極其危險的事情。即使巴克最後仍是完完全全地脫離了文明的世界，投身到狼群的夥伴中，成爲神話中的一部分，但他每年會回到約翰‧松頓罹難的地方悼念，此景卻又隱約地代表著他與這個文明世界的羈絆。

（吳凱雯／文）

庫倫戴克淘金熱

Klondike Gold Rush

　　傑克‧倫敦的小說主要以三個地方的地理和文化環境為背景：加拿大的育空、美國加州和南太平洋地區；其中流傳最廣的是以十九世紀末北美淘金潮為背景的小說，如《野性的呼喚》、《熱愛生命》等。

　　育空特區為加拿大十省三個行政區之一，面積較美國加州大，緯度比阿拉斯加州北邊，是北美唯一有公路可進入北極圈的省份。育空特區人口集中在特區首都白馬市（whitehorse），其次為道森市（Dawson City）和瓦森湖鎮（Watson Lake）。

　　育空特區的主要歷史是由早期居住此地的原住民──印第安人文化，於一八九八庫倫戴克拓荒及一九四二阿拉斯加公路興建工程的開發為主要架構，追溯至上千萬年前上一個冰河紀的長毛象時代。目前的育空是以礦業、林業和觀光業為主要的經濟來源，其中觀光業是育空政府最主要積極致力推廣的目標。

《野性的呼喚》中提到的道森，是加拿大育空地區的一座小城。
一百年前，道森是阿拉斯加和加拿大西北一帶重要的驛站。一八九七
年的秋天，傑克‧倫敦偕同幾個朋友加入庫倫戴克河（Klondike）的
淘金熱，他的黃金夢最終破滅了，卻獲得豐富的經驗和見聞，成了他
日後寫作的寶貴題材。淘金人潮來來去去，道森收留了他們，又遺忘
了他們，唯獨傑克‧倫敦例外。如今，道森的居民已經擺脫了當年淘
金潮的喧囂，每年卻有來自世界各地的遊客和作家於此憑吊傑克‧倫
敦，重溫他一篇篇膾炙人口的作品。

傑克・倫敦州立歷史公園
Jack London State Historic Park

一九○五年，傑克・倫敦與第一任妻子貝絲離婚，與第二任妻子查美安再婚後，即在加州的古連・愛倫（Glen Ellen）附近買下一片廣大牧場。此時的傑克・倫敦創作源源不絕，聲譽如日中天，而且日進斗金。後來在此定居，鎮日徜徉在大自然裡，並在這裡度過後半輩子。

一九五九年，州政府取得牧場一部分土地，建立了「傑克・倫敦州立歷史公園」，後來土地漸漸擴大，目前佔地八百英畝。公園內有傑克倫敦的墓園、狼屋（Wolf House）、博物館、牧場，還有傑克・倫敦晚年寫作居住的小屋。

地址：2400 London Ranch Road, Glen Ellen, Ca 95442

▲ 傑克‧倫敦與第二任妻子查美安（1907 年）

▲ 傑克‧倫敦與大女兒瓊恩合影（1912 年）

◀ 騎著馬的傑克‧倫敦

■ 狼屋 Wolf House

　　狼屋是傑克·倫敦籌資八萬美元，在一九一三年一手策劃興建的豪宅，全部設計以屹立千年為目的。怎料，在落成前數日，一場無名大火燒毀了狼屋，只剩下頹桓敗瓦。傑克·倫敦曾計畫重建狼屋，但一直到一九一六年去世，這個願望都沒有實現。

◀ 傑克·倫敦站在建造中
　的「狼屋」前

▼ 大火後的「狼屋」

■ 傑克・倫敦博物館 House of Happy Walls

　　House of Happy Walls 是傑克・倫敦的妻子查美安（Charmian Kittredge）在他去世三年後建造的。這間房子是仿狼屋建造的，但是規模比較小，西班牙式的屋頂，石頭堆砌牆壁，都和狼屋有些相似。查美安在這裡住了近十二年，在一九五五年去世前，她指示將這棟屋子改為博物館，以紀念傑克・倫敦。館內大部分家具都是傑克・倫敦為了狼屋特別設計的。

博物館外觀 ▶
傑克・倫敦的臥房 ▼

▲ 傑克‧倫敦的遺物

◀ 傑克‧倫敦墓園

傑克·倫敦廣場

Jack London Square

　　以傑克·倫敦爲名的「傑克·倫敦廣場」是奧克蘭有名的地點。傑克·倫敦於一八七六年生於舊金山，曾就讀於奧克蘭中學，還在那裡當過碼頭工人和水手。他曾在附近的柏克萊大學就讀一年，還沒畢業就隨著當時的克朗戴克淘金熱（Klondike Gold Rush）到阿拉斯加淘金去了。一年後傑克·倫敦空手而回，只好開始寫作謀生。傑克·倫敦在奧克蘭的故居及周圍，則被改建成「傑克·倫敦廣場」。

　　這座廣場是當地民眾舉行各種活動的場所，一年到頭都是熱鬧滾滾的。廣場裡還保存著他以前住過的低矮木屋。每個星期天，廣場內會舉辦農夫市場（Farmer Market），可以買到新鮮的蔬果、花卉和煙薰鮭魚。廣場四周有許多特別的商店，其中「巴恩斯與諾伯書店」（Barnes & Noble Bookstore）是加州數一數二的大型書店，書籍有十五萬種之多。

　　廣場邊緣設有傑克·倫敦村（Jack London Village），村內有傑克·倫敦博物館，展出傑克·倫敦當年在奧克蘭碼頭的生活。

傑克·倫敦相關網站

Jack London International

http://www.jack-london.org/

Jack London State Historic Park

https://jacklondonpark.com/

目錄

CONTENTS

第一章

前進蠻荒

前進蠻荒，
蜇伏的慾望沉潛躍動，
摩擦著束縛的鎖鏈，
流浪的渴望從漫長冬眠復甦，
狂放的野性重新燃燒沸騰。

　　巴克不看報紙，否則他早該知道這下事情糟了。不單單只有他而已，從普吉特海灣到聖地牙哥，每一隻結實健美、耐寒又熟諳水性的長毛狗都面臨了大麻煩。因爲人類在北極深處探勘時發現了黃金，加上輪船和運輸業者的炒作，成千上萬的群眾湧進了北方。他們需要狗，而且是身強體壯的大狗，要有強壯的肌肉可以拖曳重物、有厚密的毛皮可以抵禦寒冬。

　　巴克住在陽光普照的聖塔克蕾拉山谷，米勒法官的豪宅裡。房子就在大馬路旁邊，半被茂密的樹林遮掩，從樹葉的縫隙望去，可瞥見屋子四周寬敞陰涼的迴廊。屋前延伸出去是幾條碎石路，路兩旁有佔地廣闊的草坪，還有交錯聳立的高大白

楊木。後院甚至比前庭更加遼闊，寬廣的馬棚裡有上打的馬伕和侍童負責照料馬匹，成排的屋舍上纏滿了藤蔓，數不盡的倉房整齊地排列著，還有長長的葡萄籬架，綠意盎然的牧草地、果園與莓園。此外，噴水井上接了個幫浦打水到空的水泥槽裡，米勒法官的兒子們會在裡面晨泳，在酷熱的午後則躲進裡面消暑。

巴克是這大莊園裡的霸主，他在這裡出生和生活，轉眼間已過了四個寒暑。無庸置疑的，這麼大的地方當然也有其他的狗，不過他們都不足以掛齒。這些狗來來去去的，不是住在擁擠的狗屋裡，就是像日本哈巴狗杜斯或墨西哥無毛犬伊莎貝爾一樣，住在屋子偏僻的角落──這兩個怪胎幾乎都不出門的。此外還有至少二十隻以上的獵狐犬，他們會隔著窗戶對躲在女僕們的掃帚和拖把後的杜斯和伊莎貝爾兇狠地吼叫

不過，巴克可不是那種懦弱的室內犬，也不是甘於窩在狗屋裡的那種狗。這片領土都歸他管轄。他會跟法官的兒子們一塊跳進水槽游泳，或者到樹林裡打獵。晨昏時刻，他還會充當法官兩個女兒──茉莉和愛麗絲的保鑣，護衛她們外出散步。寒冷的夜晚裡，他會在書房的壁爐前窩在法官的腳邊取暖。他會讓法官的孫子們騎在他的背上嬉戲，一同在草地上打滾，或是領著他們探險，走到馬棚外的噴水池，甚至到更遠的牧場及莓園。巴克在獵狐犬的面前總是威風凜凜、不可一世的樣子，也無視於杜斯和伊莎貝爾的存在，因為他是莊園裡的霸王，不管是爬的、游的、飛的，甚至連人也一樣，只要是米勒法官家

裡的一份子，都得聽命於他。

　　他的父親艾爾墨是隻龐大的聖伯納犬，生前總是和法官形影不離，在他死後，巴克自然而然地接管了父親的地位。巴克的母親雪普是隻蘇格蘭牧羊犬，但他的體型沒有母親來得壯碩，只有一百四十磅。儘管如此，因為平時養尊處優、深受重視所養成的莊嚴氣質，讓他在一百四十磅的體重上增添不少威嚇之感。從他還是隻幼犬開始，巴克過著貴族般的生活，這四年來讓他養成了高傲的自尊，甚至有些自私自利，像個鄉紳一樣胸襟狹隘，目中無人。然而，他並非嬌生慣養、體態臃腫的家犬。狩獵之類的戶外活動，讓他除去多餘的油脂，保有結實的肌肉。就像那些冷水浴的愛好者一樣，他喜愛玩水的嗜好成了他的保健之道，讓他總是精神抖擻、身強體壯。

　　這就是巴克在一八九七年秋天的生活方式。也就是在這年的秋天，克倫戴克淘金熱吸引無數的人湧進冰天雪地的北方。但是巴克不會看報紙，他也不曉得家裡那個叫曼紐爾的園丁助手，正對他意圖不軌。曼紐爾有個戒不了的惡習，那就是沈迷中式樂透彩。當他在下賭的時候，總是堅信一套包贏的賭法，這讓他注定成為難以回頭的賭徒。玩這種包贏的賭法需要本錢，然而以他一個園丁助手的微薄收入，幾乎連養活妻小都已顯得困難重重。

　　在那個令人難以忘懷的夜晚，當法官至「葡萄農協」開會，孩子們忙於籌備一個運動俱樂部之際，曼紐爾終於背信棄義，犯下了不法勾當。沒有任何人證目擊他和巴克穿過果園而去，巴克也以爲只是像平常一樣散散步而已。他們來到一個叫做「大學公園」的車站，沒有其他人看見他們抵達，除了一個早就在那裡等待的人。那個男人跟曼紐爾談了一會兒之後，便聽見一陣錢幣碰撞聲響起。

「你應該把貨綁起來再交給我的！」那個男人粗里粗氣地罵著。曼紐爾便用一條結實的粗繩子，在巴克的脖子上繞了兩圈，在他的項圈下牢固地繫好。

「絞緊繩子，你就可以把他勒得半死了。」曼紐爾說道。那個陌生的男人隨意地咕噥一聲，表示他知道了。

巴克端莊安靜地讓曼紐爾綁上繩子，當然這是不尋常的舉動，不過他被教導應該信任他所認識的人們，應該相信人類的智慧比他來得高。但是一當繩子交到那陌生人的手上，他便發出一陣威脅的怒吼。他在暗示他的不悅，而且他自傲地認爲，他的暗示就是一項命令。然而出乎他意料之外，脖子上的繩索突然收緊，幾乎將他給勒得喘不過氣來。他怒不可遏地撲向那個男人，但是男人動作迅速地用力將繩子一拉，扯緊他的喉嚨，熟練地一轉，便將他四腳朝天、狠狠地撞到地面上。當巴克憤怒地掙扎時，繩子又被無情地收緊，他的舌頭伸出了嘴外，寬厚的胸膛痛苦急促地起伏著。在他的一生中，從未被如此卑劣的手段對待，他也從不曾這般暴怒。但是他已精疲力盡，兩眼發直，他甚至沒有察覺，在火車進站後，這兩個男人合力將他丟到放置行李的車廂裡。

巴克甦醒之後，感到舌頭隱隱作痛，他發覺自己正在某種

交通工具上因前進而顛簸著。當經過一個路口，傳來一陣尖銳的汽笛聲時，他隨即明白自己處在火車上。他以前經常與法官一同旅行，對於坐在行李車廂的感覺自然是再熟悉不過。他睜開雙眼，眼眸中散發一股狂烈的憤怒，宛如一個被擄掠的帝王。那個男人飛快地往他的脖子招來，但巴克的動作比男人更快，緊緊咬著他的手掌不放，直到他再度被繩子勒昏為止。

嘈雜的打鬥聲引來行李伕查看，男人將被咬爛的手掌藏在身後，說：「嗯，他有癲癇病。老闆叫我帶他到舊金山去看病，聽說那裡有個一流的獸醫，也許能治好這隻狗。」

在舊金山碼頭前一家酒館的小車庫裡，那個男人滔滔不絕地說著這晚火車之旅的事情。

「我只拿到五十塊錢，」他不斷地發著牢騷：「早知如此，就算給我一千塊現金我也不幹！」

他的手掌上紮著滲血的手帕，右邊的褲管從膝蓋沿路裂開到腳踝。

「另外那個同夥拿了多少錢？」酒館老闆問道。

「一百塊，」他回答：「卑鄙的傢伙，所以幫個忙吧！」

「那就是一百五十塊了，」酒館老闆盤算著：「他最好值這個價錢，我可不想當冤大頭。」

綁架巴克的男人解開他血跡斑斑的手帕，瞪著傷痕累累的手掌，說道：「我該不會得到狂犬病吧……」

「那也是你命該如此啊！」酒館老闆哈哈大笑，又補上一句：「喂，幫我一個忙再走吧！」

即使仍感到頭暈目眩，巴克忍受著喉嚨與舌頭傳來的陣陣劇痛，挺著剩下的半條命，試圖抵抗虐待他的人。然而他一再地被摔倒、被勒昏，直到他們將他脖子上沉重的銅製項圈用銼刀取了下來才停止。隨後，他們解開繩子，將他丟進一個鳥籠似的板條箱裡。

他躺在木箱內，度過這令他精疲力竭的夜晚，逐漸平復滿腔的怒火與受創的自尊。他完全無法了解這一切究竟是怎麼回事。那些陌生人到底要對他做什麼？為什麼他們將他囚禁在這狹小的木箱裡面？他不知道為什麼，但隱約有一股大難臨頭的不祥預感，沉重地壓迫著他的心頭。那晚，車庫的門有幾次喀答一聲地被推開，他猛地跳起，滿懷期待地希望看到法官或至少是孩子們。但每次總是酒館老闆那張臃腫的圓臉，藉由一盞微弱的燭光窺探著他。每每幾乎叫出聲音的歡呼，都被巴克隱忍在喉頭，轉而成為具有敵意的咆哮。

酒館老闆卻完全不理睬他。隔天一早，進來四個男人將板條箱抬了出去。看著他們猙獰的面貌、髒污的外表與破爛的衣著，巴克心想，又多了幾個凌虐他的人，於是從板條縫中對著他們齜牙咧嘴地怒吼。他們只是笑著，拿棍子戳他，巴克迅速撲上前以利齒咬住棍子，然而他發現他們就是要看這種反應，於是悶悶不樂地躺了下來，也不理會他們將木箱搬上一輛馬車。自此，巴克連同囚禁他的箱子被轉了好幾手。貨運公司的員工接手照料他，然後被另外一輛馬車運送，再被帶到裝載了各式箱子與包裹的卡車上，送到一艘渡輪上面；下了渡輪後，卡車將他載至一個規模較大的鐵路貨運站，最後終於被安置在一列快車上。

呼嘯聲轟隆作響的火車頭，拖著快車連續奔馳了兩天兩夜，而巴克也整整兩天兩夜沒吃沒喝了。列車員一開始試圖接近他，處於憤怒中的巴克對他們咆叫，惹得他們報復性地逗弄他。當他怒氣沖沖地以身體衝撞木條，氣得渾身發抖、口角起泡時，他們卻只嘲笑、奚落著他。他們學著惡犬嗥叫，學貓咪喵喵叫，還拍動雙臂模仿公雞咯咯啼。這簡直是蠢到極點，他也知道，自尊心卻仍是受到傷害，更加怒氣衝天。巴克並不在乎餓肚子，但沒有水喝讓他痛苦難耐，怒不可遏。原先已經緊繃敏感的情緒，加上乾渴腫脹的喉嚨和舌頭，這樣惡劣的對待，讓他一直處在十分激昂憤怒的狀態。

讓巴克慶幸的是：脖子上的繩子已經被取下來了。那條繩子讓人類佔盡不平等的優勢，而現在既然繩子已經拿掉了，他會讓他們明白，誰也無法將另外一條繩子套到他脖子上了，他對此已是打定主意。整整兩天兩夜，他沒吃沒喝，而這段期間所遭受的虐待，使他累積了滿腔怒火，誰膽敢第一個冒犯他的話，恐怕就會吃不完兜著走。他的雙眼充血，像極了狂暴的魔鬼，而這樣的改變，可能連法官見著了他都會認不得。當列車員在西雅圖站將巴克送下車後，他們這才終於鬆了一口氣。

四個男人小心翼翼地將木箱搬下馬車，抬到一個有著高牆圍繞的小後院。一個身穿紅色套頭毛衣、領子鬆垮垮地掛在脖子上的壯漢，出來在馬車伕的簽收單上簽了字。巴克猜想，這大概是下一個虐待他的人了，於是他猛力地以身體撞擊木箱板條。那男人毫不在乎地笑了笑，拿出一柄小斧頭和一根棍子。

「你該不會現在就要放他出來吧？」馬車伕問。

「沒錯。」那男人說著，邊將斧頭揮向木箱，將板條給撬開。

四個搬貨工人見狀立刻如鳥獸散跳到牆頭上，準備在安全無虞的距離內觀賞一場好戲。

巴克狠狠地咬住碎裂的木片，兇猛地拉扯，只要斧頭一落下，他就衝上前咆哮怒吼，恨不得立即躍身而出，而那男人卻仍若無其事地劈著木箱。

「出來吧，你這紅眼魔鬼！」那男人說道，他已將木箱劈出一個洞口，足夠巴克鑽身而出。他邊說邊將斧頭丟開，把棍子換到他的右手。

巴克真成了一個紅眼的惡魔，俯低著身子，全身毛髮倒豎，口流白沫，充血的雙眼閃著狂暴的怒光，帶著兩天兩夜蓄積的憤怒，以他一百四十磅的體重，一躍而起直撲那名壯漢。但就在半空中，當他的嘴巴即將咬中那男人的瞬間，他的身子突然遭到一記猛擊，這股劇痛讓他不禁咬緊牙關，身體也因而翻轉一圈，狠狠摔了個四腳朝天。巴克一生中從沒挨過棍子，他不明白究竟發生了什麼事。他狂吠著再度站起身來，激動地大叫，又躍身跳起，但卻又再次被重擊而摔落地面。這下他才瞭解到棍棒的可怕，然而憤怒至極的他已無視於警告，奮不顧身地又連撲了十數次，每次都被擊落於地。

在特別猛烈的一擊之後，他搖搖晃晃地站了起來，已經頭昏目眩到無法再撲上前去，他瘸著腿步履蹣跚，鮮血從他的鼻子、嘴巴和耳朵汩汩流出，原本美麗的皮毛已沾滿了血跡與口沫。那個男人走向前來，對著他的鼻子再度猛力一擊。這一擊讓他痛徹骨髓，先前所受的苦根本無法相提並論。他像隻獅子般發出怒吼，再次撲向那男人。但那個男人冷靜地將棍子從右手換到左手，再用右手攫住他的下顎，猛地往下拉再向後一

扭，讓巴克的身子在半空中翻轉了一圈半，重重地以頭跟胸部摔落地面。

巴克起身作最後一搏，男人此時揮出先前刻意保留的致命一擊，瞬間將巴克重重地擊垮在地，讓他完全失去意識。

「我就說嘛！他對馴狗真有一套！」牆頭上的其中一個男人興奮地叫出聲來。

「杜魯瑟可是每天馴服一匹種馬的啊！星期天還兩匹呢！」馬車伕邊說邊爬上馬車，趕著馬走了。

後來巴克的意識完全清醒，但體力尚未恢復時，仍舊躺在先前倒下的地方，眼睛望向那個穿著紅色套頭毛衣的男人。

「他叫做巴克，」那個男人看著酒館老闆附上的信喃喃自語，信中說明了託運的木箱和內容物。「好啦，巴克，我的小傢伙！」他用親切的口吻接著道：「我們剛剛已經小小地打了一架，而我們最好是將這件事忘記，到此為止吧！你應該瞭解自己的處境了，我也清楚自己的工作。你乖乖的話，一切就會相安無事。如果你不聽話，我就會扁得你肚破腸流。你明白了嗎？」

他一邊說著，還毫無所懼地伸手輕拍方才被他殘忍重毆的頭部，即使巴克反射性地全身寒毛直豎，仍舊是忍了下來，沒有反抗。他急躁地喝著那男人端來的水，也從那男人的手中，大口大口地吞下一塊又一塊的生肉。

他很明白自己被擊倒了，但他尚未被擊垮到一蹶不振的地步。他瞭解到一件事情，就是對於手上握有棍棒的人，自己是

絕對贏不了的。他將記取這寶貴的教訓，終身不忘。這是他即將遭遇的原始世界中所遵循的法則，他只是提前得到一個招呼罷了。殘酷的現實生活是永遠站在強者這邊的；當他不畏強權而奮力抵抗時，也激起了他體內那股潛藏的狡詐本性。日子一天天過去，陸陸續續有其他的狗被送來。有的被裝在箱子裡，有的被繩子栓著。有的很溫馴，有的像他剛到時一樣憤恨地怒吼。他看著每隻新來的狗臣服於那紅毛衣的男人。一次又一次，當他目睹必經的殘酷過程，就更加深刻地體會到這個慘痛的教訓──持有棍棒的人就是執法者，是必須服從的主人，但沒有必要刻意親近。巴克從未違背最後一點，即便他看到一些被擊敗的狗搖尾乞憐地討好著那男人；即便他也親眼目睹有隻狗在始終都不屈服的反抗下，活活地被打死。

偶爾會有形形色色的陌生人前來，或而興奮、或而奉承地討好著那紅毛衣男人。每當他們之間有金錢交易的時候，就會有一隻或以上的狗被陌生人帶走。巴克納悶他們究竟到哪裡去，爲何都一去不回。他對未知的將來感到十分憂慮，每回他沒被選中時，就不免暗自慶幸。

然而，該來的終究還是來了。一個操著破英文的乾瘦傢伙挑中了巴克，還叫著他聽不懂的奇怪喊聲。

「太不可思議了！」當他一看到巴克就叫嚷著：「眞是一條棒呆了的好狗！欸，多少錢啊？」

「三百塊，根本就等於送給你一樣。」那穿紅毛衣的男人迅速答道：「反正花的是政府的錢，你一點損失也沒有。怎麼樣，裴洛特？」

　　身為加拿大送公文使者的裴洛特露齒笑了笑，考慮到最近因狗的需求量激增而被喊到天價，三百塊對這隻難得一見的好狗來說，簡直就像糟蹋了一樣。即使這隻狗的價格看似昂貴，加拿大政府也不會吃虧，有優秀的狗加入送公文團隊，急件公文才不會有所延誤。裴洛特是個識狗行家，當他一看到巴克，就知道他是千中選一的好狗——「喔！不，是萬中選一的好狗！」他暗自讚嘆著。

　　巴克看見他們之間有了金錢交易，接著他和另外一隻叫做柯麗的溫順紐芬蘭狗，一起被那個矮小的男人帶走，對此他一點也不感到意外。這是他最後一次見到那紅毛衣的男人，而當巴克和柯麗從獨角鯨號的輪船甲板上，望著漸行漸遠的西雅圖時，也是他最後一次見到溫暖的南方。裴洛特將他和柯麗帶到船艙裡，交給一個有著黝黑臉龐的大漢——弗洪索。裴洛特是法裔加拿大人，皮膚很黑，弗洪索則是法裔加拿大人和當地人的混血，皮膚比裴洛特還黑上一倍。巴克從未見過這種膚色的人種（往後還會見到更多），雖然他對他們並無特別的好感，但卻愈發真誠地尊敬，因為他很快地發現，裴洛特和弗洪索都是正直講理的人，做事公正、處罰毫不偏袒，而且非常熟稔狗性，不會被狗給耍了。

　　巴克和柯麗被帶到獨角鯨號的夾板艙裡，和另外兩隻狗關在一起。其中一隻雪白大狗——史匹茲，是被一個捕鯨船長從挪威屬地的斯匹茲卑爾根群島帶出來的，隨後還跟隨地質考察隊深入極地荒原。這隻大狗外表看似友善，實則奸詐無比，臉上帶著笑容，心裡卻盤算著壞主意。譬如他們第一次一同進食時，他就偷吃巴克的那一份。當巴克氣得要撲過去教訓他時，弗洪索的鞭子早已從空中呼嘯而落，抽在那小偷的身上。雖然巴克搶回來的食物只剩一點點骨頭，但他認為弗洪索執法公正，自此便對這名混血兒產生尊敬之意。

另外那隻狗叫戴夫，既不跟別人親近，也無視於他人的友好表示，對於新來兩隻狗的食物更是從不覬覦。他是個陰沉孤僻的傢伙，總是一副悶悶不樂的模樣。他曾經明白地讓柯麗知道，不希望有任何人打擾他，要是有人不怕死，肯定會要他好看。他叫做戴夫，每天吃飽睡、睡飽吃，不然就是無聊地打呵欠，對任何事情都提不起興趣。當獨角鯨號行經夏洛特女王峽灣時，整條船瘋了似地左右搖晃，前後猛烈顛簸，巴克和柯麗被嚇得心驚膽跳、激動萬分，結果戴夫只是不高興地抬起頭來，冷冷地看了他們一眼，打了個呵欠，又趴下去繼續睡覺。

日復一日，夜復一夜，輪船毫不停歇地繼續航行，儘管日子一成不變，巴克卻覺得氣候漸漸地變冷了。終於有天清晨，巴克和其他的狗察覺到獨角鯨號的螺旋槳停了，船上瀰漫著一股興奮的氣氛，他知道一個重大的改變即將到來。弗洪索將他們套上繩索，再帶到甲板上。一踏上冰冷的甲板，巴克的腳便陷到一種白白軟軟、像是泥巴的東西裡面。他悶哼一聲，急忙往後跳開。那白色的東西不斷地從空中落下，飄在他身上，他甩了甩身子，結果又有更多落在他身上。他好奇地嗅了嗅，然後用舌頭舔了一下。那東西嚐起來像火一般扎舌，但下一秒又突然消失，這完全把他給搞迷糊了。他又試了試，結果還是一樣。四周的人們哄鬧大笑，害他覺得很不好意思，但他不明白人們為什麼笑他，這可是他生平第一次看到雪啊！

第二章
棍棒與利齒法則

　　巴克第一天登上位於阿拉斯加的戴伊海岸時，簡直就像一場夢魘，每一分、每一秒都充滿了衝擊與驚愕。他從文明世界的中心，突然被丟到最為蠻荒原始的中央地帶。以往那種懶洋洋地曬著太陽，無聊地到處閒晃的日子已不復存在。這裡沒有秩序，沒有安寧，更沒有片刻的安全。有的只是混亂與戰鬥，時時刻刻都有喪命或受傷之虞。隨時隨地都必須保持高度警戒，因為這裡的人和狗可不比城裡，他們像野蠻人一樣，全都不管政府頒布的法律，只遵從棍棒與利齒法則。

　　他從未見過狗打架可以像狼群一般兇殘可怕，而這第一次經驗，帶給他永生難忘的教訓。確實如此，若不是有人當了替死鬼，他也沒能活著體會到這教訓的可貴。柯麗就是那個倒楣鬼。那天，他們在木材店附近紮營，柯麗友善地對一隻愛斯基摩犬示好，他的體型跟成狼一樣大，不過還不到柯麗的一半。連個警告都沒有，那隻愛斯基摩犬突然縱身一躍，銳利的牙齒喀嚓一咬後又倏地跳開，柯麗的臉卻在一瞬間，從眼睛到下巴整個被撕裂。

這是狼群打鬥的方式──撲上前又立刻跳開，事情卻不僅如此。三、四十隻愛斯基摩犬一擁而上，將正在交戰的兩隻狗圍在中間，屏氣凝神地注視著，蠢蠢欲動。巴克不明白為何他們一副蓄勢待發，像是吃肉排時那般貪婪急切的模樣。柯麗衝向她的敵手，對方撲上前又往旁邊跳開，柯麗再度撲過去，對方擺出一種奇特的姿勢，用胸部將柯麗撞倒在地，自此柯麗就居於劣勢了，圍觀的愛斯基摩犬們所等待的也就是這一刻的來臨。他們一躍而上，將柯麗踩在腳下，興奮地喊叫著。柯麗被壓在這一大群狗的下面，發出痛苦的哀嚎聲。

　　這一切發生得太過突然了，絲毫沒有預警，巴克徹底地被震懾住了。他看到史匹茲露出深紅色的舌頭竊笑著，然後又瞧見弗洪索揮舞著斧頭衝進一團混亂的狗群中，還有三個男人持著棍棒過來幫他驅離狗群。從柯麗倒下，到最後幾隻攻擊的狗被棍子驅離，前後不過兩分鐘的光景，柯麗卻已軟綿綿地癱倒在地，倒臥在一片滿是血跡、泥濘的雪地上，失去任何生命氣息，她幾乎是被撕咬到碎屍萬段的地步。那個黑臉的混血兒站在柯麗的屍體前面，咬牙切齒地咒罵著。這一幕後來經常出現在巴克的夢中折磨著他。生命就是這麼一回事，沒有所謂公平的競爭，一旦倒下，就得面臨自己的末日。就是這樣，他必須時時警惕自己，絕對不可以倒下！史匹茲又伸出舌頭竊笑著，從那一刻起，巴克就對他深惡痛絕，誓不兩立。

　　尚未從柯麗的慘劇平復過來，巴克又得面臨另一項令他震驚的事情。弗洪索為他套上一副有著環扣的繩索，那是一種拖

拉物品用的馬具，他在家鄉曾經看過馬伕將這種東西套在馬匹
的身上，好讓馬匹拉車，而現在他也要開始這項工作了。弗洪
索駕著雪橇到山谷間的森林裡砍柴，再將一整車生火用的木材
帶回來。即使因為被當作拖運貨物的牲口，而讓他的自尊受到
莫大的損害，巴克仍識趣地未做任何抵抗。雖然這項工作對他
而言十分生疏，他依舊全力以赴，盡心負責。弗洪索非常嚴
格，以他的皮鞭為輔，要求絕對且立即的服從。戴夫是隻經驗
老到的壓陣狗，只要巴克一出錯，就往他的後腿咬上一口，以

示警告。史匹茲則是領隊狗，同樣閱歷豐富，雖然咬不到巴克來教訓他，但會以時常怒吼來大聲斥責，或是巧妙地以身體的重量扯動繩索，將巴克拉回他應該前進的方向。巴克學得很快，在他兩位同伴與弗洪索的協同教導之下進步神速。在他們還沒回到營區之前，巴克就已經學會了聽到「喝」要停下，聽到「駕」要起步；轉彎時的角度要大，而當載滿木材在下坡從後急墜時，不能擋到壓陣狗的路，以免被撞上。

「這三隻狗真是讚啊！」弗洪索對裴洛特說：「尤其是巴克，拉得真好！教他什麼馬上就學會了！」

下午，裴洛特為了不讓急件公文的遞送進度落後，帶回了另外兩隻狗。他喚他們「比利」和「喬」，是兩隻血統純正的愛斯基摩犬。雖然他們倆是出自同一個母親的親兄弟，個性卻有如天壤之別。比利的缺點就是太過善良，而喬卻恰恰好相反，既刻薄又內向，動不動就對人怒吼和瞪視。巴克接納他們作為夥伴，戴夫則是不理不睬，而史匹茲更是來個下馬威，攻擊了一個，再痛毆另一個。比利搖尾乞憐以示討好，當他發現沒有效果時，趕緊轉身就跑，而在史匹茲的利齒咬進他的側腹時，哀嚎之餘還不忘繼續搖尾求饒。但喬就不是這麼一回事了，當史匹茲繞著他轉時，他也跟著轉，始終都面向著他，毛髮直豎，兩耳後貼，顫著嘴咆哮著，不斷地上下猛烈咬合，目露兇光，一副準備交戰的模樣。他兇狠的樣子讓史匹茲打消教訓他的念頭，但為了掩飾他的困窘，只好轉而對不會反抗、還哀哀叫的比利出氣，一直將他趕到營地外圍才罷休。

到了晚上，裴洛特又弄來一條狗，這是隻年紀大的愛斯基摩犬，身形削長、骨瘦如柴，臉上佈滿戰鬥留下的疤痕，唯一存留的一隻眼睛閃爍著警告意味，與不容小覷的威嚴。他叫作索列克，意思就是「狂暴的狗」。像戴夫一樣，他不奢求也不施予，不冀望任何事情，當他緩慢地走到狗群中間時，連史匹茲也不敢招惹。巴克在一次倒楣的情況下，發現了他的一個怪癖——他不喜歡有人接近他瞎了眼的那一邊。巴克在毫不知情下犯了這個大忌，他只記得下一秒索列克就撲到他的身上，將他的肩膀撕咬出一個三吋深的傷口，深可見骨。從此之後，巴克就記得要避開他瞎眼的那邊，而在他們結束同伴關係之前，再也沒有發生任何紛爭。跟戴夫一樣，他唯一的願望就是不希望有人打擾他。不過後來巴克才知道，其實每隻狗都有一兩樣無以取代的心願。

　　那天夜裡，巴克面臨了怎麼睡覺的大難題。點著燭火的營帳，在一片白雪皚皚中顯得格外的溫暖，當他理所當然地要鑽進帳篷裡睡覺時，裴洛特和弗洪索卻對他破口大罵，還拿炊具扔他，當他從驚愕中回神過來後，才充滿屈辱地逃到酷寒的黑夜裡。一陣寒風吹來，像針般扎到身上，他肩膀上的傷口更是像被毒液侵蝕般痛苦難當。他躺在雪地上試圖入睡，結果凍得他全身發抖。他哀傷地在營帳間遊蕩，發現每個地方都一樣寒冷，還有惡犬兇狠地想撲向他。他聳立起頸部的毛髮咆哮著（這招他可是很快就學會了），那些惡犬便乖乖地讓路。

　　最後他終於想到一個辦法——回去看自己的夥伴究竟是怎

麼解決這問題的。他驚訝地發現，他們全都消失了。他再度遊蕩在營帳之間，尋找他們的蹤跡，最後還是無功而返。他們有沒有可能在帳篷裡面？不，這不可能，否則他就不會被趕出來了。那他們究竟到哪去了？他渾身發抖，尾巴無精打采地垂著，悽涼絕望到極點，漫無目標地在營地四處遊蕩。驀地，他前腳陷入鬆軟的雪地裡，整個身體跟著陷下，腳碰到一團蠕動的物體。他趕緊跳開，寒毛直豎地吼著，被這不明物體嚇得半死。他隨即聽到一個友善的叫聲，這才放下心來，趨前察看。一股熱氣撲鼻而來，原來是比利蜷縮成一團，溫暖舒適地躺在雪地下面睡覺。比利討好地嗚嗚叫，蠕動著身軀示好，還大膽地用他溼熱的舌頭舔向巴克的臉龐，以求相安無事。

又學到了一課。原來，他們都是這樣睡的啊！巴克選了一個可靠的地方，手忙腳亂地花了許多的力氣，才替自己挖了一個洞鑽進去。才一瞬間，洞裡就充滿了他的體熱，他也沉沉地進入夢鄉。這天既漫長又艱辛，他總算能好好地睡上一覺，儘管惡夢讓他在熟睡中不時發出吼聲，動來動去。

一直到全營的人和狗都起來了，巴克才被嘈雜的聲音驚醒，睜開雙眼。一開始，他完全忘了自己身在何處。夜裡下過雪，將他徹底淹沒在雪堆裡。四面八方全都是雪，像銅牆鐵壁一樣將他困在裡面。一陣極度的恐慌倏地籠罩著他——如同野生動物對陷阱的本能反應，這也象徵著他即將回歸到祖先生活，由於他是在文明世界過度馴化的狗，根據過去的經驗，他完全不知道什麼是陷阱，也無從恐懼起。然而此刻，他全身的肌肉卻不由自主地不停收縮，頸背上的毛髮聳立。他發出一聲兇暴的怒吼，猛地衝出雪洞，迎面而來的白雪如燦爛的雲朵飛逝而去，終於，耀眼的陽光灑在臉上。腳還未站穩，他看到眼前盡是被白雪覆蓋的營帳，才猛然記起自己身處何方。回想起從曼紐爾帶他出來散步的那天，一直到昨夜他為自己挖了一個地洞，一幕幕的景象浮現腦海。

巴克一出現，弗洪索就發出一聲歡呼。「我就說吧！」這個駕狗人對裴洛特喊著：「這個巴克學啥都快的不得了啊！」

裴洛特一本正經地點點頭。身為加拿大政府的信差，肩負著遞送急件公文的重責大任，他非常需要最優良的狗來協助，而擁有巴克這樣的好狗，他感到十分的欣慰。

一個鐘頭內，隊伍又增加了另外三隻愛斯基摩犬，現在總共有九隻之多。不到一刻鐘的時間，他們已經套上了挽具，奔馳在通往戴伊峽谷的雪道上。巴克很高興終於啓程了，儘管工作很辛苦，但他發現自己並不會特別討厭。他很驚訝地看到，上路後整個隊伍就被生氣勃勃的熱切氣氛包圍，連他都受到感染。更讓他詫異的是，戴夫和索列克的轉變。在套上挽具之後，他們簡直就變成了另外一條狗。以往的被動與冷漠已不復見，他們變得積極靈活，一心渴望工作能順利進行，無法忍受任何延誤或混亂造成工作的延宕。挽具下的苦差事，似乎是他們生命中最重要的價值，彷彿是爲此而活，也是唯一能帶給他們樂趣的事情。

　　戴夫是壓陣狗，在他前面的是巴克，然後再來是索列克。其他的狗成一路縱隊往前排去，而最前面的領隊位置則是由史匹茲擔任。巴克被刻意安排在戴夫和索列克的中間，好接受他們倆的指導。雖然巴克反應敏捷、學習迅速，但他們倆也是教導有方，從不讓他發生同樣的失誤，否則就會用銳利的牙齒施以教訓。戴夫十分公正且生性聰穎，絕不無緣無故咬他，但一有必要也絕對不會放他一馬，況且還有弗洪索的鞭子作爲靠山，巴克發現與其反抗報復，倒不如改進自己的缺點還來得划算些。有一次，在片刻的休息後，巴克被挽繩纏住而延誤了出發的時間，戴夫和索列克便一起衝上前狠狠地教訓他一頓。雖然這反而使得挽繩纏得更緊了，但巴克從此就小心翼翼地不讓挽繩纏繞在一起。這天尚未結束，巴克已經對他的工作遊刃有餘，同伴也不再挑剔他，連弗洪索鞭子落下的次數也變少了，裴洛特甚至還抬起巴克的腳掌仔細檢查，賦予他莫高的榮譽。

這天行程極為艱辛，他們爬上峽谷，穿越牧羊人的露營拖車陣，經過山峰與樹林小徑，橫越凍結百呎深的冰河，最後通過廣闊的奇爾庫特分水嶺。這條分水嶺不但區隔了淡水與鹹水，更為孤寥的北方大地提供了一道險峻的天然屏障。他們經過一連串死火山湖泊，路程十分順暢，深夜時刻抵達了伯奈特湖泊的大營區，那裡有上千的淘金客正打造著船隻，好在春天雪融時航行。巴克這晚疲倦至極，為自己挖了雪洞後便沉沉入睡。但隔天凌晨天色都還未亮就被喚醒，在寒冷的天氣中和夥伴繼續一同上路。

這天走的雪道因已有人事先通過壓實，他們總共趕了四十哩路；但從第二天開始，接下來好幾天的路程都必須要自己開路，不僅耗時也較為辛苦。通常是裴洛特在隊伍的最前面開路，用寬底的雪靴將雪踏平，以利通行。弗洪索則用雪杖控制著雪橇的方向，有時會與裴洛特互換工作，但並不頻繁。裴洛特急於趕路，他相當自豪己深諳冰雪特性，這於此處是不可或缺且實用的知識，因為在秋天冰層較薄，而且水流湍急的地方也結不了冰。

日復一日，巴克和夥伴們辛苦地拉著雪橇，這樣的日子好似永無止境。他們往往在天還未亮時就啟程，等到天際第一道曙光出現，他們已經趕了好幾哩路了。而總是天黑之後，他們才能休息紮營，吃過一點點的魚乾糧後，再鑽進洞裡睡覺。巴克永遠處在飢餓的狀態，因為配給到的一磅半鮭魚乾糧，根本就不夠他塞牙縫。他從來就不曾吃飽過，總是痛苦地挨餓著。其他的狗因為體重輕，且過慣了這種日子，儘管他們只吃一磅的魚乾，已足夠維持良好的體力。

巴克很快地改掉以往養成的挑食習慣。他原本進食時十分優雅有家教，但他發現每次同伴先吃完後，就會過來搶他的食物，讓他防不勝防，因為等他打退了其中兩三隻後，回頭一看，食物早已進了其他夥伴的肚子裡。為免悲劇再次發生，巴克只好吃得跟其他夥伴一樣快。原本他總是不屑偷搶別人的食物，如今迫於強烈的飢餓感，他也開始去偷竊不屬於他的食物，並且暗中觀察學習。派克是一隻新來的狗，最擅長裝病和偷東西，有回他趁著裴洛特轉過身去時，狡猾地偷到一片培根肉。隔天巴克也如法炮製，把一整塊肉都給偷走，引起一陣喧嘩騷動。但巴克並未被懷疑，反而是那隻笨狗杜柏，每次偷東西都被抓個正著，這回就成了巴克的代罪羔羊，無端受罰。

巴克第一次的偷竊行為，代表他能在北方惡劣的環境存活下去。這也顯示出他有足夠的應變能力適應環境的改變，若缺乏這種能力，勢必會迅速慘死。同時，這也意味著巴克原有的道德良知正在逐漸衰退與消逝。在殘酷無情的生存鬥爭中，這樣的德性反而是有害無益。在南方，大家遵守的是愛與友誼法則，尊重私有財產與個人情感，這再正確不過；但在北方，奉行的卻是棍棒與利齒法則，要是還有誰遵從南方的那一套，肯定是個傻子。而根據巴克的觀察，這樣的傻子絕對是活不成。

這並非巴克推理出的結論，他只是在順應環境，在不知不覺中適應了新的生活方式。綜觀他的一生，無論情勢多麼險惡，他從未臨陣脫逃。然而，那個身穿紅色套頭毛衣的男人，用棍子將更基本、更首要的生存法則，重重地打進了他的內心深處。受過文明洗禮的他，可以捨生取義，可以死在米勒法官執法的馬鞭之下。但是現在，他已經徹底野蠻化，為了保護自己的性命而棄道義於不顧。他並不是為了要找樂子而偷竊，而是為了要填飽肚子。他不是公開搶奪，而是暗地裡狡猾地去偷取，這完全是因為他遵守棍棒與利齒法則。總而言之，他之所以幹這些勾當，是因為做比不做會讓生活更好過。

他進步（倒不如說是在退步）得很快，渾身肌肉變得鋼鐵般堅硬，對於一般的傷痛，已經不以為意了。他無論內在或外表，都發展得十分符合經濟效益。他什麼都吃，不管東西有多噁心、多難以消化，他都可以吞得下去。一旦吃進肚裡，他的胃就會吸收養分直到最後一滴被榨盡，然後他的血液會將養分送到全身最遠的每個角落，轉化成最堅韌最結實的身體組織。他的視覺和嗅覺也變得十分靈敏。尤其是聽覺，敏銳的程度甚至讓他在睡夢中也能聽見最微弱的聲響，並且準確地判斷其中所蘊含的吉凶。他學會了用牙齒咬掉凍結在腳趾縫中的冰；口渴時，如果遇到水面上結了一層厚厚的冰，他會以後腳站起來，然後用前腿把冰敲碎。而他最為出色的本領，是能嗅出風向，而且是在前一個晚上就能預測得到。即使當他在樹旁或堤

岸挖洞時連一絲風也沒有，到了半夜也絕對會刮起風，而他早已在背風處睡得安安穩穩了。

　　他不僅從經驗中學習，那股喪失已久的野性本能也再度復甦了，連同歷代以來因被人類馴養而形成的習性，也正一點一滴逐漸地消逝。他依稀有個模糊的印象，那是他這個族群期的生活模樣，當時他們是成群結隊的野狗，在原始的森林裡穿梭，以追趕捕殺獵物維生。對他而言，以利齒倏地撕咬、像狼一般快速攫奪的戰鬥方式，並不需要刻意地學習，因為被遺忘的祖先們就是這樣與敵人作戰的。他體內潛伏的原始本性已經逐漸甦醒了，而祖先們代代相傳的求生伎倆，也就是他的伎倆，就像是與生俱來一般，不須花費任何的氣力學習。在寂靜

野性的呼喚

寒冷的夜裡，當他像狼一般仰鼻長聲嗥叫的時候，那也正是他早已化爲灰土的祖先，越過了這許多個世紀，透過他仰起鼻子對著星辰長嗥，嗥叫出與祖先相同的音調，於中訴說著他們的悲哀，在那寒冷的黑夜中所深藏的孤獨。

就這樣，像是在悲嘆生命猶如一齣傀儡戲，那首古老的歌，從他的內心流洩而出。然而，巴克也因此回歸了最純眞的自我。而這一切的改變，只因爲人類在北方發現了一種黃色的金屬，只因爲一個叫曼紐爾的園丁助手，賺的薪水不夠養活他的妻兒。

第三章

原始獸性的統治慾望

　　巴克的血液裡流淌著原始獸性裡統治與支配的強大慾望，這本性在拉雪橇的嚴苛生活中不斷地滋長。但這樣的渴望是暗地裡壯大的，他新習得的狡詐個性，使他懂得偽裝與自我約束。他正忙著適應新的生活，無暇顧及內心那股不自在的感覺。他不僅不去主動挑起爭端，更是極力避免；他相當地謹慎沉著，絕不操之過急，更不輕舉妄動。即使他對史匹茲懷著深仇大恨，但從未顯露出急躁的態度，盡可能避免一切挑釁的動作。

　　另一方面，也許史匹茲直覺地認為巴克是個危險的敵人，一逮到機會，便對他齜牙咧嘴地警告示威，甚至時常無緣無故地欺侮巴克，想想激怒他並進行生死決鬥。若非發生一件非比尋常的意外，這場戰爭早在旅程開始不久就該爆發了。那晚，結束一天的工作之後，他們在拉霸傑湖畔紮營。當時大雪紛飛，寒風刺骨，猶如熾熱的刀子刺入。四週一片漆黑，他們被迫摸黑尋找可以紮營的地方。他們從未遇過比這更糟糕的情況。為了減輕負擔，裴洛特和弗洪索早遺棄帳篷在戴伊峽谷。

此刻背後高高地聳立著一座陡峭的懸崖，他們只好挨著崖壁，撿來幾根漂到岸邊的樹枝，在結冰的湖面上生火、打起地舖。然而火堆很快地被融化的冰水熄滅，他們只好在一片黑暗中吃著晚飯。

巴克緊挨著可以遮風蔽雨的峭壁，挖了個雪洞當窩。窩裡既安適且溫暖，當弗洪索分發用火烘烤過的魚乾時，他甚至有些捨不得離開。當巴克吃完飯回到雪洞時，他發現自己的窩被霸佔了，聽到裡面傳來一聲警告性的咆哮，他知道入侵者正是史匹茲。到目前為止，巴克總是避免與史匹茲發生摩擦，但這一次他實在太過分了。他體內的獸性大發，憤恨地怒吼一聲向史匹茲撲去。這個狂暴的舉動讓雙方都感到意外，尤其是史匹茲，因為根據以往的經驗，他一直認為他的對手不過是隻膽小如鼠的狗，只不過身材高大勉強替他保留點面子罷了。

弗洪索更是驚訝。他看見他們從崩毀的雪洞一路扭打出來，便猜到爭執的起因。「哎哎哎！」他對巴克大叫：「讓給他吧！看在老天爺的份上，讓給那個卑鄙的小偷吧！」

史匹茲早希望有這樣決鬥的時機。他憤怒至極，大聲地吼叫，來回兜著圈子，想伺機撲上前去。巴克也一樣怒氣難消，小心翼翼地兜著圈子，企圖找到有利於自己的時機。然而，就在此時，一件意外發生了，這次爭奪霸權的決鬥便因而延宕至多日之後，一直到經過了許多令人疲憊的旅程和苦役才到來。

裴洛特倏地咒罵一聲，隨即響起棍子打在骨瘦如柴身軀上的聲音，接著傳來一聲慘痛的尖叫，一場大騷動就要爆發了。

營地裡突然擠滿了一群鬼鬼祟祟、毛茸茸的東西——大約有八、九十隻飢餓的愛斯基摩犬，從印地安村落裡循著營地的氣味而來，趁巴克和史匹茲在打架的時候悄悄接近。當裴洛特和弗洪索揮著粗大的棍子衝進狗群時，他們就齜牙咧嘴地反抗。食物的香味已讓這些狗失去理智。裴洛特發現一隻狗的頭埋進了食物箱裡，他揮起棍子重重地打向那隻狗瘦到突出的肋骨，結果食物箱也跟著翻倒在地，剎那之間，二十幾隻飢餓的狗蜂擁而上，爭相搶奪掉在地上的麵包和培根肉。棍子打在他們身上根本毫無作用，他們在如雨點般的棍擊下

慘叫，卻仍舊不減瘋狂地搶奪食物，直到最後丁點的麵包屑都吞下肚後才散開。

就在同時，雪橇隊的狗也驚慌地跳出雪洞，但只有被這些兇狠的入侵者襲擊的份。巴克從沒見過這樣的狗。他們的骨頭好像快要戳破出皮膚一樣，每隻狗都骨瘦嶙峋，鬆垮垮的皮膚掛在骨頭上，眼睛閃閃發光，牙齒上沾著欲滴的唾沫。長期的飢餓讓他們瘋狂至極，令人害怕且難以抵禦。雪橇隊的狗才剛要進攻，就被逼退到崖壁底下。巴克被三隻愛斯基摩犬圍攻，才一瞬間，他的頭部和肩膀就被撕裂多處。搏鬥的喧鬧聲令人恐懼，比利一如往常般嚇得哀啼。戴夫和索列克英勇地並肩作戰，身上幾十處的傷口不斷地淌著血。喬則像個魔鬼般亂咬，一次，他的牙齒咬住了一隻愛斯基摩犬的前腳，喀擦一聲連骨頭都咬碎了。裝病鬼派克就跳到這隻斷了腳的傢伙身上，牙齒一亮，快速地一扭，將對方的脖子咬斷。巴克咬住一隻口吐白沫的狗的喉嚨，當他的利齒將對方的頸動脈咬斷時，鮮血濺了他一身，而嘴裡那股溫熱的血腥味，更激發了他的兇猛。他向另一隻狗撲去，就在那一刹那，卻感覺到自己的喉嚨被人給咬住了，原來是史匹茲趁火打劫，從側邊向他襲擊。

裴洛特和弗洪索將營地裡的愛斯基摩犬趕走之後，趕緊過來搭救自己雪橇隊的狗。面對他倆，那群餓到發狂的瘋狗稍微退開了一些，巴克便得以趁機脫身，於是兩個人又跑回去搶救糧食。但維持不到片刻，那些愛斯基摩犬又捲土重來攻擊雪橇狗。比利被嚇過頭反而勇敢起來，奮不顧身地衝出野狗的包圍，倉皇地逃向結冰的湖面。派克和杜柏緊隨在後，隊裡其餘的狗也跟著逃走。正當巴克要跟著同伴突破重圍時，眼角的餘光卻看到史匹茲正向他衝了過來，顯然是要將他撞倒。巴克知道，一旦栽倒在這群瘋狂的愛斯基摩犬腳下，一切就完蛋了。於是他站穩腳根，硬是撐住自己，頂住史匹茲的衝撞，再追上夥伴，往湖面逃去。

之後，雪橇隊裡的九隻狗聚在一起，在樹林裡找了個藏身之地。雖然不再有任何追兵，但他們仍舊傷勢慘重。每隻狗身上都至少有四、五處的傷口，其中幾隻的傷勢十分嚴重。杜柏的一條後腿受到重創；在戴伊峽谷那邊最後加入的朵麗，喉頭被撕下了一大塊肉；喬成了獨眼龍；而個性善良的比利，一隻耳朵被咬得稀巴爛，嗚咽地哭了整個晚上。天一破曉，他們小心翼翼、一拐一拐地回到營地，發現那些打劫的傢伙已經走了，而兩個男人心情大壞，因為那群愛斯基摩犬將糧食整整吃掉了一半，連雪橇上的皮帶和帆布蓋也嚼爛了。事實上，不論有多難下嚥，所有的東西都沒能逃過一劫。他們吃掉了裴洛特的一雙鹿皮靴、一段皮韁繩，甚至連弗洪索的鞭子末端，都給吃掉了兩呎。弗洪索暫時從皮鞭受損的悲傷中抽離，過來仔細檢查他受傷的狗兒們。

「啊！我的朋友們！」他輕輕地說：「這麼重的傷，會不會將你們變成瘋狗呢？不會全瘋了吧？你說呢，裴洛特？」

那個信差搖了搖頭，沒有把握。距離多森還有四百里的路程，他可禁不起狂犬病在他的狗群中肆虐。他們邊咒罵著，邊努力收拾營區，費了兩個小時才將挽具整理好，而這群片體鱗傷的狗又繼續上路，痛苦地掙扎向前，邁向這段前往多森旅途中最為艱辛的路程。

眼前是「三十哩河」寬闊的河道，它湍急的水流尚未結凍，只有在水渦處和水流平緩的地方才有結冰。他們整整花了六天的時間，才走完這驚險的三十哩路。大家極其驚恐，不論人或狗，踏出的每一步都冒著生命危險。裴洛特小心翼翼地在前開路，有十幾次都踩破冰層、跌進河裡，每一次都是藉著竿子橫撐在洞口，他才得以活命。但此刻正巧有寒流來襲，氣溫降到零下五十度，為了保住性命，每次一掉進河裡，就必須生火將衣服給烤乾。

然而沒有一件事情可以令他氣餒，而這也是他獲選為信差的原因。他不怕任何的危險，從昏暗的黎明到漆黑的深夜，他乾瘦瘦小的臉龐堅定不移地對抗嚴酷的霜雪，沿著結冰的河岸向前奮進。每踏一步，腳下的冰層便崩塌碎裂，他們不敢多做逗留。有一次，雪橇拖著巴克和戴夫一起掉到冰河裡，等到被拖上來的時候，他們已被凍得半僵，身上結了一層厚厚的冰，幾乎快被淹死。於是為了救命，兩個人照例又生起火來，讓他們不斷地繞著火堆跑，好流下汗水來融冰。由於他們離火太近，連身上的毛也被熊熊烈火給燒焦了。

還有一次，史匹茲掉進河裡，把後面整支隊伍都拖了下去，巴克趕緊將前爪抵在滑溜的碎冰邊緣，用他全身的力量使勁地往後拉，四周的冰層不停地顫動破裂著，他後面的戴夫也用盡渾身力氣往後拉，雪橇後面的弗洪索，更是拉到渾身筋骨喀喀作響。

此刻，他們前後的冰層都裂開了，除了爬上陡峭的懸崖，別無他法。正當弗洪索祈禱神蹟降臨時，裴洛特竟然奇蹟式地爬了上去，將所有的皮帶、繩索和挽具搓成一條長繩，把狗一隻隻地吊上懸崖。等雪橇和所有的物品都吊上去之後，弗洪索才壓隊爬上去。接著，他們必須尋找一個下去懸崖的路徑，而最後還是憑藉那條長繩，才終於下

到結冰的河道，而這時，早已是暮色蒼茫。這天，他們只走了
四分之一哩的路程。

當他們抵達虎特林克後，湖上的冰層已十分厚實，巴克早
已疲憊不堪，其他的狗也好不到哪裡去。但裴洛特為了彌補先
前耽擱的時間，仍舊逼著他們繼續趕路，天未亮就啟程，直到
天黑才休息。第一天走了三十五哩路，來到了大鮭魚河；第二
天同樣走了三十五哩路，來到小鮭魚河；第三天走了四十哩
路，總算接近了五指山。

巴克的腳掌並不像愛斯基摩犬一樣結實堅硬。從他最後一
代野生的祖先被穴居或河居的人馴養的那一刻起，歷經數代，
他的腳已經軟化了。每天他都痛得一瘸一拐地跑著，營地一紮
好，他躺下來就像隻死狗一樣，動也不動。即使饑腸轆轆，也
不願起身領取自己那份魚乾，弗洪索只好親自送到他的面前。
另外，每天吃完晚餐後，弗洪索都會為巴克按摩半個小時的
腳，還割下他自己的鹿皮靴的靴統，為巴克作了四隻鞋套，大
大減輕了巴克的痛苦。一天早晨，弗洪索忘了幫巴克穿上鞋
子，他就躺在那裡，四隻腳不停地在空中揮動哀求著，不穿上
鞋子的話就不上路了。裴洛特見到這個情景，他乾癟瘦小的臉
龐都不禁露齒一笑。後來，他的腳已經硬得足以勝任艱辛的旅
程，早已破損不堪的鞋套，也就棄而不用了。

在貝里河口的一天清晨，正當他們準備套上挽具出發的時
候，從來不出風頭的多麗突然發瘋了。她發出一聲令人心碎的
長嗥，嚇得每隻狗都寒毛直豎。倏地，她朝巴克撲了過去。巴

克從沒見過瘋狗，對於瘋狗的可怕也一無所知；但他知道事情
非常不對勁，於是驚慌地逃開。他一路狂奔，而多麗口吐白
沫、氣喘吁吁地在後面追著，只要她往前一躍就撲得到；但他
始終拼命地往前奔逃，多麗也無法追上；而喪失理智的多麗，
瘋狂地追趕，讓巴克怎麼也甩不掉。就這樣，多麗追不上他，
他也甩不開多麗。巴克逃進一座島中央的樹林裡，又往低窪處
狂奔，跨過一條覆蓋碎冰的小水道，逃到另外一座島，接著又
跑上第三座島，最後又繞回來大河道上，拼命地往前衝。即便
他自始至終都沒有回頭張望，但他聽到多麗的吼叫與喘氣聲，
知道她就在一躍可及的距離。弗洪索在四分之一哩路的地方喊
他，然後他又再度折回，始終保持著一個躍身的距離，痛苦地
大口喘著氣，全心全意地希望弗洪索可以拯救他。弗洪索將手
中的斧頭高高地舉起，當巴克一經過他的身邊，斧頭便隨即劈
落，剛好將發瘋的多麗的頭顱給敲碎。

　　巴克步伐蹣跚地走向雪橇，精疲力竭地靠在上面，嗚嗚咽
咽地喘著氣。這時，史匹茲見機不可失，便撲到巴克的身上，
接連兩次用他的利齒咬進毫無抵抗能力的敵人，將巴克的肉撕
裂到深可見骨的地步。此刻弗洪索的鞭子呼嘯而至，狠狠地抽
在史匹茲的身上，巴克於是在一旁滿意地看著，隊裡有史以來
最為嚴厲的毒打。

　　「史匹茲真是個惡魔！」裴洛特說道：「他總有一天會咬
死巴克的。」

　　「巴克才是惡魔中的惡魔！」弗洪索答道：「我一直在觀

察他，對他再瞭解不過了。你等著看吧，我敢說他總有一天會發起瘋來，把史匹茲撕成碎片，再將他吐在雪地上。」

從此之後，史匹茲和巴克之間就不斷發生戰鬥。不論是身為領隊狗，或是作為隊伍裡所有公狗認同的領袖者，史匹茲感到自己的威權與地位正被這隻奇怪的南方狗威脅著。對史匹茲而言，巴克是個異類，因為他所看過的南方狗中，從沒有像巴克這樣，能在營地與苦役中有如此出色的表現。他所知道的南方狗都很柔弱，不是被辛苦的勞動累死，就是被餓死或凍死。而巴克卻是個特例，不但能挨餓受凍，連體力、狠勁和狡獪的個性，都足以和愛斯基摩犬相互匹敵。換句話說，他絕對是塊統治者的料。而他之所以變得如此危險、令人恐懼，是因為那個穿紅色套頭毛衣的男人，用棍子打掉了他支配欲中的那種盲目的勇氣與輕率的作風，轉而變成懂得狡點遮掩的野心者，憑著耐性，等待機會的來臨。

爭奪領導權的衝突遲早會爆發。這正是巴克所渴求的，這種渴望出自他的天性，來自於挽下辛勤工作而產生的那股自豪，這股難以言喻的情緒，緊緊揪住了他的心頭——為了這份自豪之情，狗兒可以獻上他們的性命，辛苦地工作直到嚥下最後一口氣，甘願死在挽具之下；如果不讓他們工作，反而會使他們感到心痛欲碎。也正是這股自豪，讓戴夫樂於當隻壓陣狗；讓索列克不遺餘力地賣命拉著雪橇。每次拔營上路時，這股自豪便駕馭、支配著他們，讓他們從一群乖戾殘暴的野犬，轉而成為勤奮上進、積極進取的良犬。白天，這股自豪驅使著

第三章

他們勇往直前，但當黑夜來臨，紮營休息時，這股自豪卻又消失殆盡，讓他們再度沉浸在陰鬱的不安與不滿之中。這股自豪，激發了史匹茲強烈的責任感，加以懲罰那些在行程中搗亂、偷懶，或在早晨該套上挽具時偷溜的傢伙。因為這股自豪，他害怕巴克會取代他的地位成為領袖狗，相對的這也正是巴克深感驕傲之處。

他開始公然挑戰史匹茲的領袖地位，故意在史匹茲和應該受懲戒的傢伙們間挑撥離間。有天夜裡下了場大雪，隔天早上，裝病鬼派克卻不見了，安然地躲在積雪一呎深的雪洞裡，任憑弗洪索怎麼喊他、找他，也徒勞無功。史匹茲簡直氣瘋了，怒氣沖沖地跑遍整個營區，四處嗅著，挖掘每一個可疑的藏身之處。他憤怒的咆哮聲，嚇得派克躲在雪洞裡渾身發抖。

最後，史匹茲還是將派克從雪洞裡挖了出來。當史匹茲正要撲上前去懲罰他時，巴克卻突然也同樣怒不可遏地衝到他們之間。由於事出意料，加上巴克的動作十分敏捷，史匹茲因而被撞得四腳朝天，往後倒栽。原本卑躬屈膝、渾身顫抖的派克，一看到這樣公開的反叛，也壯起膽子來，撲向倒在地上的領袖身上。而巴克，早就忘了什麼叫做公平的遊戲規則，也向史匹茲撲上前去。目睹這個突發事件，弗洪索心裡竊笑個不停，不過仍是毫不遲疑且公正地執法，揮起鞭子朝巴克身上打去。但這猛力的一抽，仍舊無法將巴克從倒臥在地的史匹茲身上驅離，於是弗洪索改用鞭子的手柄猛敲，打得巴克暈頭轉向，頭暈目眩地往後退開。史匹茲也將一再犯錯的派克給結結

實實地教訓了一頓。

接下來的幾天，隨著多森愈來愈近，巴克依舊妨礙史匹茲執法；不過他學聰明了，都趁弗洪索不在的時候才幹。由於巴克暗地裡的反抗行為，狗隊裡的動亂也隨之越來越盛，只有戴夫和索列克不為所動，其他的隊員則是愈加放肆，行為越變越糟。他們爭執不斷，麻煩事層出不窮，而這一切的主謀都是巴克，搞得弗洪索手忙腳亂的，擔心兩隻狗之間的生死搏鬥遲早會發生；有好幾個夜晚，當他聽見狗群的喧鬧聲時，總是趕緊鑽出被窩察看，唯恐是巴克和史匹茲在決鬥。

然而，時機一直沒有成熟。在一個陰暗的下午，他們抵達多森，這場大戰卻還在醞釀。多森裡不僅人多，還有數不清的狗，巴克發現他們都在工作著，就好像是狗天生註定要工作一樣。他們排成一列列縱隊，整天拉著挽繩在街上來來往往，甚至到了深夜，都還聽得到他們身上的鈴鐺叮噹作響。他們將木屋材料和柴火運到礦場裡去。這些工作，在聖塔克蕾拉山谷裡全是由馬匹來做的。巴克偶爾遇到南方來的狗，不過大多數仍是那些像狼一般的愛斯基摩犬。每天晚上九點、十二點、以及清晨三點，這些狗會準時高聲唱起一種神祕的夜頌，有著奇特且詭異的調子，巴克也十分高興地加入他們。

天上的北極光閃耀著冷冽的光芒，繁星隨著紛飛的雪花跳動著，在冰雪的覆蓋下，大地一片麻木死寂，而這群愛斯基摩犬的歌聲，像是對生命的反抗，只是陰沉的小調，伴隨著深長的嘆息與嗚咽的抽泣，更像是在傾訴著生命的哀傷，以及生存的痛苦艱難。這是一首古老的歌曲,和他們的族群一樣古老,是遠古世界裡最早出現的一首悲歌。曲調中蘊含著無數世代的悲慟,使得巴克莫名地心神不寧。當他嗚咽哀泣時,就如同他原始的祖先們傾訴著內心的哀痛;他對於嚴寒與黑夜的恐懼,也正是祖先們曾經懷有的恐懼與神祕感受。這首歌之所以深深地引起他的共鳴,正說明了雖然他前幾代的祖先曾受到爐火與房屋的庇護,但是現在,他正朝著本性回溯,回歸到他的祖先們在野蠻的時代所開創的最原始的生活。

　　抵達道森後的第七天,他們沿著貝勒庫斯旁陡峭的河岸上了育空雪道,朝戴伊峽谷和鹽水鎮前進。裴洛特回程所運送的公文,似乎比來程帶的公文還要緊急,加上他自豪於自己的旅途經驗,使得他決心挑戰本年度的旅程紀錄。對此,有幾件事情都對他有利。經過一個星期的休養,狗兒們已經恢復體力、情況良好。而他們先前所開闢的雪道,也已經被之後的旅客踏得更結實了。除此之外,警方也設了兩三個休息站,放置了人與狗的糧食,所以他們可以輕裝踏上回程了。

　　他們第一天就跑了五十哩路,來到「六十哩河」;第二天,又飛快地奔馳在育空河道上,直往貝里而去。然而,對弗洪索來說,這樣出色的成績,並不代表一路上就沒有需要他操心的麻煩事。巴克暗中主導著叛變,已經將狗隊的團結破壞殆盡,不再像以前一樣萬眾一心地拉著雪橇了。巴克帶給這些反抗者種種不良的示範,史匹茲再也不是令他們敬畏的領袖了,取而代之的是大家對他威權的挑釁。一天晚上,派克在巴克的庇護下，搶了他半條魚吞進肚裡。又有一晚，杜柏和喬聯合起來攻擊他，逼迫他放棄原本他們應受的懲罰。甚至連一向溫馴的比利，脾氣也沒那麼好了，嗚嗚的討好聲也不像以前那麼巴結奉承了。每次巴克接近史匹茲的時候，總是毛髮直豎、齜牙咧嘴地怒吼著以示威脅。事實上，巴克的態度已近乎欺凌霸道了，時常在史匹茲的面前，目中無人、趾高氣昂地走來走去。

紀律的敗壞，也影響了狗與狗之間的關係。他們的吵鬧越來越頻繁，營區時常爆發一片亂哄哄的嘈叫。戴夫和索列克仍舊不為所動，但也常被毫無停止跡象的喧鬧惹得心煩意亂。弗洪索氣得大聲咒罵，暴跳如雷地在雪地上急跺腳，還揪著自己的頭髮。他的鞭子從沒停止抽打狗群，但絲毫起不了什麼作用，只要他一轉過身子，他們又開始鬧了起來。他用鞭子來為史匹茲撐腰，而巴克卻同時在暗地裡支持其他的狗。弗洪索知道這一切都是巴克在暗中搞鬼，巴克也知道弗洪索明白內情，但他十分機警狡猾，絕對不再給他當場逮個正著的機會。套上挽具，他忠實勤懇地工作，因為這項苦役早已變成他的樂趣。不過，暗中煽動夥伴打上一場、將挽繩攪得糾纏不已，似乎更加有趣。

一天夜裡，在塔基納河口吃過晚飯之後，杜柏發現一隻雪兔，他笨拙地撲了過去，沒有抓到。一瞬間，狗隊所有的狗吵鬧地追了起來，連百碼外西北警局營地裡的五十隻愛斯基摩犬，也加入追逐的行列。那隻兔子沿著小河逃了下去，轉進一條小溪，在冰凍的河面上輕快敏捷地奔馳著，而狗群一跑就陷入積雪裡，追得十分吃力。巴克率領著這六十隻狗竭盡所能地追著，轉了一圈又一圈，卻還是抓不到兔子。他俯身疾馳，熱切焦急地低吼，健美的身軀在銀白皎潔的月光下飛馳、跳躍著。而那隻雪兔彷彿是白雪的精靈，一蹦一跳地始終在巴克的面前飛跑著。

由於古老本能的驅使，人類離開喧囂的城市，走向森林或原野，使用化學製造的鉛彈大肆殘殺生命。這種嗜血的慾望和殺戮的樂趣，正是巴克此刻的寫照，更是他內心深處早已具備、再熟悉不過的激情。他正率領著隊伍追捕著獵物，想用自己的利齒撕裂這個活生生的軀體，將嘴巴深深浸入溫熱的血液裡，進而沾滿整個臉龐。

那種狂喜象徵生命的巔峰，也是生命難以超越的狀態。這就是生活中的矛盾之處。這樣的瘋狂狀態，只有當一個人最為生氣蓬勃的時候才會顯露，然而，此時此刻，也正是一個人將生命完全置之度外之時。如此迷亂忘我的狀態，讓藝術家點燃烈焰並任其吞噬自己；讓戰場上打得發狂的士兵，拒絕撤退；而也正是這種狂喜的緣故，巴克領著隊伍，如狼般嗥叫，在月光下拼命追趕那隻迅速奔逃的獵物。他從內心深處潛藏的本性裡發出叫聲，那叫聲帶領著他回溯到遠古生命的最初。純粹的生命之源與感官的震撼全然地支配他，每塊肌肉、每個關節、每條韌帶，都感受到至高無上的狂喜，那種興奮之情既狂熱又猛烈，使他在繁星夜空下、死寂的大地上恣意地奔馳。

然而，即便是最為興奮的狀態，史匹茲依舊能保持冷靜且精於算計。他脫離隊伍,從河流轉彎處抄捷徑到了前面。巴克對此並不知情,當他轉過河灣時,依舊跟在那白色鬼魅般飛奔的兔子之後,他看到另一個更大的白色魅影,從突出的河岸上飛身而下,攔住了兔子的去路。那是史匹茲。兔子來不及轉身,雪白的利齒在空中咬碎了牠背脊,牠發出像人類被擊中時的巨大哀嚎聲。那哀嚎,就像是死神在生命的最高峰處奪走性命時的宣告。巴克後頭的狗群,聽到這聲哀嚎,頓時爆出陣陣愉快的狂吠。

巴克並沒有叫喊出聲,也不停下腳步,直接往史匹茲衝了過去。但由於衝勁過猛,肩膀撞在一塊,反而沒有咬到史匹茲的喉嚨。他們交纏在鬆軟的雪地上接連翻滾,史匹茲很快地穩住身子站了起來,彷彿從沒被撞倒過一樣,迅速地咬住了巴克的肩膀又跳開。他後退站穩腳步,牙齒像是捕獸夾的鋸齒一般緊緊鉗住,嘴唇斜斜地往上翻,齜牙咧嘴地怒吼著。

在那一瞬間,巴克突然明白了,他和史匹茲決一死鬥的時機已然來臨。他們彼此兜著圈子,耳朵往後倒貼,互相咆哮著,伺機尋找有利的機會以便出手。眼前這個情景,讓巴克驀地產生一種似曾相識的熟悉感——那片白雪皚皚的樹林、大地與月光,還有令人顫慄的奮戰。一種陰森恐怖的靜穆籠罩著這片雪白與寂靜,空氣中連一絲最微弱的風也沒有,所有的東西彷彿都靜止不動,連樹葉也都寂然,狗群呼出的熱氣清晰可見,裊裊上升,在冰冷的空氣中縈繞不散。這群像狼一般、充滿野性的狗,早已迅速地解決了那隻雪兔;而現在,他們圍成

一個圓圈，同樣靜靜地等待著，只有眼中閃爍著熱切的光芒，與緩緩上升的氣息。對巴克而言，這幅彷若遠古時代的景象，一點兒也不陌生，好像習以為常般地，毫無新奇之處。

史匹茲是個經驗豐富的戰士，從史匹茲柏根群島到北極，橫越了加拿大和貝倫斯荒地，無論面對何種敵人，他總是能堅守陣地，更能成功地奪取主導權。他滿腔怒火，但絕對不盲目。當他一心想要撕裂敵人、摧毀他們的時候，也絕不忘記他的敵人同樣地渴望消滅自己。尚未準備好迎接襲擊前，他絕不襲擊敵人；尚未準備好抵禦攻擊前，他絕不莽撞攻擊敵手。

巴克企圖咬住這隻大白狗的脖子，卻都徒勞無功，任憑他的利齒對準的是柔軟的血肉，總是會受到史匹茲尖牙的阻擋。雙方利齒互相撞擊在一起，咬得唇破血流，然而巴克還是無法突破對方的防線。他再度做好準備，將史匹茲包圍進他設下的突擊範圍，一次又一次地想咬住那雪白的喉嚨，那裡是最靠近生命之泉的部位，但每一次都是史匹茲咬中他後又安然退開。接著，巴克假裝要往喉嚨攻去，頭卻突然往後收，改從側邊攻擊，用肩膀撞向史匹茲的肩膀，想要像鐘錘一般將他撞倒。不料，情況卻正好相反，每一次都是史匹茲咬傷巴克的肩膀，再輕巧敏捷地跳開。

史匹茲毫髮未傷，巴克卻渾身是血、氣喘吁吁。這場戰爭漸漸到了攸關性命的時候，外圍狼樣的狗群則靜靜等待其中一方倒下，結束戰事。當巴克上氣不接下氣的時候，史匹茲不斷地猛攻衝撞，使他幾乎站不穩身子。一次，巴克被撞得翻了個觔斗，圍繞成圈的六十隻狗倏地挺直身軀，不過他幾乎在半空中就已經穩住自己，於是那些狗又再度俯低身子繼續等待。

然而，巴克擁有一項天生的卓越資質——想像力。他能憑著本能戰鬥，也可以靠頭腦打仗。他衝上前去，像是在重施故技要撞向肩膀，但在最後那一刹那，卻突然將身子壓得極低，貼著雪地衝了過去，一口咬住了史匹茲的左前腿，一時間傳出骨頭碎裂的喀擦聲，而這隻大白狗就只剩三隻腳來對付敵人了。巴克接下來又試了三次，假裝要撞倒他時又故技重施，將他的右前腿也給咬斷。史匹茲痛苦不堪，處境絕望，拼命掙扎想要爬起站穩。他看到那圈靜靜等待著的狗群，眼神發亮，舌頭伸得長長的，呼出的白色熱氣裊裊上升，漸漸地收攏過來，向他逼近，就像過去他擊敗對手時的景象。只不過，這次他成了那個戰敗者。

史匹茲已經沒有任何希望了。此時的巴克變得冷酷無情，計畫著最後一擊。過去保有的憐憫心，就讓它留在溫暖的南方吧。他感覺到圈子逐漸收攏，左右兩邊都能察覺那些愛斯基摩犬的呼吸。他可以看到史匹茲背後與兩旁的愛斯基摩犬，伏低著身子，眼睛緊緊地盯在史匹茲的身上，一副蓄勢待發的模樣。時間似乎在刹那間停止了，所有的狗彷彿變成了石頭，動也不動，只有史匹茲渾身顫抖、前後搖晃，全身毛髮聳立，發出威脅的怒吼，似乎想要嚇退已經逼近眼前的死亡。這個時候，巴克倏地撲了上去，終於用肩膀撞到了對方的肩膀。然後，在灑滿月光的雪地上，原本黑暗的圓圈收攏成一個黑點，

野性的呼喚

史匹茲自此消失無蹤。巴克站在一旁冷眼旁觀著，這個勝利的
戰士，這個擁有原始統治慾望的野獸，完成他的第一次屠殺，
嚐到了殺戮與勝利的甜美滋味。

第四章

勝者為王

「我說的沒錯吧！巴克才是魔鬼中的魔鬼！」

隔天一早，弗洪索發現史匹茲不見蹤影，而巴克渾身是傷的時候，他這麼說道。他將巴克拉到火堆旁邊，藉著火光一邊指著他佈滿全身的傷痕。

「史匹茲打起架來還真狠！」裴洛特檢視著那些撕裂的傷口，這麼說道。

「這個巴克打得更狠吧！」弗洪索答道。「這下我們總算能平靜了。沒有了史匹茲，當然也就沒有麻煩了。」

裴洛特將營具收好放到雪橇上，弗洪索則是為狗套上挽具。巴克快步走到原先史匹茲擔任領隊狗的位置上，但弗洪索並不理會，他判斷索列克應是目前狗隊中最佳領隊狗，反而將索列克帶到這個令他垂涎的位置。巴克憤怒地撲到索列克身上，將他趕走，自己站到領隊狗的位置上。

「欵？欵！」弗洪索大聲喊著，愉快地拍拍大腿。「你看巴克！這傢伙以為幹掉史匹茲，就可以取代他的位置啦！」

「噓！走開！」他叫道，但是巴克拒絕挪動身子。

　　弗洪索才不管巴克威脅的怒吼聲，拎起他頸背上的皮，將他拉到一旁，再度換上索列克。這隻老狗不喜歡這個新位置，也明顯地表示出害怕巴克的模樣。弗洪索非常固執己見，但是他一轉身，巴克就又趕走了索列克，而索列克也很樂意離開那個位置。

　　弗洪索火大了。「去你的，看我怎麼修理你！」他大叫，回來時手裡多了根粗棍子。

　　巴克想起了那個穿紅色套頭毛衣的男人，慢慢地往後退了開來。當索列克又被帶到前面時，他不再企圖擠上去，不過卻待在棍子正好打不到的地方，憤怒難當地咆哮著。他一邊圍著弗洪索繞著圈子，一邊緊緊盯著那根棍子，好在弗洪索打過來時趕緊閃開，因為他實在太瞭解棍子的厲害了。

　　弗洪索繼續他的工作，然後叫巴克回到原來的位置，也就是戴夫的前面。巴克向後退了兩三步，弗洪索向前追上去，巴克又往後退。幾次反覆之後，弗洪索以為巴克是害怕挨打，便丟掉手中的棍子。巴克卻公然起而反抗，並非因為怕挨棍子，而是要得到領隊狗的位置。那是他的權利，是他掙來的，不給他應得的他心有不甘。

　　裴洛特也過來幫忙，兩個人追著巴克跑來跑去，折騰了半個多小時。他們用棍子丟他，他就敏捷地閃開。他們大聲咒罵他，從他的祖宗八代，罵到他的子孫以及更遙遠的後代，甚至詛咒他身上的每一根毛髮、血管裡的每一滴血液，巴克則以咆哮聲回敬，始終保持在他們逮不到的距離。他並不想逃跑，只

在營地裡繞來繞去，清楚明白地表示，只要如他所願，他就會乖乖歸隊。

弗洪索坐下來，直抓頭皮。裴洛特看了看錶，大聲咒罵了起來。時間飛逝，他們早該在一個小時前就上路了。弗洪索又抓了抓頭皮，搖搖頭，朝裴洛特傻傻地笑了笑。裴洛特也聳了聳肩，表示他們被打敗了。於是，弗洪索走到索列克的位置，招呼巴克過去。巴克笑了，用一種狗特有的方式，可是還是保持距離。弗洪索解開索列克的挽繩，帶他回自己的老位置去。現在狗隊已經套好挽具，在雪橇前排好縱隊準備上路了，除了最前面的領隊位置，已經沒有其他地方留給巴克了。弗洪索再次叫巴克過去，結果他笑了笑，還是不過來。

「丟掉你的棍子。」裴洛特吩咐道。

弗洪索扔了棍子，於是巴克快跑步過來，露出勝利的笑容，大搖大擺地站到隊伍的最前面。等他一套好挽繩，兩個男人也催駕了起來，雪橇隊伍旋即奔馳在河床的雪道上。

弗洪索對巴克的評價原本就很高，認為他有魔鬼般的能力，而這天啟程才不久，弗洪索就發現自己還是低估他了。當上領隊的巴克，盡心盡力作好自己份內的工作，他的判斷力強，反應靈敏，動作極為迅速，表現明顯地凌駕於史匹茲之上，而弗洪索原先以為史匹茲已經是他見過最棒的狗了。

尤其是在制定規則要求同伴遵守這點上面，巴克更為出色。戴夫和索列克毫不關心領導權的變更，那種事根本就和他們無關。他們只管賣命工作、辛勤地拉雪橇就夠了，除非工作受到干擾，否則他們才不在乎，就算是好脾氣的比利來當領袖都沒關係，只要他能維持秩序就好。但是在史匹茲最後一段執權的日子裡，隊裡其他的狗已變得無法無天了，現在巴克要開始整頓他們，他們莫不大吃一驚。

派克的位置緊跟在巴克之後，往常工作時懶惰成性，除非逼不得已，否則從不肯多花一絲力氣拉雪橇。可是現在不斷受到巴克的處罰，這天都還沒結束，他已經是空前地賣力了。第一天晚上在營地裡，脾氣最乖戾的喬也被狠狠地教訓了一頓，這是以往史匹茲做不到的。巴克只消利用體重的優勢，壓得他喘不過氣來，再咬得他停止亂動、嗚咽求饒才罷休。

狗隊很快就恢復了昔日的團結一致，在挽繩下的夥伴，又像從前一樣，像一條狗似的保持相同步調奔馳了。到達林克急流區時，又加入了兩條當地的愛斯基摩犬迪克和庫納，巴克迅速地收服了他們，讓他們進入情況，快得連弗洪索都不敢置信。

「有哪一條狗比得上巴克啊！」弗洪索叫道。「沒有，絕對沒有啊！他甚至值得一千塊呢！你說是不是啊，裴洛特？」

裴洛特點點頭。這天他已經刷新旅行的紀錄了，而且速度一天比一天快。雪道的狀況良好，堅硬結實，而且最近沒有下雪，天氣也不會太過寒冷，氣溫降到零下五十度之後便維持穩定，直到全程結束為止。兩個男人輪流坐雪橇，狗兒們全速向前奔躍著，途中極少停下休息。

「三十哩河」的河面覆著厚實的冰層，他們只花了一天的時間就走完這段路，而來時卻整整花上十天。他們一口氣跑了六十哩路，從拉霸傑湖到白馬急湍，穿越馬許、塔基斯和博奈特（綿延七十哩長的湖泊區）。他們前進的速度飛快，所以在雪橇後面的人，都緊緊抓住繩子尾端，任由雪橇拖著向前奔馳。第二個禮拜的最後一個晚上，他們爬上了白峰嶺，藉著腳下史蓋圭市和海上船隻的燈光，沿著海岸的斜坡下山。

這趟旅程打破了以往的紀錄。十四天以來，他們平均日行四十哩路。足足三天的時間，裴洛特和弗洪索昂首挺胸地走在史蓋圭市的大街上，大夥都爭先請他們喝酒，狗隊也變成鎮上所有馭犬夫注目的焦點，受到眾多的讚賞。後來，有三、四個西部來的壞蛋企圖洗劫鎮上，反而被子彈打得渾身是傷，滿身窟窿像胡椒瓶似的，大家的注意力才被轉移。之後，政府的公文又下來了，兩個男人必須調至他處。弗洪索將巴克叫到腳邊，緊緊地摟住他，伏在他身上痛哭著。這是巴克最後一次見到弗洪索和裴洛特，從此之後，他們就像其他人一樣，永遠從巴克的生命中消失了。

一個蘇格蘭混血兒接管了照料巴克和他的同伴，與其他十幾支狗隊一同上路，再度踏上那條枯燥乏味的旅程回去道森。因為這是一輛郵車，裝載著來自世界各地的郵件，要寄給那些在北極淘金的人們。所以，這回沒有辦法輕鬆地奔馳，也沒能刷新紀錄，只有拖著一車沉重的負擔，每天痛苦艱辛地拖行。

巴克不喜歡這種工作，但他仿效戴夫和索列克那種以工作為榮的精神，除了盡好本分，也監督同伴盡忠職守，不管他們是否也以此為榮。每天的生活極其單調乏味，像是機器運轉般

規律，日復一日，一成不變。每天早上到了一定時候，廚伕就
會起床生火，然後就是早餐時間。接著吃完早餐，有的人拆
營，有的人將狗套上挽具，在破曉前一小時就上路。夜裡紮營
時，有的人搭帳篷，有的人砍著柴火或削木屑舖床，其他的人
就幫忙廚伕挑水運冰。當然，還會有人餵狗。這對狗兒們而
言，這才是一天中的大事。吃完魚後，他們可以和其他狗隊的
狗一起溜達，散步個一小時左右。那些狗總共有一百多條，其
中不乏兇猛好戰之士，在巴克和其中最兇猛的那隻鬥過三次之
後，隨即取得主宰的霸權地位，只要他一聳立毛髮，齜牙咧
嘴，其他的狗便慌忙閃避。

　　但巴克最喜歡的事，莫過於躺在火堆旁邊，蜷曲著後腿，
前腳向前伸展，仰著頭，望著跳動的火光，若有所思地眨著眼
睛。有時，他會想起那個陽光普照的聖塔克蕾拉山谷，裡頭那
棟米勒法官的大宅院，想起那個水泥砌成的游泳槽，那隻墨西
哥無毛犬伊莎貝爾，還有那隻日本哈巴狗杜斯。然而，他更常
想到那個身穿紅色套頭毛衣的男人、柯麗的死與史匹茲之間的
生死決鬥，以及他吃過或想吃的美味食物。他並沒有得思鄉
病，記憶中那片陽光明媚的家鄉模糊且遙遠，對他而言早已毫
無感覺。相較之下，那種遺傳在血液中的記憶卻更加強而有
力，即便從未見過的景物，竟是那麼地熟悉、似曾相識。那曾
經一度消失的本能，因循著腦海中祖先的印記幻化成習性，如
今在他的體內甦醒過來，再次復活了。

　　有時，他蜷縮在火堆旁邊，望著火焰眨著眼睛，眼神迷

矇，感覺眼前的火焰像是另外一堆火，而混血兒廚伕也變成了
另外一個完全陌生的人。那個人短腿長臂，筋肉糾結而不圓
腫，長長的頭髮糾纏在一起，覆蓋了整個頭部，只露出一雙眼
睛。他發出奇怪的聲音，似乎懼怕黑暗，不斷地窺向暗處，長
長的手臂垂到小腿邊，手裡抓著一根尾端綁著一塊大石頭的棍
子。除了肩頭掛著一塊焦黑破爛的獸皮，他幾乎是赤裸著身
體。他身上毛髮濃密，像是胸肩之處，還有手臂和大腿外側，
看起來像是另外一塊獸皮。他並不是挺直著站立，而是前傾著
上半身，雙膝彎曲。他的身體像貓一樣極富彈性，警覺性靈

敏，對有形無形的事情都滿懷恐懼。

　　有時，這個毛茸茸的人蹲在火堆旁邊，抱頭埋在兩腿間睡覺。這時，他會將雙肘靠在膝蓋上，兩手緊抱著頭部，彷彿在用毛髮濃密的胳膊遮著雨。在火堆後那片漆黑裡，巴克看見許多閃閃發光的炭火，總是兩個兩個一起，他知道那是野獸的眼睛，他能聽見他們穿越樹叢的劈啪聲，以及黑暗中發出的騷動聲。在育空河畔，他又瞇視著火焰懶洋洋地做夢，這些聲音和景象還是讓他頸背上的毛髮直聳，不禁發出低吟，輕聲咆哮著，直到那個混血兒廚伕對他喊著：「喂！巴克，醒一醒！」於是，那另一個世界便從眼前消失，真實的世界重回眼簾。他爬起身子，伸一伸懶腰，打個呵欠，彷彿大夢初醒一般。

　　這趟旅程十分艱辛，身後沉重的郵件拖得他們精疲力竭、疲憊不堪。當他們抵達道森的時候，體力已經透支，身形也削瘦不少，起碼需要七到十天的休息時間才能恢復。但是，兩天之後他們又啓程了，負載著一整車寄往外地的郵件，從貝瑞克斯順著育空河岸往下走。狗兒們疲憊至極，趕狗的人也是滿腹怨氣，更糟糕的是，每天都下雪，讓地面十分鬆軟，摩擦力更大，狗兒需要花更多的力氣拖拉雪橇。幸而趕狗的人始終都待他們不錯，盡最大的努力來照顧他們。

　　每天晚上，都是狗兒們比馭犬夫還先吃晚餐。此外，每個人都先將自己的狗從頭到腳檢查一遍之後，才會更衣睡覺。即便如此，狗兒們的體力仍舊逐漸衰退。入冬以來，他們已經趕了一千八百哩的路程，即使是最健壯的狗，也經不起這樣的折

磨。巴克儘管疲憊不堪，仍是硬撐著自己，督促同伴工作、維持紀律。比利每天晚上睡覺時總是會嗚咽哀嚎。喬比以前更乖戾了，而索列克現在無論是不是瞎眼的那邊，都不讓其他狗接近了。

然而，最為痛苦的就是戴夫了。他的身體有些不對勁，變得更加陰鬱暴躁，一紮營就立刻挖洞躺下，趕狗的人必須拿食物到窩裡去餵他。只要挽具一卸下，他就會臥倒在地，一直到隔天早上套挽具的時候才會起來。有時當雪橇突然煞住或啟動，而稍微用力牽動挽繩時，他就會痛苦地大叫。趕狗的人仔細檢查他全身上下，仍是找不到原因。所有的馭犬夫都十分關心他的病情，不管是吃飯或是睡前抽最後一根煙時，都在討論著這件事。一天晚上，大家幫他做了一次會診，將他從窩裡面移到火堆旁邊，在他身上這裡壓壓、那裡戳戳的，痛得他哀嚎連連。他身體裡面確實出了點問題，但是大家連根斷骨頭也找不到，不曉得究竟是哪裡出了毛病。

抵達卡西亞沙洲的時候，他已經衰弱得一再地摔倒在挽繩底下。那個蘇格蘭混血兒叫雪橇隊停下，將他從隊伍裡拉出來，讓原本在他前面的索列克頂替他的位置。他想讓戴夫先休息一下，跟在雪橇隊後面跑就好了。但即使病成這樣，戴夫卻對被拉出隊伍感到十分憤怒，當挽具被卸下的時候，他發出不滿的噪叫聲；而看到索列克站在他長年工作的位置時，更是心碎地哭泣著。他一向以在雪道上辛勤地拉著雪橇奔馳而自豪，即使病死，也不能忍受別的狗頂替他的工作。

當雪橇開始滑動後，他在雪道旁鬆軟的雪地上奮力地跑著，一邊用牙齒去咬索列克，衝撞著他，想將他推到另一邊鬆軟的雪中，拼命地想跳進韁繩裡面，插進索列克和雪橇之間，卻不斷痛苦地哀嚎著。那個蘇格蘭混血兒試圖揮著鞭子趕他走，但他卻無視於鞭痛，而那個男人也狠不下心用力打他。戴夫不肯乖乖地跟在雪橇後面，在已被輾平的雪道上輕鬆地跑，卻繼續在最難走的鬆軟雪地裡拼命掙扎前進，直到筋疲力盡、不支倒地為止。當長長的雪橇隊經過身邊，他躺在跌倒的地方，悲傷地長嗥。

　　他用殘餘的一點精力爬起來，蹣跚地跟在隊伍的後面跑，直到雪橇隊再次停下休息時才趕上。他掙扎著越過幾輛雪橇，回到自己的車隊，站到索列克旁─那原本屬於他的位置。馭犬夫跟後面的人借火點菸，因而耽擱了一會兒。當他回來準備趕狗上路時，狗兒們向前一衝，發現毫不費力，大夥驚訝地停了下來，不安地回頭看，馭犬夫也吃了一驚，因為雪橇根本就沒移動，還停在原地。他叫同伴過來看發生了什麼事——原來戴夫咬斷了索列克兩端的挽繩，自己站在雪橇前面，他本來的崗位上。

　　他帶著懇求的目光，希望馭犬夫能允許他留在自己的位置上。馭犬夫不知該如何是好，他的同伴說道，如果拒絕讓狗工作的話，他會因此心碎而死。他們還回想起記憶中的這類例子，有些狗因年邁或傷殘，不適合工作後被解下挽繩，結果卻因此死去。既然戴夫遲早會死，就應該讓他心滿意足且無憾地

死在挽繩下。於是他又再次套上了挽具，如同往常般驕傲地拉起了雪橇。雖然不只一次，體內的劇痛讓他忍不住哀嚎出來。有幾次他跌倒後被韁繩拖著往前走，甚至有一次被雪橇輾過，讓他瘸了一條後腿。

　　儘管如此，他仍堅持跑到紮營的地方。馭犬夫在火堆旁邊為他做了一個窩，隔天清晨，發現他已經衰弱到無法再上路了，套挽具時，他卻企圖走到馭犬夫跟前。他全身抽搐著掙扎地想站起身來，但隨即搖搖晃晃地又倒下了。他慢慢地朝著正在套著挽具的同伴爬去，用他的前腳往前伸，再拖著身體往前挪動幾吋。但他已經耗盡所有的力氣了，同伴們最後一眼看到他躺在雪地中喘著氣，依依不捨地望著他們。即使他們走到河邊樹林，看不到他了，卻仍舊可以聽見他悲傷的哀嚎聲。

　　雪橇隊停了下來，那個蘇格蘭混血兒慢慢地走回剛才離開的營地。所有的人停止談話，聽到「砰」地一聲槍響。過了不久，那個男人快步跑回來，鞭子又劈啪地揮了起來，雪橇上的鈴鐺也叮噹作響，隊伍繼續沿著雪道往前邁進。然而，巴克知道，所有的狗也都知道，剛剛在樹林後面發生了什麼事。

第五章

挽繩與雪道

　　離開道森一個月後，巴克和夥伴們拖著鹽水鎮的郵件雪橇，終於抵達了史凱威。他們的狀況淒慘，個個筋疲力盡，幾近潰倒的地步。巴克的體重原本有一百四十磅，現在瘦得只剩一百一十五磅，其他的狗本來體重就比較輕，相對減少的體重也比他還多。那個裝病鬼派克，以往經常佯裝腳痛，現在則是真的瘸腿了。索列克也是一瘸一拐的，杜柏則是扭傷了一邊的肩胛骨。

　　他們的腳疼痛至極，已經失去了任何彈力，步伐沉重地落在雪道上面，全身痛得劇烈震動，因而倍感疲累。他們沒有生病，只是疲乏到了極點。這種疲乏不是短時間過度勞累造成、休息個幾小時就可以恢復，而是一連好幾個月來的苦工，使得體力慢慢消逝，甚至連復原的力量也已經消耗殆盡，一滴也不剩。每一塊肌肉，每一根纖維，乃至每一個細胞，都已經累垮了，徹底的累了。這當然事出有因。他們在不到五個月的時間裡，總共跑了兩千五百哩路，而在最後一千八百哩的旅程之中，他們只休息了五天。抵達史凱威時，他們已然精疲力盡，幾乎拉不直韁繩，在下坡的時候，也只能讓雪橇先行滑下，如此才不至於被壓到。

「繼續走吧，可憐的痛腳！」他們蹣跚地走在史凱威的大街上時，馭犬夫激勵著他們。「這是最後一段路了，然後就可以休息個夠了。這是真的，我們可以休息好一陣子！」

馭犬夫滿心待期待一段長期的休息，因為他們自己也是走了一千兩百哩的路，才得到兩天的休息，按理說自然應該好好休個假。然而，湧入庫倫戴克的人實在是太多了，而隻身前來沒有隨行的情人、妻子、和親戚陪伴的人更是無法估計，因此堆積的信件幾乎像阿爾卑斯山那般地高，更別提還有往返的政府公文。所以，一批從新赫德遜灣來的狗，要取代這群已經不中用的狗了；而這群沒有利用價值的狗，就只能賤價賣出。

三天過去了，巴克和他的夥伴們才知道自己累到什麼地步。第四天早上，兩個美國來的傢伙，沒花幾個錢就買下了他們和挽具及所有的東西。這兩個人彼此稱呼對方為「哈爾」和「查理斯」。查理斯是個中年人，膚色蒼白，兩隻眼睛水汪汪地卻缺乏神彩，往上翹的鬍子與那鬆弛下垂的嘴角恰好形成強烈對比。哈爾是個年方十九、二十的小夥子，腰帶上掛著一把柯爾特左輪手槍和一把獵刀，子彈閘也鼓鼓的裝滿子彈。這條皮帶是他身上最引人注目的東西，充分顯露出他的不成熟。這兩個與此地格格不入的人，為什麼會到北方冒險，實在令人難以理解。

巴克聽到討價還價的聲音，又看到他們把錢交給政府雇

員，就清楚地明白到，那個蘇格蘭混血兒，還有那些駕駛郵件雪橇的馭犬夫，正如同裴洛特、弗洪索和其他之前離開的人一樣，也要繼他們之後從此走出他的生命。巴克和他的夥伴一起被趕到新主人的營地，只見眼前一片狼藉，帳篷只搭了一半，碗盤也沒洗，一切都凌亂無序；他還看到一個女人，男人叫她美希黛茲，是查理斯的太太，也是哈爾的姊姊 —— 還真是美滿的一家子啊！

巴克憂慮忡忡地看著他們開始卸下帳篷，把所有的東西都搬上雪橇。他們看起來一副賣力工作的樣子，卻是毫無條理。帳篷被笨拙地捲了起來，比應該捲成的體積還大上三倍；錫製碗盤連洗都沒有就收了起來。美西黛茲不斷地在兩個男人之間晃來晃去，一直嘮叨個不停，還不時提出忠告和主意。他們將一隻裝衣服的大袋子放在雪橇前面，她卻認為應該擺在後面。因此他們照辦將之擺在後頭，又在上面堆了兩捆其他包裹，她這時卻發現一些剛剛遺漏的東西，非得擺在那只袋子裡面不可，他們只好又將行李給通通搬下來。

隔壁的帳篷裡走出三個男人，在一旁看著熱鬧，彼此擠眉弄眼地嘲笑著他們。

「你們的行李已經裝得夠多啦！本來我是不應該多管閒事的，不過，我如果是你們的話，我就不會帶著帳篷走的。」其中一個說。

「這簡直太難以想像了！」美希黛茲優雅地揮著手，做作地驚呼著。「沒有一頂帳篷的話，我可得怎麼辦啊？」

「現在是春天了，天氣不會再轉冷了。」那男人答道。

她堅決地搖了搖頭。於是，查理斯和哈爾又將最後一些零星的物品，放到已經是堆積如山的雪橇上面去。

「你們覺得這樣拖得動嗎？」三個男人中的一個又問。

「為什麼不行？」查理斯相當不耐煩地反問。

「喔，可以、當然可以！」那個人趕緊順著他的意思說：「我只是好奇罷了！它看起來有點頭重腳輕。」

查理斯轉過身子，盡量將捆行李的繩子往下拉緊，但一點作用也沒有。

「這些狗肯定是能拖著那玩意兒跑個整天囉！」那些男人立刻回應。

「那是當然的了。」哈爾禮貌性的回答，口氣卻十分冷淡。他一手握著雪橇的舵桿，一手揮動鞭子，大聲喝道：「走！起跑吧！」

所有的狗都抵著胸前的挽繩，拼命地往前拉，用力的拉了一會兒以後就停了下來。他們根本就拉不動雪橇。

「這些懶惰的畜生！非得給你們一點顏色瞧瞧不可！」他叫著，準備用鞭子抽打他們。

但是美希黛茲衝過來阻止，大喊著：「喔！哈爾，你不能這麼做！」她抓住鞭子，把它搶了過來。「可憐的小寶貝們！現在你必須答應我，以後絕不再虐待他們，否則我就不走。」

「妳還真瞭解狗啊。」她的弟弟諷刺地冷笑。「妳不要管我可以嗎？我告訴妳，這些狗懶得要命，妳得抽個幾下鞭子，

他們才會做事。他們就是這樣，妳不相信的話自己去問其他人。問那些人看看。」

美希黛茲懇求地看著他們，美麗的臉龐上寫滿不捨的哀痛。

「如果你想知道的話，我就告訴你們吧！其實他們已經累垮了，」其中一個男人答道，「徹徹底底地累垮了，就是這樣。他們需要的是休息。」

「休息個屁！」一句咒罵從哈爾沒長鬍鬚的口中吐了出來。美希黛茲聽到這句咒罵，難過地叫了一聲。

但她是那種胳膊向裡彎的人，所以立刻為自己的弟弟辯解。「不要管他！」她尖聲說道。「趕狗的人是你，你覺得怎麼樣好，就怎麼做吧！」

哈爾的鞭子再度抽打在狗兒的身上。他們傾身向前抵住胸帶，腳踩進了壓平的雪地裡，身體貼住地面，用盡全身的力量往前拉。而雪橇就好像嵌在地底的鐵錨一般，動也不動。他們試了兩次之後，停下來喘著氣。鞭子又殘酷地揮了下來，美希黛茲再度過來干涉。她跪在巴克的面前，眼眶含淚，兩手緊緊摟住他的脖子。

「喔，可憐的小寶貝！你們這些可憐的小寶貝！」她同情地叫著，「為什麼不出力拉呢？這樣你們就不會被鞭子抽了啊！」巴克不喜歡她，但是抵抗她的話好像又太過分些，因而將她也當成這天苦差事的一部分。

在旁邊圍觀的其中一個人，原本緊咬著牙一言不發，這時

忍不住大聲地說道：「我才不管你們會怎麼樣，可是為了這些狗，我想告訴你們，你們必須先幫他們個大忙，先把雪橇鬆動開來才行。雪橇的滑板被凍住了，你們得用全身的力量扳動舵桿，左右兩次就可以鬆開雪橇了。」

狗隊第三次嘗試著要拉雪橇，而這一次，哈爾終於聽進勸告了，他先將凍住的滑板鬆一鬆，超載笨重的雪橇這時開始前進了。在如雨點般的鞭抽之下，巴克和夥伴們只得掙扎地往前邁進。在前方一百碼的地方有個彎道，陡峭地通到大街上，這時就必須依賴一個經驗老到的駕駛，才能穩住頭重腳輕的雪橇，但哈爾並不是這樣的好手。當他們轉進彎道時，有一半的物品從鬆脫的捆繩中甩了出去，但是狗隊並未停下腳步。變輕的雪橇以側面著地，在狗隊背後一蹦一跳地被拖著前進。因為剛才飽受虐待，加上過重的行李，狗兒們十分憤怒。巴克怒氣沖沖地往前飛奔，領著隊伍拼命地往前跑。哈爾大聲地吆喝著：「停！停下來！」但他們毫不理會，結果哈爾摔了一跤，還被雪橇輾過去。狗隊一直衝到大街上，雪橇上所剩的東西沿著史凱威的街道灑了一地，為市上添了不少笑話。

好心的市民幫忙攔下狗隊，撿起散落一地的物品，還勸告他們，如果想去道森的話，就得將行李減半，狗的數量也要加倍。哈爾和他的姊姊、姊夫不情願地聽著，重新搭起帳篷，把所有裝備檢查一遍。看到罐頭食品被翻出來的時候，周遭的人哄堂大笑，因為帶罐頭食品在雪地中長途跋涉，簡直是異想天開。「毯子夠一整個旅館用的了。」一個幫忙的人笑著說。

第五章

「連一半都還嫌太多！還有帳篷也應該丟掉，碗盤也是，誰要洗啊？天啊！你們以爲是在坐火車旅行呀！」

　　就這樣，一件件多餘的物品被無情地剔除了。看到自己的衣袋被扔在地上，東西一件又一件被丟掉時，美希黛茲難過地哭了。她不僅爲了被丟棄的東西哭泣，也爲了這整件事情哭泣。她雙手環抱著膝蓋，傷心地前後搖晃著。她發誓不再前進半步，即使有一打查理斯也不走。她向每個人和每件物品懇求，最後，她一面拭淚，一面狠下心來將所有非必備的東西都扔了。她越扔越起勁，扔完自己的東西後，轉而進攻那兩個男人的物品，一陣旋風似的將它們一掃而光。

　　東西扔完之後，整個裝備已經少了一半，但體積仍是十分龐大。晚上，查理斯和哈爾買了六條從外地來的狗，加上原來的六隻，還有一起創下紀錄的兩隻愛斯基摩犬，迪克和庫納，湊了一支有十四隻狗的隊伍。雖然這些外地狗一登陸就受過訓練，但一點作用也沒有。其中有三條是短毛獵犬，一條是紐芬蘭犬，另外兩隻則是血統不明的雜種狗。這些新來的狗一副茫然無知的樣子，巴克和同伴都很討厭他們，雖然他很快就讓他們知道自己的處境以及不該做的事，卻怎麼也教不會他們什麼才是應該做的事情。除了那兩隻雜種狗外，身在這個陌生野蠻的環境，以及遭受的虐待，都使他們茫然不知所措，顯得十分害怕。那兩隻雜種狗則是一點精神都沒有，有的只是一身隨時都可能折斷的瘦骨。

　　這些新來的狗毫無希望可言，而原來的幾條狗，早就因爲

兩千五百哩路的長途跋涉而疲憊不堪了，他們的前景顯然不太光明。然而，那兩個男人卻非常興奮，甚至十分得意，對自己擁有十四隻狗的隊伍感到驕傲萬分。他們看到許多從關口前往道森的雪橇，以及從道森來的雪橇，從沒有見過有哪輛雪橇是由十四隻狗拉的。事實上，在北極之所以不用十四條狗來拉雪橇，是有其緣故的，因為一輛雪橇根本裝不下十四隻狗所需的食物。但是，查理斯和哈爾不懂這一點，他們只在紙上用鉛筆簡單計算了一下，一隻狗吃多少食物，有多少隻狗，行程有幾天，總共需要多少食物等等。美希黛茲從他們的肩頭看過去，點點頭，表示明白，事情就是這麼的簡單！

第二天臨近中午的時候，巴克才領著這支長長的隊伍走在街上。他和夥伴們一點也興奮不起來，整個狗隊死氣沉沉的，還沒出發就疲憊不堪。他們已經在鹽水湖和道森之間來回走了四趟了，現在又要踏上相同的旅程，讓他苦不堪言。巴克毫無心思工作，其他的狗也差不多。新來的狗是膽小害怕，原來的狗則是對主人沒有任何信心。

巴克依稀感覺到，這兩男一女根本不能信賴，他們什麼也不懂；幾天過去了，顯然他們什麼也沒學會。他們做什麼事情都馬馬虎虎，沒有任何秩序與章法可言。都快半夜了他們才搭好一個亂七八糟的帳篷，隔天快中午的時候才拆掉營地，然後草率地將行李裝上雪橇，結果沿途必須不斷地停下來重新整理。有些時候，一天走下來連十哩路都不到。而其他時候，他們壓根兒也出發不了。儘管他們在預算狗食時，確定了每天的

里程，卻沒有一天達成一半進度。

　　不可避免的，他們即將面臨狗食短缺的情形，但是他們還是過量餵食，更加速了糧食的消耗，使狗食短缺的日子提前來臨。那些外地狗的食慾特別旺盛，還沒經過長期的挨餓來訓練自己的消化能力，沒有辦法吃得少又充分地吸收營養。此外，那些累壞的愛斯基摩犬拉雪橇時顯得有氣無力，哈爾以為是因為他們吃得太少，於是將食物量加倍。更糟的是，美希戴茲那美麗的雙眼會盈滿淚水，發出顫抖的懇求聲，勸哈爾再多加些狗食，如果他不聽從，她就會偷偷從袋子裡拿魚乾餵他們。然而，巴克和愛斯基摩犬要的不是食物，而是休息。儘管他們前進的速度十分緩慢，但沉重的負擔仍舊壓榨著他們的體力。

　　終於，狗糧短缺的問題出現了。哈爾發現狗糧已經吃掉一半，而預定的路程才走了四分之一，而且現在用盡各種方法也無法取得狗食了。因此，哈爾決定削減狗兒每日的飯量，然後增加每日的行程。他的姊姊和姊夫都很贊同，但由於他們沉重的行李和自己的無能，計畫仍舊失敗。要減少狗食很簡單，但絕不可能讓狗隊跑得更快，況且要他們早上提早出發，根本辦不到。他們不僅不懂得怎麼讓狗工作，連自己應該做什麼工作都不知道。

　　最先被犧牲的是杜柏。這個可憐的笨賊，老是被逮到，免不了受處罰，但他工作的時候還是十足認真勤奮。他扭傷的肩胛骨始終沒能得到治療和休養，情況越來越糟，最後哈爾只好用那枝柯爾特左輪手槍將他擊斃。當地人都知道，外地狗如果

吃得跟愛斯基摩犬一樣多的話，一定會餓死。而巴克率領的那
六隻外地狗，每天吃得只有愛斯基摩犬的一半，肯定是死路一
條。最先餓死的是那隻紐芬蘭犬，接著是三隻短毛獵犬，兩隻
雜種狗雖然頑強地試圖抓住生命，最後仍是難逃死劫。

　　這時，南方人特有的溫文儒雅，在這三個人身上消失殆盡
了。北極之旅的誘惑魅力與傳奇性色彩消褪之後，對他們這樣
的男人與女人來說，只是一件嚴苛殘酷的現實。美希戴茲不再
為狗哭泣了，因她忙著為自己悲泣，忙著與丈夫和弟弟爭吵。
只有爭吵這件事，他們永遠不會感到厭倦。他們的暴躁易怒加
劇了不幸的程度，而不幸的遭遇只讓他們更加暴躁。有些人具
有極佳的耐性，在長途跋涉時，能忍受艱苦的工作和痛苦，還
能保持溫和的口氣，和顏悅色。但是他們連一絲一毫這樣的耐
性都沒有。他們凍得身體僵硬，而且到處都疼痛不堪，肌肉
痛、骨頭痛，甚至連心都痛；也因為如此，從早到晚他們口中
所講出的每一句話，無不尖酸刻薄，難以入耳。

　　只要美希戴茲一讓查理斯和哈爾給逮到機會，就會又開始
爭吵起來。每個人都堅信自己做了超量的工作，一有機會就會
忍不住出聲抱怨。美希戴茲一會兒偏袒丈夫，一會兒又站在弟
弟那邊，結果變成了一場永無休止、可看性十足的家庭鬧劇。
一開始只是查理斯和哈爾兩人爭吵著應該由誰來劈柴生火，結
果連家裡其他的成員也被扯進來，從爸爸、媽媽、叔叔、伯
伯、表哥、表妹……幾千哩遠的人、連早已不在世的人都被他
們給罵了進去。好笑的是，哈爾對藝術的見解或他舅舅寫的社

會劇作，能跟砍柴生火扯上什麼關係，真是令人費解。而現在
爭吵的焦點，好像又轉到查理斯的政治成見上面了。查理斯的
姊姊愛搬弄是非的習性，又和育空河畔生火有啥關聯，這恐怕
只有美希黛茲才知道了，她對這個話題正滔滔不絕地高談闊論
著，還講到她夫家裡面一些成員惹人厭的怪癖。就這樣，火一
直都還沒有生，帳蓬只搭了一半，連狗也沒有餵。

　　美希戴茲滿腹委屈，那是因性別的不同而引起的辛酸。她
既美麗又溫柔，總是受到大家的殷勤款待，但是現在，丈夫和
弟弟對她的態度卻再也談不上禮貌周到了。以往那種令人憐惜
的無助模樣，現在只落得他們抱怨連連。既然他們對她基本的
女性特權加以責難，她索性讓他們的生活苦不堪言。她再也不
為狗兒著想了，而且因為自己渾身酸痛疲累，堅持要坐在雪橇
上。即使她嬌弱可人，體重也有一百二十磅，這對拖著沉重負
擔、虛弱無力又挨餓受凍的狗兒來說，簡直是雪上加霜。她在
雪橇上坐了好幾天，直到狗兒們撐不住倒在韁繩下，雪橇一動
也不動。查理斯和哈爾苦苦哀求她下來用走的，她只是一逕對
著上天哭泣，哀訴他們的殘酷無情。

　　有一次，他們卯足了力硬是將她拖下車，不過他們再也不
敢這麼做，因為她像個耍賴的小孩一樣，故意癱在雪地上不走
了。他們兩個繼續往前走，她卻動也不動。直到他們走了三哩
路，才無奈地將雪橇上的行李卸下，回到原處找她，再用力將
她抬上雪橇。

　　他們自己的處境悲慘，對於狗兒們的痛苦就更加視若無

睹、冷酷無情。哈爾主張對狗要心狠手辣，他曾向姊姊和姊夫
宣導這個理念，但並不被接受，於是他將這個理論實施在狗兒
身上，用棍子將狗打得悽慘。在五指山的時候，狗食終於耗盡
了，一個無牙的印地安老婆婆提出一項交易，用幾磅凍得發硬
的馬皮，跟哈爾交換他腰際獵刀旁邊的那枝柯爾特左輪手槍。
這些馬皮是半年前從牧羊人餓死的馬上剝下來的，凍得硬梆梆
的像是鍍鋅的鐵片一樣，成了狗兒粗劣的替代食品。狗兒勉強
把它吞進肚子裡，也只是溶成一條條毫無營養價值的細薄皮
繩，以及一大團的短毛，既傷胃又難以消化。

　　這些日子以來，巴克始終都步伐蹣跚、跟蹌地走在隊伍的
前面，簡直像是一場夢魘。他還有力氣的時候，就繼續拉雪
橇，力氣用完了，就仆倒在地上，直到被棍子或鞭子打得他不
得不再站起來。他美麗的毛皮早已失去原有的光澤與彈性，邋
邋鬆軟地垂著，被哈爾棍子打過的地方，還糾結著凝乾的血
跡。他強健結實的肌肉萎縮了，佈滿一條條細長的青筋疙瘩。
原本壯碩的身子已不復見，皮膚鬆弛皺褶，使得每根肋骨以及
骨架上的每一塊骨頭，都清晰可見。這樣的情景讓人心碎，但
是巴克並沒有被打倒，如同先前那紅衣男人所證明的一般。

　　巴克的情況如此，其他的同伴也不例外，活像是一具具行
屍走肉般的骷髏。包含巴克在內，這個隊伍一共有七隻狗。在
他們從未曾有過的悲慘不幸中，對於鞭子的抽打、棍棒的毒
打，都已經毫無知覺了。被打時的疼痛感已變得遙遠模糊，如
同他們耳聞目睹的一切那般隱約而遙遠。他們半死不活的，有

些甚至只剩下四分之一條的性命。瘦骨嶙峋的身軀，像是一堆裝在皮袋裡的骨頭，生命的火花微弱地在他們體內閃動著。雪橇停下休息的時候，他們連同挽繩倒在地上，像是死了一樣，生命之火更是黯淡無光地抖著，彷彿即將熄滅。當棍棒和鞭子打在他們身上的時候，生命之火才又微微抽動了幾下，他們巍巍顫顫地站起身來，蹣跚地往前拖行。

終於有一天，溫馴的比利不支倒地，再也爬不起來。哈爾的手槍已經換成馬皮了，他就用斧頭砍向比利的頭顱，將屍體從挽具下解下來，拖到一旁丟棄。巴克目睹一切，他的夥伴們也看到了，他們明白這一天離自己也不遠了。第二天，庫納也死了，只剩下五隻狗了。喬，早已衰弱得沒力氣發狠；派克一瘸一拐的走著，意識不清，沒有心思可以裝病了；而獨眼的索列克，仍舊盡忠職守地拉著雪橇，對自己虛弱的體力感到悲傷；迪克，由於他去年冬天並沒有跑過太遠的路程，相較之下是個新手，因此比別人挨了更多棍子。而巴克依然是領隊狗，但再也不維持紀律或勉強其他狗遵守了，他有一半的時候都虛弱得兩眼昏花，只憑藉著雪道朦朧的影子和腳底模糊的感覺繼續往前拖行。

明媚的春天已經降臨，但沒有任何狗或人察覺到這一點。太陽每天早早升起，晚晚落下。凌晨三點，曙光就已經出現了，而到了晚上九點，天邊還有晚霞逗留著。漫長的白晝陽光燦爛，陰森死寂的冬天遠離，取而代之的是萬物復甦、喧囂騷動的春天。這樣的喧囂來自於大地，洋溢著生命的喜悅；來自於再度生機盎然的萬物，它們在漫長的冰天雪地中沉寂著，近乎死去一般。松樹的樹液在枝幹中湧動；楊柳冒出了新芽；灌木與藤蔓換上綠色的新裝。夜晚，蟋蟀鳴唱；白晝，各種爬行動物在絢爛的陽光下蠕動著。森林裡，鶴鶉啼叫，啄木鳥叩叩地敲著。松鼠啾啾，鳥兒啁啾地唱著歌。頭頂上，從南方飛來的野雁排成精巧的人字形，呼嘯地劃過天空。

山坡上流水潺潺，隱匿未現的泉水發出美妙的音樂。萬物紛紛解凍，一切都在溶解、發出劈啪的聲響。育空河正奮力地掙脫冰塊的束縛，河水從底下沖蝕著冰層，陽光則從上面溶化瓦解。氣孔形成了，產生的裂縫越來越大，冰層較薄的地方，冰塊成片碎裂，掉進了河裡。而在燦爛的陽光下，陣陣如嘆息般的微風中，當萬物甦醒、冰雪融化、生命開始悸動的之際，那兩男一女與幾隻愛斯基摩犬，彷彿是步向死亡的過客，蹣跚地往前行進。

狗兒不斷地跌倒，美希戴茲坐在雪橇上哭泣著，哈爾無意義的出聲咒罵，查理斯的雙眼憂愁地泛著淚光。他們就這樣搖搖晃晃地走到了白河口，走進了約翰‧松頓的營地裡。當他們停下來休息的時候，那幾隻狗全部都倒在地上，像是被人打死了一樣。美希戴茲拭乾淚水，看了看約翰‧松頓。查理斯因為全身僵硬，緩慢吃力地坐在一塊大木頭上面休息。只有哈爾開口說話。約翰‧松頓正在為他用白樺木做的斧頭柄作最後修飾。他邊削邊聽，發出「嗯」般簡短的聲音，被問到事情時，就簡潔地提出忠告。他太瞭解像他們這樣的人了，即使他提出

勸告，也不一定會被接受。

「在上面的時候，那些人早就告訴過我們，雪道底下的冰層已經開始崩落了，最好是先停下來，不要往前走。」當松頓勸告他們不要在正解凍的冰層上面冒險時，哈爾這樣答道。「他們也說我們到不了白河，但我們這不是已經到了嗎？」說到最後一句話時，還得意地的冷笑著。

「他們說的可是實話，」松頓答道。「雪道隨時都可能會崩落，只有傻瓜才會笨到想去碰運氣。我坦白跟你說，即使給我阿拉斯加所有的黃金，我也不會冒著生命險走在冰上。」

「那是因爲你不是傻瓜吧，我想。無論如何，我們要繼續往道森前進。」哈爾說，揮起了鞭子喝道：「起來了，巴克！喂！起來啊！要走了！」

松頓繼續削著他的木頭。他知道，想叫一個傻瓜別幹傻事，只是在浪費時間和力氣，就算是兩個或三個傻瓜湊在一起，也沒有辦法停止愚蠢的行爲。

狗隊並沒有聽他的命令站起身來，長久以來，他們都是要等到挨了打才會站起來。鞭子揚了起來，無情地四處落下。約翰・松頓咬緊了嘴唇，不發聲響。索列克首先站起來，迪克跟著站起來，接著是喬疼痛哀嚎著站起來。派克痛苦地掙扎著，兩次都爬到一半又倒了下去，第三次才勉強站了起來。而巴克，連試也不試，靜靜地躺在先前倒下的地方，鞭子一次次地抽打在他的身上，但他既不哀叫，也不掙扎。有好幾次，松頓忍不住想開口制止，話到了嘴邊又收回去，淚水潤溼了他的眼眸，**鞭子仍是無情地繼續抽著**，他站起身來，猶豫不決地來回踱步。

巴克不肯站起來，光是這一點，就足以使哈爾大發雷霆。他放下鞭子，拿出慣用的棍子，如雨般的重擊落在巴克的身上，但巴克仍舊拒絕移動。其實他可以像他的夥伴一樣，勉強地爬起身來，但是他痛下決定，無論如何都不起來。他隱約感覺到大難即將來臨，在他將雪橇拉上河岸時，這種感覺就很強烈，到現在都還沒有消失。這一整天，他都感到腳下那層薄薄的雪道正在融解，他覺得災難近在眼前，而他的主人卻不斷逼他走到那片冰層上。他拒絕起身。他遭受太多的痛苦與折磨，身體早已孱弱不堪，所以根本不覺得棍子打得有多疼痛。棍子不斷地打，巴克體內的生命之火也顫抖著，彷彿即將熄滅。他感到一陣異常的麻木，模模糊糊地知道自己正在挨打。最後，連痛覺都已經消失了，他失去了所有的知覺，雖然隱隱約約聽到棍子打在身上的聲音，但那好像已經不是他的身體了，連聲音也變得十分遙遠。

突然，約翰‧松頓毫無預警地發出一聲怒吼，含糊地像是野獸一般，直直撲向那正在揮舞著棍子的男人。哈爾像是被一株倒下的樹木給擊中一樣，被撞得往後退了好幾步。美希戴茲大聲尖叫，查理斯則是哀愁地看著，揉一揉濕潤的雙眼，因為身體僵硬而沒有站起來。

約翰‧松頓挺身護衛在巴克的前面，他竭力地克制住自己，氣得全身顫抖，說不出話來。

最後，他好不容易哽咽地說出話來：「如果你再打這隻狗，我就殺了你！」

「那是我的狗！」哈爾回答，走了過來，邊擦著嘴角的血跡。「滾開，別多管閒事，否則我就先修理你！我要往道森去！」

松頓站在哈爾和巴克的中間，一點也沒有打算要讓開。哈爾抽出他那把長獵刀，美希戴茲見狀驚叫了一聲，又哭又笑的，陷入了歇斯底里的狀態。松頓用斧頭柄敲了哈爾的指關節，把他的獵刀打落在地。哈爾準備彎下腰去撿，卻又被松頓敲了一記。然後，松頓自己彎下身撿起那把獵刀，揮了兩下，將巴克身上的挽繩割斷。

哈爾鬥志全無，況且他的雙手也被姊姊抓住，準確的說，是兩隻手臂都被緊緊地抱住。巴克也已經奄奄一息，根本沒有辦法再拉雪橇了。幾分鐘後，雪橇從堤岸滑入河面上。巴克聽到他們離開的聲音，抬起頭望著，看見派克領著隊，索列克當壓陣狗，中間則是喬和迪克，他們一瘸一拐的蹣跚前進。美希戴茲坐在裝載行李的雪橇上，哈爾操縱舵桿控制方向，查理斯則是跟蹌地跟在後頭。

巴克望著他們遠去的時候，松頓跪在他的身邊，用粗糙溫柔的雙手撫摸著他，檢查他身上有沒有斷掉的骨頭。檢查完後，他發現巴克除了傷痕累累和極度的飢餓外，並沒有什麼大礙。此時，雪橇隊伍已經走了四分之一哩遠，巴克和松頓一起看著雪橇在冰上緩緩行進。倏地，他們看到雪橇的後端往下

陷，好像陷到溝裡一樣，哈爾手握著舵桿，被拋到半空中。美希戴茲的尖聲傳來，他們看見查理斯轉身往回跑了一步，整片冰裂了開來，所有的狗和人跟著消失不見，只剩一個張著大口的冰洞。雪道的底層化開了。

約翰·松頓和巴克彼此望著。

「你這可憐的傢伙。」約翰·松頓說。

巴克舔了舔他的手。

第六章

摯愛的人

　　去年十二月，約翰‧松頓凍傷了腳，夥伴們替他療傷，將他留下來休養，然後就溯河而上，前去砍木造筏，準備到道森去。松頓救巴克的時候，腳還有點跛，隨著氣候逐漸回暖，終於完全康復了。巴克就在這裡度過了整個漫長的春天。他臥在河畔，望著潺潺的流水，懶洋洋地聽著鳥兒的歌聲與大自然的吟唱，漸漸恢復了體力。

　　在跋涉了三千哩路之後，能得到一陣充分的休息，是再好不過的事了。隨著傷口的癒合，巴克的肌肉又長了出來，再次遮蓋了他的骨頭，但必須承認的是，他也變得懶散了。其實應該是說，巴克、約翰‧松頓、思姬特、尼格，他們全部都無所事事，只等著木筏的到來，將他們載往下流的道森去。思姬特是一隻愛爾蘭長毛獵犬，她很快就跟巴克變成好友。巴克當時生命垂危，也無力拒絕她的接近示好。像某些狗一樣，她具有療護的特性，像是母貓舔著小貓似的，舔淨巴克的傷口。巴克每天吃完早餐時，她就會過來執行這項她給自己指定的工作，最後，巴克甚至開始期待她的照顧，就如同他期待松頓的愛護

一般。尼格是一隻大黑狗，是警犬和獵鹿犬的混血，和思姬特
一樣十分友善，只是比較不善於表達，眼睛裡總是含著笑意，
表現出善良的本性。

　　使巴克感到驚訝的是，這兩隻狗對他沒有絲毫的妒意，似
乎樂意與他一同分享著約翰‧松頓的仁慈與寬容。當巴克身體
稍微健壯之後，他們就誘使他玩各種滑稽的遊戲，連約翰‧松
頓都忍不住加入他們的行列。就在這樣的氣氛中，巴克輕鬆地
度過了他的療養期，進入了一種全新的生活。生平第一次，他
感受到真正的愛，由衷且熱情的愛。這種愛，即使是在陽光燦
爛的聖塔克蕾拉山谷，米勒法官的家裡，也未曾體驗過。陪伴
著法官兒子們打獵散步，是工作中的夥伴之情；陪伴著法官的
孫子們，是一種自傲的監護之責；至於陪伴著大法官本人，則
是一種莊重威嚴的友誼之情。可是，只有約翰‧松頓才能喚醒
巴克體內股狂熱赤誠的愛，那是崇拜，那是瘋狂。

　　這當然和這個男人救了他的性命有極大的關聯，但更重要
的是，他是一個完美的理想主人。別人照顧狗是因為出於責任
和商業利益，然而，約翰‧松頓對待狗彷彿是在照顧自己的孩
子，是一種天性。他很周到，從不忘記親切地對他們打一聲招
呼，或是一句鼓勵的話，他常會坐下來跟他們娓娓長談（他稱
之為閒扯淡）。此時此刻，他和狗兒們一樣感到很快樂。他會
粗魯地用雙手抱住巴克的頭，再將自己的頭靠在上面，前後搖
晃推揉著巴克的身子，嘴裡胡亂喊著一些像是在罵人的字眼，
可是對巴克而言，這就像是充滿愛意的字眼一樣。當巴克被粗

魯的擁抱、低聲咒罵著時，總是感到一陣無比的狂喜。每次被約翰‧松頓前後的推揉著時，他總覺得自己的心狂喜得要跳出胸口。當松頓一放開手，他就會跳起來用後腳站著，咧著嘴笑，眼中蘊含著千言萬語，喉頭顫抖著吐不出聲音，就這樣動也不動地站在原處。約翰‧松頓由衷地贊嘆道：「天哪！除了不能說話，你什麼都懂！」

巴克用他特有的方式表達自己的愛，這種方式近於傷害。他用嘴咬住松頓的手，非常兇猛用力，使得手上留下深深的齒印，要好一段時間才會消失。就像巴克知道那些咒罵是愛的話語一樣，松頓也將這佯裝的咬手行為，當作是一種親密的撫觸。

不過，巴克通常還是用崇敬的方式來表達愛意。當松頓撫摸他或與他說話的時候，他會欣喜若狂，但他並不會主動博取主人的寵愛。他不像思姬特，喜歡將鼻子伸到松頓的手下，拼命的摩蹭，直到松頓撫摸她才肯罷休。也不像尼格，總是喜歡悄悄地走近松頓，把自己的大頭放在松頓的膝蓋上。巴克只要遠遠地看著松頓，就感到心滿意足。他會在松頓的腳邊趴上好幾個小時，抬著頭熱切渴望地注視著松頓的臉龐，仔細地端詳觀察，饒富興味地捕捉他每一種稍縱即逝的表情。偶爾，他會躺在比較遠的地方，在松頓的旁邊或是後面，凝視著他身體的輪廓與他的一舉一動。彷彿是心電感應一般，巴克的凝視散發著一種力量，常常吸引松頓將頭轉過來，然後默默地報以同樣的凝視，眼中流露出的愛意，正如同巴克眼中所閃耀的一樣。

巴克獲救後之後，有好長一段時間，他都不能讓松頓離開他的視線。從早到晚，即使松頓只是離開帳蓬一下子，他都會緊緊跟隨在後。進入北國以來，巴克的主人一再的更換，這讓他心生恐懼，擔心沒有一個主人可以恆久不變，害怕松頓會像裴洛特、弗洪索、和那個蘇格蘭裔的混血兒一樣，從他的生命中永遠消失，甚至晚上做夢也常常被這種恐懼驚醒，更時常會做這樣的惡夢。這時，他會用力地驅走睡意，在寒風中爬到帳蓬的垂簾旁邊，站在那裡傾聽著主人的呼吸聲。

　　巴克對約翰‧松頓的依戀，似乎表現了文明影響下溫柔的一面，但是他被北方生活所激發出的原始本性，依舊在他的體內活躍著。他既有從南方火爐的溫暖與遮風蔽雨的屋頂而產生的忠實與虔誠，同時，也保有著狂野與狡獪的本性。與其說他生長在溫暖的南國，有著世代文明的烙印與教化，不如說他是一隻來自於荒原的野獸，是約翰‧松頓把他救出來，現在坐到了他的火堆旁。他深切愛著主人，所以不會偷他的東西；但若是其他營地的人，他便會毫不遲疑地下手，而且，他的機靈狡詐，使他不會被逮到，可以完全逃脫。

　　他的臉上和身體，佈滿了其他狗所留下來的齒印，他現在打起架來更是兇猛萬分，比起以前有過之而無不及。然而思姬特和尼格都是好脾氣的狗，不會與人爭吵，更何況，他們是約翰‧松頓的狗。如果是陌生的狗，不管血統或膽量如何，都不得不臣服在巴克的威權之下，否則會馬上發現自己必須和一位可怕的對手，拼個你死我活。巴克是冷酷無情的，他早已徹底

領悟棍棒與利齒的法則，當他對戰時，決不放過任何一個有利的機會，也絕不會對一個已經走上死路的敵人手軟。他從史匹茲、警局和郵件車隊的狗那裡記取了教訓，知道不是支配別人就是被別人支配，沒有所謂的中庸之道。仁慈是一種懦弱的表現，而在蠻荒的世界裡，仁慈根本就不存在。那是一種弱點，會被視為恐懼害怕，而這樣的誤解會導致自身的死亡毀滅。殺或是被殺，吃或是被吃，他必須遵從這自遠古時代就流傳下來的法則。

　　他的靈魂比他所經歷的歲月、呼吸過的空氣都還更年邁。他貫通了遠古與現代，在他體內的永恆力量以強而有力的律動震顫著，支配著他，就如同潮汐與季節一樣。蹲在火堆前面、約翰‧松頓的身旁，是一隻有著寬厚胸脯、潔白牙齒的長毛狗；但是，在他的背後，卻隱藏著各式各樣的狗、半狼的狗、以及野狼的影子，慫恿著他，鼓動著他，與他一同享受著肉的美味、喝水，與他一起嗅風的味道，教導他傾聽著森林的聲音，左右著他的情緒、主導著他的行動。他臥在地上時，他們便一同躺下共眠，一起入夢，而且超出他的形體之外，變成了他夢中的題材與影像。

　　這些影子獨斷蠻橫地召喚著他，因而他的內心與人類以及人類的想法日益疏遠。他經常聽到森林裡傳來一種聲音殷勤地呼喚著他，這種聲音既神秘又動人心弦，誘惑著他不由自主地轉過身去，背對著火堆和週遭熟悉的土地，拋開所有的事物，不斷地往森林急奔而去。然而，每當他走到未曾有人開墾過的鬆軟土地時，看見濃密的樹蔭，又會想起約翰‧松頓的愛，此刻又將他拉回了火堆旁邊。

只有松頓一個人令他戀戀不捨，其他人在他的眼裡簡直毫無是處。偶爾，路過的旅客會稱讚他幾句或撫拍他，他只是冷淡地接受而已。如果有人對他過分地親暱討好，他就會站起身來，轉身離開。松頓的夥伴，韓斯和彼得，乘著那艘期盼已久的木筏到來時，他理都不理。直到後來知道他們是松頓的好友，才勉強接納了他們。他接受了他們的好意，好像是在給他們面子一樣。他們和松頓一樣高大，也是腳踏實地、思想單純、目光敏銳的人，當木筏還沒抵達道森鋸木廠附近的大漩渦時，他們就已經十分了解巴克的個性，也不強求他一定要和思姬特和尼格一樣跟他們親近了。

然而，他對松頓的愛卻似乎不斷增長著。在夏季旅行的時候，走在人群之中，只有松頓能將行李放在巴克的背上讓他馱著。只要是松頓提出的要求，無論如何繁重，巴克絕對不會皺一下眉頭。當時，他們以木筏作為抵押，得到的資金要從道森往塔納那河而去。一天，人與狗一同坐在一座懸崖上休息，那座懸崖高約三百呎，聳立在赤裸岩石的河床之上。約翰‧松頓靠懸崖邊坐著，巴克則挨在他的身邊。突然，他閃過一個荒誕輕率的想法，他叫韓斯和彼得注意，想對巴克做個試驗。他一揮手臂，指向懸崖底下的深谷，命令道：「巴克，跳！」剎那間，他已經和巴克扭成一團，在懸崖的邊緣上掙扎著，韓斯和彼得趕緊將他們拖回安全的地方。

「太危險了！」驚魂甫定後，彼得這麼說道。

「不！真是太了不起了！而且也太可怕了，你知道嗎？有時候我會非常擔心。」松頓搖搖頭說。

「只要有他在你身邊，我可不敢動你一根寒毛！」彼得邊對巴克點點頭，做出這樣的結論。

「啊哈！我也不敢啊！」韓斯也這麼說道。

這年年底，在瑟寇城，彼得的疑慮終於被證實了。黑人柏頓是個脾氣暴躁、心腸狠毒的人，在酒館裡面跟一個新來的淘金客發生爭執，松頓好意上前勸架。如同以往一般，巴克趴在一個角落裡，頭枕在前腳上，注視著主人的一舉一動。柏頓毫無預警，猛地就揮拳打了過來，松頓被打得暈頭轉向，抓住了酒吧圍欄上的欄杆才沒有跌倒。

這時，那些旁觀的人只聽到一種聲音──既不像吠聲，也不是嚎叫，最恰當的說辭應該是怒吼，接著看見巴克從地板上飛身躍起，撲向柏頓的喉嚨。柏頓反射性地伸出手臂擋住，他撿回一條命卻被撞倒在地。巴克撲在他的身上，鬆開咬住手臂的利齒，轉而再次朝他的喉嚨進攻。這次柏頓只擋到了一點點，喉嚨就這樣被咬破了。眾人一擁而上，急忙趕走巴克。外科醫生為傷者上藥止血時，巴克在旁邊竄過來竄過去的，還想再撲上去，結果被大家拿著棍子打走。於是，他們當場召開一次礦工會議，宣判巴克的發怒是有充分理由的，因而獲判無罪。從那天起，巴克因此聲名大噪，威名傳遍了阿拉斯加的每一個營地。

那年秋天，他又再一次地，以另一種完全不同的方式救了
約翰·松頓的性命。當時，他們三人駕著一艘狹長的撐篙船，
順流而下，在「四十哩河」一帶湍急的險灘中航行。韓斯和彼
得沿著河岸，用一根細長的繩子順著前進的方向，將船以繩子
繫在樹上，再換到另一棵樹上，用來剎住船身，以免被急流沖
走。松頓則留在船上撐篙划船，一邊大聲地指示岸上兩人的行
動。巴克在岸邊焦慮不安地隨著船身向前走，眼睛自始至終一
刻也不離開主人。

　　當他們來到一處特別險惡的急流時，河中處處都是暗礁，
一塊礁石突出水面，松頓將船撐進河流之中，於是韓斯放鬆繩
子，手抓著繩子沿著河岸往下跑，準備等船一通過暗礁再勒緊
繩子，將船停住。然而，船在風車送水般的急流中飛馳而下，
經過暗礁的時候，韓斯趕忙拉緊繩索，誰知這一拉用力過猛，
整個船被拽翻，翻成了底朝天，松頓則是被拋出船外，落在水
中，被急流沖到最險惡的急湍處，那裡一片驚濤駭浪，沒有人
得以倖免。

　　巴克見狀立即跳入水中，游了三百碼，在一個洶湧澎湃的
漩渦中趕上了松頓。當他一感覺松頓抓住了他的尾巴之後，便
竭盡全力，奮力向岸邊游去。然而，他靠向岸邊的速度十分緩
慢，而往下飄的速度卻快得驚人。而下游的急湍更是瘋狂奔
竄，沖在梳齒狀的巨岩上，激起了洶湧的怒濤，浪花四濺。急
流沖在最後一座陡峭的岩石上，那吸力大得驚人，他猛地被一
塊岩石擦了過去，又撞到了第二塊石頭，最後更是猛力地衝撞

到第三塊岩石。松頓知道要從這裡游上岸是不可能的事，他放開巴克，雙手死命抱住第三塊光溜溜的岩石頂部，在激烈澎湃的急流中大喊著：「走！巴克，快走！」

巴克支撐不住，被急流沖向下游。他拼命地掙扎，想游回去救松頓，卻怎樣都游不回去。他聽見松頓再一次地命令著他，就努力地讓身體浮出水面，將頭抬得高高的，好像是要看他最後一眼似地，才轉身服從地朝岸邊游去。他拼命地游著，就在他幾乎撐不住要滅頂的時候，正好被彼得和韓斯抓住，將他拖回岸邊。

他們知道一個人在急流的衝擊之下，抱著一塊光滑的岩石，只能夠支撐幾分鐘的時間。他們沿著河岸趕緊往回跑，跑到和松頓平行的地方，用原本控制船的繩子繫住巴克的脖子和肩膀，他們綁得十分小心，既不能緊到讓他喘不過氣來，又不能鬆到讓繩子妨礙他游泳。然後，再將他放入水中。巴克勇敢地往前游了出去，然而，他並未筆直地朝著松頓游過去，但等到發現的時候為時已晚。他游到與松頓平行的位置，只差再滑幾下的距離而已，卻仍是無能為力，被水流給沖了下去。

韓斯趕緊拉住繩子，好像巴克是一條船一樣。這突然的一拽，繩子便緊緊地勒住了巴克，整個身體被猛力拽到水底下，一直沉了下去，直到身體撞上河底才又被拉了上岸。這時，巴克已經是被淹得半死不活了，韓斯和彼得趕緊撲在他身上做人工呼吸，一邊將空氣灌進去，一邊壓出他肚子裡的水。巴克蹣跚地爬起身來，馬上又不支倒地。同一時間，他們聽見松頓微弱的呼救聲，雖然聽不清楚他在講些什麼，但是很明白他已瀕臨絕境。主人的呼叫聲，像是閃電一般打在巴克的身上，他猛地跳了起來，趕在韓斯和彼得之前，沿著河岸又跑向上游剛剛落下水的地方。

　　他們再次將繩子栓在巴克的身上，放他下水。他再度奮力地游了出去，而這次他游得非常筆直，因為他已經失誤了一次，這次決不能重蹈覆轍。韓斯小心翼翼地放出繩子，不讓它太鬆，彼得則是留意著不讓繩子糾成一團。巴克直直地游了過去，和松頓成同一直線之後，才以特快車般的速度，轉身衝向松頓。松頓看見巴克撲了過來，用盡了全身僅剩的力氣，伸出雙臂緊緊地抱住巴克毛茸茸的脖子。韓斯趕緊將繩子繞著樹幹栓緊，巴克和松頓被勒得喘不過氣來，被拖到水面下，一會兒人在上面，一會兒狗在上面，就這樣在崎嶇不平的水底被拖著走，沿路撞上水底一塊塊暗礁和岩石，最後終於被拖上岸來。

　　松頓遍體鱗傷，韓斯和彼得將他腹部朝下，放在一截漂木上，前後用力地推拉著他，幫他擠出肚子裡的水，過了好一會兒，他才緩緩地醒了過來。他第一眼便是忙著尋找巴克，只見他軟綿綿地躺在地上，毫無生氣。尼格在他身邊發出哀嚎，思姬特則是舔著他溼漉漉的臉龐和緊緊閉著的雙眼。松頓自己滿身是傷，仍是拖著腳步走到巴克的身旁，仔細檢查他的身體，發現巴克斷了三根肋骨。

　　於是，他宣布道：「就這麼決定了，我們在這裡紮營吧！」

他們就在這裡搭起了帳蓬，一直住到巴克的肋骨痊癒，可以旅行了，他們才再度上路。

在道森的那年冬天，巴克又立下一件功勞。這件功勞也許沒有上一次那樣英勇，卻也讓他聲名大噪，名字被高高地刻在阿拉斯加的圖騰柱子上。三個人也為此尤其興奮，因為，他們因此湊足了所需的裝備，可以到渴望已久、尚未開發的東部去實現夢想，那是礦工們至今尚未開採過的地方。而這件事情的起因，是因為愛爾多拉度酒館裡的一句話。在酒吧裡，大夥兒總是喜歡吹噓自己的愛犬，而由於巴克過去的輝煌紀錄，自然而然地成為了大家的話題焦點，松頓當然極力為自己的狗辯護。經過半個鐘頭的爭論之後，一個人說他的狗能拉得動五百磅的雪橇，而且還可以走；接著，又有一個人說自己的狗可以拉動六百磅；然後第三個人說他的狗能拉到七百磅。

「呸！這算得了什麼？巴克拉得動一千磅！」約翰‧松頓這麼說道。

「拉得動一千磅？能拉得走嗎？能拉著走上一百碼嗎？」剛剛吹噓自己的狗可以拉到七百磅的人，就是伯納札的金礦大王，馬休斯。

「能！拉動雪橇，再走一百碼！」約翰‧松頓冷冷地說。

馬休斯為了讓在場的每一個人聽得清清楚楚，便從容不迫地說：「好！我就用一千塊來跟你賭！我賭他拉不動！」說著，他往桌子砰地扔出像一袋義大利臘腸那麼大的金沙。

屋子裡鴉雀無聲。松頓的大話——或許真的只是大話，現

在恐怕得被迫實現了。松頓感到一股熱血往臉上倒衝，剛剛只為了逞口舌之快，他根本不確定巴克能不能拉得動一千磅。半噸重啊！如此龐大的數字嚇壞了他。他只知道巴克的力氣很大，也認為他應該拉得動這麼重的負擔。但是，他並不知道巴克能不能拉到一千磅。他從來沒有像這樣得真的去試。十幾雙眼睛緊緊地盯著他看，靜靜地等著他開口。更何況，他也沒有一千塊啊！哈斯和彼得也沒有。

「我現在正好有一輛雪橇停在外頭，上面裝著五十磅一袋的麵粉，總共有二十袋，你不用操心了。」馬休斯直率地說。

松頓沒有回答，他不知道該說什麼才好。他彷彿喪失了思考能力，茫然若失地望著每一張面孔，到處尋找可以重新啟動腦筋的東西。接著，他看到了吉姆·歐布萊恩的臉孔，那是曼斯頓金礦的金礦大王，也是他從前的好夥伴。這好像是在暗示著松頓，叫他去做一件作夢也沒想過的事。

「你可以借我一千塊嗎？」他幾乎是悄聲地問。

歐布萊恩答道：「沒問題！」同時將一袋沉甸甸的金子，扔到馬休斯的口袋的旁邊。「不過，約翰，我不大相信那隻狗能幹得了這件事啊！」

愛爾多拉度酒館的桌子全都空了，大家一窩蜂地擁上街頭來看這場賭局。賭錢的人紛紛下注，準備好看結果如何。好幾百個穿著皮衣、戴著手套的人，在雪橇旁邊不遠的地方圍成了一圈。馬休斯那輛載著一千磅麵粉的雪橇，在外面停了兩個多小時。外面是零下六十度的嚴寒，雪橇底部的滑板，早就牢牢地跟地上的冰雪給凍在一塊兒了。人們以一賠二的賠率，賭巴克拉不動雪橇。而這時大家對於「拉動」這模稜兩可的字眼下了不同的定義。歐布萊恩主張松頓可以先將雪橇凍結的地方先鬆開，再讓巴克將雪橇從完全靜止的狀態拉起；而馬休斯則是堅持認為，「拉動」就必須包括將滑板本身從冰凍的情況下拉出來。大部分的人多半支持馬休斯，因為他們根本不認為巴克能辦得到。於是賠率便提高到了一賠三，大家都賭巴克必輸。

沒有人下注賭巴克贏；所有的人都不相信巴克有這樣的能耐，因此沒人接受挑戰。松頓過於草率地與人打賭，本來已是憂心忡忡，現在又看到雪橇前面趴著十隻狗。擺在眼前的事實，令他愈難以相信巴克能完成任務了。而馬休斯卻更加地洋洋得意。

「我賭一賠三！」他大聲地宣布。「我再另外跟你賭一千塊。松頓，你說如何？」

松頓一臉充滿疑慮的模樣，但是，內心那種超越勝負的好戰個性被激發了出來，這時，他再也顧不了輸贏，也管不了雪橇能不能被拉動，他什麼也聽不進去了。他把韓斯和彼得叫過來，但他們也沒多少錢，連同他自己的，三個人只湊到了兩百塊。當時是他們手頭最拮据的時候，這兩百塊已經是三個人全部的財產了，然而，他們卻毫不猶豫地孤注一擲，去賭馬休斯的六百塊錢。

人們解開了雪橇上的十隻狗，巴克戴上自己的挽具，被栓在雪橇上面。那種興奮之情也感染了他，他明白自己要為約

翰‧松頓做一件天大的事情。他儀表堂堂、出類拔萃的體態，早讓四周的人們不禁發出讚嘆。他的狀態十分良好，全身上下沒有一絲贅肉，一百五十磅的體重，是如此地勇猛與英挺。毛皮閃閃發光，如絲綢一般，順著脖子而下的大片鬃毛披滿雙肩，靜止且半聳立著，彷彿會隨之起舞。他的精力似乎過於旺盛，連身上的每一根毛髮也有著十足的生命力。而他的胸脯寬厚、前腿粗壯，與身體的其他部位，顯得十分相稱協調。皮下的筋肉渾厚結實，大家伸手一摸，都說堅硬如鐵。因而賭注的賠率降為一賠二。

「天啊！先生！天哪！先生！」最近剛發跡的暴發戶之一，一個坐頭把交椅的販狗大王，結結巴巴地說：「我給你八百塊錢買他，比賽前，先生！光看他站在那裡，我就出八百塊錢買他！」

松頓搖了搖頭，走到巴克的身邊。

「你必須離他遠一點！讓他自己幹活兒！不能影響他！」馬休斯抗議著。

群眾安靜了下來，只有賭徒枉然地叫著一賠二的聲音。大家都公認巴克實在是一隻十分出色的狗，然而，二十袋的麵粉，每一袋有五十磅之重，在他們看來實在是太重了，他們不敢白白扔錢給別人。

松頓在巴克的身邊跪了下來，兩手捧著他的腦袋瓜，和他臉貼著臉。但他並不像平常一樣，既不開玩笑地搖晃著他的頭，也不是小聲地罵著他，而是在他的耳畔輕輕地低喃著：

「我愛你，巴克！就像你愛我一樣！我愛你就像你愛我一樣！」巴克壓抑住滿腔的熱情，嗚咽地叫了幾聲。

群眾好奇地看著他們，覺得事情看上去很是神祕，就好像是在施魔法一樣。松頓一站起身，巴克就立刻咬住了他戴著手套的手，用力地咬了一會兒，才慢慢地、依依不捨地放開。這個回答並不是言語可以形容的，那都是愛啊！松頓後退幾步。

「現在開始吧，巴克！」他說。

巴克拉緊挽繩，再放鬆幾吋。這是他從經驗中習得的技巧。

「向右！」松頓的聲音響起，在一片靜謐中顯得格外尖銳。

巴克將身體往右邊斜衝，直到衝力繃緊了挽繩，一百五十磅的身軀猛地一拉，滑板下面傳來一陣劈啪的破冰聲。

「向左！」松頓又命令道。

巴克重複了一遍剛剛的動作，只不過這次的方向是往左。只聽見冰雪劈啪的破裂聲，變成了一種猛爆的斷裂聲。雪橇旋轉了，滑板往旁邊滑動了幾吋。雪橇動了！每個人都屏氣凝神地，甚至都忘了呼吸！

「現在，走！」

松頓的命令像是槍聲一般響起。巴克往前奮力地拉著，挽繩倏地繃緊，發出刺耳的聲音。他因使盡了最大的力氣，全身緊緊地縮在一團；絲絹一般的毛皮下，肌肉扭動、糾結在一起，像是有生命似的；他的頭往下壓低，寬厚的胸脯低低地貼

近地面，四肢爪子瘋狂地往前扒著地面，在堅硬的地上刮出了
兩條平行的凹痕。雪橇受到震動，輕輕地晃了起來。突然，他
的一隻腳滑了一下，有人大聲呻吟了一下。之後，雪橇開始搖
搖晃晃地向前移動，看起來有點像停停又走走的樣子，事實上
從未完全停頓下來。雪橇不斷地移動著……半吋……一吋……
兩吋……，雪橇停頓的感覺漸漸減少。而當有足夠的衝力時，
巴克立刻穩住了震動，直到雪橇可以平穩地向前移動。

　　圍觀的人們都忘了自己曾經在那一瞬間停止呼吸，現在喘
了一口氣之後，又開始平順地呼吸起來。松頓跟在雪橇的後面
跑著，用簡短有力的話語激勵著巴克。規定的距離早就先量好
了，當他接近標記一百碼位置的木柴堆時，歡呼的聲音越來越
大。當他走過了木柴堆，聽到停止的命令時，人群的歡呼聲更
是震天價響。每個人都興奮欲狂，紛紛脫下帽子和手套激動地
丟向空中，就連馬休斯自己也不例外。大家激動地互相握手，
也不管是在跟誰握，亂七八糟、興奮地亂喊亂叫，現場氣氛熱
鬧到了極點。

　　只有松頓跪在巴克的身邊，頭靠著頭，將他來來回回地用
力搖晃著。有些跑過去圍觀的人們，聽到松頓在罵著巴克，罵
得既溫柔又親暱，熱烈且長久！

　　「天啊！先生！天哪！先生！」那個坐頭把交椅的販狗大
王，又語無倫次地說：「我給你一千塊！先生！喔，不！我出
一千二買他！」

　　松頓站起身來，雙眼泫然，淚水當眾毫無顧忌地流著。他

對那個販狗大王說：「不，先生，我不賣。你去死吧！先生，這就是我的回答。」

巴克用牙齒咬住了松頓的手，松頓則抱住他，不斷地來回撫摸著他的身子。圍觀的人很有默契地退開了一步，再也沒有人魯莽地上前打擾了。

第七章

回歸本性

　　短短五分鐘的時間，巴克就幫約翰・松頓贏得了一千六百塊錢，不僅讓他的主人得以清償債務，還可以讓他與夥伴們前往東部，尋找傳說中一處地點不明的金礦。那金礦的年代和當地的歷史一樣久遠，許多人曾前往探尋，少數的人有所發現，但更多的人一去不復返。

　　這失落的金礦變成了一個悲劇，籠罩在一種神秘的氣氛當中。沒有人知道最先發現金礦的人是誰，即使最古老的傳說，也不能追溯到這件事。傳說中，那裡有間頹圮老舊的小木屋，奄奄一息的人們，甚至在臨終前發誓它的存在，指出若找到小木屋的話，就能找到金礦。而且他們還拿出一塊塊的金子以茲證明，那些金子的等級完全不同於任何產於北方的金塊。

　　然而，從來沒有任何活著的人曾經找到這座寶藏，死的人也已經不在世上了。於是，松頓、彼得、和韓斯，帶著巴克和其他六條狗，一同踏上這趟未知的東方之旅，想要完成許多人與狗都未能實現的夢想。他們駕著雪橇，沿著育空河上溯了七十哩路，再向左轉，進入史都華河域，途經馬約與麥奎斯遜，繼續前進，直到史都華河變成了一條小溪，再穿越大陸脊背分水嶺，一座座高聳入雲的山中。

約翰·松頓對人或大自然都是無所苛求，也不畏懼身處荒原，只要有一撮鹽巴、一把來福槍，他就能深入蠻荒，想到哪裡就到哪裡，想待多久就待多久。由於不急著趕路，他像印地安人一樣，每天在旅途中打獵為食；如果打不到獵物，也像印地安人一樣，繼續往前邁進，相信總會有找到獵物的時候。因此，這次進入東部的長途旅行中，菜單上清一色都是肉，雪橇上主要裝著的是工具和彈藥，而時間表則是在無限期、無止盡的未來。

對巴克而言，這是趟充滿無窮樂趣的旅程，不論是打獵、捕魚、或是在陌生的地方毫無目標地遊蕩。他們有時會連續走好幾個禮拜都不休息，日復一日；有時則是隨地紮營，一停留就是好幾個星期。狗兒到處隨心所欲地閒逛，那三個人就以火在冰層上燒出洞來，用火的熱度將無數的髒碗盤清洗乾淨。有時候他們必須餓肚子，有時候則是盡情吃喝，完全根據打獵運氣的好壞和獵物的多寡。夏天到了，人和狗將東西馱在背上，乘著木筏，渡過碧綠的山頂湖泊；或是坐在樹木做成的細長小船中，在不知名的河流裡逆流而上，或是順流而下。

時光流逝，幾個月來，他們在那片茫茫無際的荒山野嶺中，曲折蜿蜒地前進；如果那座如果那座小木屋真實存在，應該有人到過，但這裡卻杳無人跡。他們冒著夏季的暴風雨，穿越了一座座分水嶺。在森林邊界與終年積雪的荒山禿嶺上，半

夜裡陽光依然燦爛，他們卻冷得直打哆嗦。他們也曾進入處處
都是蚊蠅的夏日山谷中，而在山的陰影之處，可以採到如同南
方一樣甜美艷麗的草莓和花朵。那一年秋天，他們深入到一片
怪異的湖沼之地，那裡凄涼寂靜，讓人毛骨悚然，除了野鳥棲
息過的痕跡，毫無其他生命跡象，只有呼嘯而過的寒風，隱蔽
的湖面凍結的冰雪，凄涼的漣漪聲拍打著寂寥的湖岸。

　　又一個冬天過去，他們在那些人煙已無的小徑上四處流
浪。一次，他們來到一條林間小路，一條古老的道路，感覺那
座小木屋彷彿近在不遠處。但是這條道路不知從哪開始，也不
知通往何處，和開闢它的人、以及為何開闢它一樣，仍然是一
個謎。另一次，他們無意間發現一座時間久遠、殘圮的獵人小
屋，約翰‧松頓還在腐爛的毯子中，找到了一枝長管火石簧扳
槍。他知道這是哈德遜灣公司的產品，是早期西北部使用的槍
械，當時一把槍的價值如同堆得跟它一樣高的海狸皮。但線索
就只有這樣而已，至於當年誰建造了這間獵人木屋，誰在毯子
裡留下了這把槍，都無從得知。

　　又一個春天來臨了，他們在流浪多時之後，終於有了結
果。他們並未發現那座小木屋，卻在一片寬闊的山谷之中，發
現了一條淺淺的沙金沖積的礦床。金子亮澄澄地像黃色的奶油
一般，在淘金盤底閃閃發光，當然，他們就不再到別處搜尋
了。每工作一天，他們可以得到價值數千元的純淨金砂與金
塊，而他們天天工作，淘出來的金子裝在麋鹿皮做成的袋子
裡，每五十磅裝成一袋，一袋袋地像柴火一樣，堆在赤松木搭

起的小屋外面。他們像巨人般辛勤地工作著，日子如做夢般一天天飛逝，他們的財富也越堆越高。

狗兒們除了有時將松頓打到的獵物拖回來之後，就沒有任何事情可以做了。巴克成天趴在火堆旁邊沉思，時常看到那個毛茸茸的短腿男人，而現在既然沒啥事情可以做，巴克就更常臥在火堆邊，眨著眼睛出神，跟那個毛茸茸的男人，一同在記憶中的另一個世界裡漫遊。

那個世界裡最要緊的事情，彷彿只有恐懼。他望著那個毛茸茸的男人坐在火堆旁邊睡覺，兩手抱著頭顱，埋在雙膝之間。巴克看見他睡得極不安穩，時常驚醒，向黑暗中驚恐地窺視，同時又擺了更多的柴火在火堆上面。他們有時會走在海邊，毛人一邊撿拾貝殼，一邊將之吃掉，眼睛不時地四處張望，擔心有沒有潛藏的危險，準備好一聽到什麼風吹草動時，隨時可以拔腿就跑。他緊跟在毛人的後面，在森林裡無聲無息地潛行著。他們保持高度的警覺，也特別提高警戒，不時地抽動著耳朵，擴張著鼻孔，那人的嗅覺和聽覺，就像巴克般敏銳無比。毛人可以縱身上樹，在樹上行動自如，如履平地般迅速。他用雙臂從這邊的樹枝盪到那邊的樹枝，有時甚至離了好幾十呎遠，也能一放一抓，從不曾失手跌落。事實上，毛人在樹上簡直就和地上一樣，從容自在；巴克想到有幾個夜晚，那個毛人緊緊抓住樹幹睡覺，而他就在樹底下守夜。

和長毛人的景象密切相扣的，是森林深處傳來的呼喚聲音。那聲音激發他心中一股不平靜的奇妙衝動。那聲音讓他隱

隱約約地感到一種甜蜜的喜悅，並且對他毫不知情的那個聲音，產生了一股瘋狂的渴望與莫名的騷動。有時，他會循著聲音到森林裡找尋，彷彿將它當成可以觸摸的實體一樣。隨著內心的起伏變化，時而輕聲叫喚，或是大膽地挑釁怒吼。有時，他會將鼻子伸進蔭涼的青苔當中，或是雜草叢生的黑土裡面，愉快地嗅著肥沃的大地氣息。有時，他會躲在生滿菌類的樹幹後面，一蹲便是好幾個小時，彷彿在埋伏著要打仗一樣，眼睛睜得大大的，耳朵豎得高高的，仔細地傾聽周遭的動靜。他這樣潛伏著，也許是想要嚇一嚇那不能理解的呼喚，但他不明白自己會什麼會有這樣的行為，只是不由自主地被驅使這麼地做，完全不知所以然。

　　一股壓抑不住的衝動襲上心頭，緊緊地攫住巴克。在暖和的白日裡，他會懶洋洋地躺在營地裡打盹，睡夢中他倏地抬起頭來，豎起耳朵，全神貫注地傾聽著，然後猛地一躍而起，衝了出去，穿越林間小徑，越過灌木叢生的曠野，一口氣跑上好幾個小時。他喜歡沿著乾涸的河道奔馳，在樹林中壓低身體匍匐前進，偷偷地窺視鳥兒們的生活。有時，他會臥在灌木叢裡，看著一群群鷓鴣咕咕叫著，趾高氣昂地跳來跳去，一躺便是一整天。而他最喜歡做的，是在夏日午夜裡，盡情恣意的在朦朧的微光中奔跑，聆聽著森林中如夢囈般的輕喃之聲，就如同人們讀書似地，辨別著各種符號與聲音，尋覓著那無論是他醒著或睡著，都一直召喚著他前去的神秘呼喚。

　　一天夜裡，巴克倏地從睡夢中驚跳而起，眼神熱切焦躁，

127

顫動著鼻翼嗅著，他的鬃毛聳立，如波浪般起伏著。從森林深
處，傳來了呼喚的聲音（或是其中一種音調，因為呼喚聲裡有
許多不同的音調），從來不曾這樣清晰明確。那長長的嗥叫
聲，與愛斯基摩犬的叫聲不盡然相同，卻彷彿是他聽慣了的聲
音。那聲音就像他以前聽過的那熟悉的呼喚。於是，他穿越沉
睡中的營地，迅速且安靜地衝進了森林。當他接近呼喚聲的時
候，漸漸地放慢了速度，小心翼翼地移動著腳步，走到林間的
一片空地，往裡頭一望，看見一隻身形瘦長的灰狼，直直地蹲
著，鼻子朝向天空。

　　巴克並未發出任何聲響，那匹灰狼卻停止了嗥叫，拼命地
嗅著，想找出巴克的藏身之處。巴克昂首闊步地走向空地，身
子半蹲半伏地蜷縮著，尾巴直直地挺著，腳步放得格外小心，
一舉一動既帶著威脅，又帶著友善求和般那樣複雜的態度。這
是猛獸相遇時，向對方傳遞休戰訊息的方式。然而，那灰狼一
看見他轉身就跑，巴克瘋狂地直起猛追，最後將他逼進一條無
路可退的溝裡，那條溪床被一堆木頭擋住了去路。就像喬和所
有被逼上絕路的愛斯基摩犬一樣，那匹灰狼以後腳轉身過來，
毛髮聳立，齜牙咧嘴，咆哮怒吼著，牙齒咬得喀喀作響。

　　巴克並沒有攻擊，只是圍著他繞著圈子，以一種友好的態
度攔住、趨近他。灰狼既懷疑又懼怕，因為巴克的體重足足有
他的三倍重，他的頭也勉強構到巴克的肩膀而已。他抓住機會
再次逃跑，於是一場追逐又重新展開。有好幾次巴克已經追上
了，又被他趁機脫逃，很明顯地他已經是筋疲力竭了，否則巴

克也不可能如此輕而易舉地追上他。他不停往前奔，直到巴克的頭都跑到他的側腹邊，他停下來，轉過身，一逮到機會要拔腿就跑。

最後，巴克的不屈不撓終於得到了回報。那匹灰狼發現巴克並無惡意，就用鼻子和巴克互相嗅了嗅，接著雙方便十分友好，半羞澀半大方地一同嬉戲著，這是猛獸隱藏兇狠本性的方式。過了一段時間之後，灰狼用輕鬆的步子跑開，表示要到某一個地方去，像是在示意著巴克跟他一起走。於是，他們肩並肩地跑到朦朧的夜色中，沿著溪床往上游直奔，來到河道的源頭，並且跨越了那座荒涼的分水嶺。

順著分水嶺另一面的斜坡而下，來到了一處平坦的原野，一片片森林綿延不絕，溪流縱橫。他們繼續往前奔馳，一個小時接著一個小時，跑著跑著，太陽已高高地升起，天氣也變得更暖和了。巴克欣喜若狂，他知道自己終於回應了那呼喚著他的聲音，現在，他正與森林中的兄弟一同奔向那呼喚聲。往日的記憶驀地浮現心頭，不由得情緒激昂，就如同他曾經激動過的現實一樣，而他們僅僅是現實中的幻影。從前，他在那朦朧的國度裡曾經做過這樣的事，而今，相同的景象又要重新上演，在遼闊的原野中自由自在地奔馳著，腳下踩著未曾被人走過的大地，頭頂上則是無際的天空。

他們在一條奔騰不息的溪水旁邊停下來喝水。一停下腳步，巴克便想起了約翰·松頓，於是他遲疑地坐了下來。那匹灰狼繼續朝那呼喚的聲音奔去，一會兒又跑了回來，嗅了嗅巴

克的鼻子，作出各種姿勢，彷彿是鼓勵著巴克繼續跟他走一樣。然而，巴克卻轉過身去，緩緩地走上回家的路。那荒野中的兄弟輕聲嗚咽著，跟著他跑了半個多小時，最後，他只得坐了下來，鼻子仰天而嘯，聲音悲涼。隨著巴克堅定不移地往回走，他聽見那長嚎聲愈行愈遠，直到消失在遠方。

巴克衝進營地的時候，約翰·松頓正在吃午飯。他滿懷著如癡如狂的愛意撲向約翰·松頓，將他撲倒在地，趴在他的身上，又舔他的臉、又咬他的手。「真像個大傻瓜！」松頓這麼說著，同時一邊摟著巴克，前前後後搓揉搖晃著，親暱地罵他。

連續兩天兩夜，巴克寸步不離營地，一刻也不讓松頓離開自己的視線。巴克跟著他去工作，盯著他吃飯，晚上看著他鑽進毯子裡，早上又看著他鑽出來。然而，兩天之後，森林裡的呼喚聲又再度響起，這次似乎比以前更加的急切。一股不安的情緒又重新襲上巴克的心頭，想起荒野中那位兄弟的一切，分水嶺那邊風光明媚的土地，還有那並肩快意的奔馳，穿越片片遼闊的森林。這些回憶一直在他的腦海裡縈繞不去。於是，他又開始在森林裡四處遊蕩，但是那荒野的兄弟並未再度出現。儘管在漫長的夜晚裡不眠不休地守候，側耳傾聽著，但那悲涼的哀嚎聲，卻再也不曾響起。

他開始在外頭夜宿，一連好幾天都不回營地。有一次，他到達小溪的源頭，越過了分水嶺，走進那片林木蒼鬱、溪流縱橫的地方，四處遍尋那荒野兄弟的蹤跡，花了一個星期，卻仍是一無所獲。他一路晃蕩，一邊捕食獵物，邁著輕鬆自如的腳步，似乎永不知疲累爲何物。他在一條注入大海的河中捕捉鮭魚，在河邊殺死了一頭黑熊。這頭黑熊在捕魚時被蚊子螫瞎了眼，絕望無助地在林中到處怒吼奔竄。即便如此，這仍是一場硬仗，而這場搏鬥激起了巴克潛藏的兇殘本性。兩天後，他回到咬死熊的地方，發現十幾隻狼獾正在爭搶熊的殘骸。於是他兩三下就將他們給驅離，留下來的兩隻，也不敢再來爭食了。

　　他對於殺戮的渴望，從來沒有像此刻一樣如此地高張。他成了殺生獵食的野獸，獵殺落單、無助的小動物，依靠著自己的氣力與勇敢，在這敵意環伺、只有強者才得以生存的環境中，成功地存活了下來。因此，他爲自己是個勝利者而自豪，這股自豪像是傳染般地展現在他的肉體上，從他的一舉一動中，從每一塊活動自如的肌肉中，便可一目瞭然。這股自豪顯現在他的外表上，讓他的皮毛光彩奪人，更加炫麗燦目。若不是口鼻與眼睛之處，有著些許的棕毛，胸前還有一片白毛，人們肯定會將他誤認爲一匹比任何狼種都還要巨大的狼。他的外型和重量遺傳自他聖伯納種的父親，骨架卻遺傳了牧羊犬的母親。他的嘴形長得就像長形的狼嘴，只不過比任何一隻狼都還要大；而他的頭顱也像是狼頭，只是稍微寬大一些。

　　他的狡猾則是屬於狼性般那樣野蠻的狡獪；他的智慧綜合了聖伯納犬和牧羊犬，加上來自於險惡環境中所得到的經驗，使他成爲了荒野上最爲可怕的野獸之一。作爲一個完全依靠肉食生存的食肉動物，他正處於身體最健壯的巔峰，年輕力壯，精力旺盛。當松頓順著他的背脊往下撫摸的時候，手所到之處，發出陣陣的聲響，每一根毛髮也因碰觸而釋放著蘊藏的磁力。身體的每一個部位，大腦、肌肉、神經、筋骨，都達到最敏銳的巔峰狀態，而各部位之間，依然維持著最佳的平衡，有著絕妙的協調性，對於視覺、聽覺以及突發事件的必要反應都快如閃電。即使愛斯基摩犬防禦或攻擊時候的速度已經十分迅速，但他至少還要快上兩倍。他對動靜的反應時間比別的狗還少，而且他察覺、判斷、與反應的這三個動作，幾乎是同時發生的。當然這三個動作是有先後的順序，只是因爲間隔非常地短暫，才會讓人看起來像是同時發生的一樣。他的筋肉充滿了生命的活力，動起來彷彿彈簧般迅速敏捷。他的生命力在他體內洶湧澎湃地流動著，充滿了喜悅，無法遏止，那如癡如狂的狀態，彷彿要將身體撐破一般，不斷地流瀉到這個世上。

「從來沒有見過這樣的狗！」一天，當他們三個看著巴克走出營地時，約翰・松頓如此說道。

「上帝在造他的時候，模子肯定撐破了！」彼得說。

「天啊！我也是這麼的想！」韓斯表示同意。

他們只是看到他大步走出營地的樣子，卻沒有見過他一旦置身於森林深處時，那種驚人的可怕變化。他不再快步前進，而是立刻變成一隻荒原中的野獸，鬼鬼祟祟、躡手躡腳，偷偷地潛行，像是林蔭中一閃而逝的魅影，時隱時現。他像蛇一般匍匐前進，再倏地跳起毫不猶豫襲擊。他可以從窩裡抓走松

132

雞，殺死熟睡中的兔子，跳到空中咬住來不及逃到樹上的小栗鼠。對他而言，在沒有結冰的池水中，魚游得不比他快；而築壩的海獺也不如他來得機警。他為了果腹才殺生，並不是出於胡作非為、恣意濫殺。他只是比較喜歡吃自己所捕殺的獵物罷了。因此，他有時會鬼鬼祟祟的惡作劇，特別喜歡悄悄地接近松鼠，在幾乎要抓住他們的時候，再故意放他們走，嚇得他們吱吱喳喳地叫著逃到樹梢上，這讓巴克大感痛快。

那年秋季到來的時候，出現了成群的麋鹿。為了度過寒冬，他們緩緩地移往地勢較低的溫暖山谷。巴克逮到了一隻脫離群隊的小麋鹿，但他極度盼望能抓到一隻更大、更兇狠、難以對付的麋鹿。一天，在小溪源頭的那座分水嶺上，終於讓他碰到機會了。一群二十幾隻的麋鹿從一處溪流縱橫、森林密佈的地方而來，首領是一隻體型壯碩的雄麋鹿，身材高達六呎多，看來兇性十足，正好是巴克日夜所期待的理想對手。雄麋鹿來回搖晃著他那兩根掌形的大鹿角，上面有著十四根的枝叉，兩端張開的距離足足有七呎之寬。他一看到巴克，兩隻小眼睛中便燃起了仇恨的光芒，怒氣難當地大聲咆哮。

他之所以如此窮凶惡極，是因為他的側腹邊，插著一根露著尾端羽飾的箭。受了原始時代所遺留下來的狩獵本能指引，巴克開始企圖要將這頭雄麋鹿從鹿群中引誘出來。但是，這當然不是一件輕而易舉的事。他在雄鹿的面前又叫又跳的，卻又不能太靠近，只能站在那雙可怕的大叉角和巨蹄接近不到的距離。雄麋鹿無法擺脫這個尖牙利齒的傢伙，不禁大發雷霆，於是本能地向巴克猛衝過去。巴克狡猾地後退，假裝一副逃脫不掉的模樣，誘使雄麋鹿追過去好讓對手與鹿群隔開。但是，每當雄麋鹿要離開夥伴時，就會有兩三隻較年輕的雄麋鹿，向巴克背部衝撞而來，以便讓那隻受了傷的大雄鹿趁機回到隊伍之中。

野獸深具耐性，頑強不屈、百折不撓，堅持到底。這種耐性可以讓蜘蛛守在網上、蛇盤繞起來、豹子潛伏伺機，長時間一直蟄伏不動。而這樣的耐性，只能見於那些以獵取動物為生的猛獸中。巴克就擁有這樣的特性。他絕不善罷甘休，緊跟在鹿群旁邊，阻攔他們前進，激怒年輕的雄鹿，折磨帶著小麋鹿的雌麋鹿，也讓那隻受傷的大麋鹿失了對策，暴跳如雷。這樣情形持續了有半天之久，巴克突然加速從各個方向進攻，旋風般將鹿群圍繞在圈子裡面，在他的目標回到鹿群之前飛快地攔住他，將那群受害者的耐性逐漸磨光。受攻擊者的耐性，總是遠不如攻擊的一方。

白天漸漸流逝，夕陽落到西北方向的安樂窩去了（黑夜又降臨大地，秋天的黑夜只有六個小時之短）。年輕的雄麋鹿，愈來愈勉為其難地回來援助被困的領袖，他們對逐漸下降的氣溫感到痛苦，急著趕往地勢較低的地方去，卻似乎永遠擺脫不了這個不知疲倦的傢伙的糾纏。此外，並非整個鹿群的生命皆受到威脅，也不是年輕的雄鹿，而只是一隻受傷的麋鹿罷了。因而，與自己的性命相較之下，輕重不言而喻。最後，他們甘願將老雄麋鹿作為安全通行的過路費。

第七章

　　薄暮降臨時，年老的雄麋鹿低頭站著，望著他的夥伴們——那熟識的雌麋鹿，他親生的小麋鹿，以及他曾統治過的年輕雄鹿，在逐漸黯淡的暮色之中，倉皇匆忙地離他而去。他無法跟上前去，因為眼前這隻長著利齒的傢伙，正兇狠地跳躍著，阻止他的離去。他重達半噸又三百磅，經歷了漫長且威風的一生，不知有過多少次的戰鬥，而現在，竟然要在一個頭部遠不及他粗大膝蓋那般高的敵人利齒下送命。

　　從那時開始，巴克不分晝夜地糾纏他的獵物，寸步不離，絕對不給他片刻喘息的機會，也不讓他有機會吃上一口樺樹的葉片或楊柳的嫩芽，或是在度過潺潺小溪時，喝上一口水以解他焦躁如焚的乾渴。被逼到走投無路時，雄麋鹿常常會猛然之間就拔腿奔馳，而巴克並不加以阻攔，而是跟在後頭，輕快地緩緩跑著，非常滿意這種戲弄獵物的遊戲方式。當雄麋鹿站著不動時，巴克就臥下來休息；當他想要吃東西或喝水時，就上前兇狠地攻擊。

　　雄麋鹿長著樹枝狀鹿角的頭越垂越低，蹣跚的腳步也更加軟弱無力。他開始長時間地站著，鼻子貼近地面，耳朵喪氣地垂著，而巴克則因此有了更多的時間喝水和休息。此時，巴克吐著紅紅的舌頭喘著氣，目不轉睛地盯著大雄鹿，感到事物好像發生了什麼變化，他可以感覺到這片土地出現了新的騷動。當那群麋鹿來到這地方的時候，好似有其他的生物也隨之而進，而森林、河流、和空氣，彷彿因為那些生物的出現，而顯得悸動不安、恐懼顫抖。他不是依靠視覺、聽覺或嗅覺來獲知這些訊息，而是根據一種極其微妙又敏銳的感覺而得知。他並沒有看見什麼，或是聽到、嗅到什麼，但他感覺到這片土地不知爲何產生了變化，有了一種新的騷動，他決定先解決眼前這件事，再去查個水落石出。

最後，在第四天的黃昏，巴克終於將這頭大雄鹿撂倒在地。在這隻被咬死的麋鹿旁邊，他吃飽睡、睡飽吃，休息了一天一夜。在休息之後，他恢復了體力和精神，隨即轉身往營地和約翰‧松頓的方向奔去。他輕鬆地邁開步伐往前奔馳，一個小時接著另一個小時，一路不曾停歇，從不曾因爲錯綜複雜的路徑而搞混方向，他越過陌生的地帶，筆直往家的方向跑去，其精確無比的方向感，足以令人和指南針爲之羞愧。

當他繼續往前跑的時候，越來越強烈地感覺到這片土地上的新騷動。有外來的新生物進入了這片土地，和整個夏天都存在這裡的生命有很大的不同。這並不是再由微妙神秘的感覺而得的，而是明顯到連鳥兒都在啾啾地談論著，松鼠吱吱喳喳地議論紛紛，甚至連陣陣微風也在輕聲細語地低訴著。有好幾次，他停下腳步，大口大口地吸著早晨新鮮的空氣，但從中察覺到的訊息卻使得他加快前進的速度。那是一種大禍臨頭的感覺，若非已經發生，就是正在發生中。他越過最後一座分水嶺，沿著山谷往營地奔去，腳步更加小心翼翼。

在距離營地三哩遠的地方，他發現了一道新的足跡，直直通往營地與約翰‧松頓的所在處。巴克頓時毛髮直豎，迅速而隱蔽地往前飛奔。他的神經緊繃，警戒地觀察著眼前所有的細節,而這些跡象除了沒有說明結局之外,再再都顯示了一件意外。他用鼻子嗅出了那些生物如何經過他現在腳下的這些地方。他發現,森林裡一片死寂,鳥兒全都飛走了,松鼠也躲了起來。他只看到一隻毛色光亮的灰松鼠,趴在一根灰色的枯枝上,看起來就像是樹枝的一部分,一個長在樹枝上的樹瘤。

像一道急速掠過的影子,巴克形跡隱匿地往前潛行,突然,鼻子彷彿被一種力量緊緊拽向一旁似的,一股新的氣味將他引到灌木叢裡,在那裡發現了尼格。他的屍體側躺著,像是受傷後忍痛爬到這裡才死去的。一支箭貫穿了他的身體,箭的頭尾分別露在身體的兩側。

再往前一百碼,巴克發現了一隻松頓在道森買的雪橇狗,躺在路的中間抽搐著,作垂死的掙扎。巴克從他的身旁繞過,並不多加停留。這時,一陣微弱的嘈雜聲從營地裡傳了過來,單調的歌唱聲此起彼落著。巴克匍匐前進著,爬到營地的邊緣,發現韓斯身上滿滿都是箭,看起來像是一頭豪豬,臉朝下趴在地上。他立刻往赤松木所搭蓋而成的小屋望去,那種景象讓他頸背上的毛髮,倏地全都豎立了起來,一陣狂暴的怒氣橫掃全身。巴克不由自主地吼叫了一聲,那吼聲極其兇猛殘暴。這是他一生中,最後一次讓憤怒與激情取代了他的狡猾與理性,這都是因為他對約翰‧松頓的那份真摯深厚的愛,使他昏了頭。

葉海特族印地安人正圍著小木屋的廢墟跳著舞,猛地聽到一陣可怕的怒吼,接著就看到一隻從未見過的怪獸朝著他們撲了過來。那就是巴克，像是一陣憤怒的颶風，瘋狂地想將他們毀滅。他撲到最前面的那個人身上（這個人是葉海特族的酋長），將他的喉嚨撕裂出一道大口子，血如泉湧般從頸部的靜脈中噴灑了出來。巴克不管這個受害著是死是活，又縱身一跳，撕裂了第二個人的喉嚨。沒有人抵擋得了他。他衝到人群中，又撕又咬，毀滅所有的事情。而他動作如此的迅速敏捷，因此射向他的箭完全落空，更因為印地安人擁擠不堪，射出的箭反而傷到了自己人。一個年輕獵人將一枝標槍擲向半空中的巴克，結果卻刺穿了另一個獵人的胸膛，力道大得矛頭穿出了那個人的後背，露在外面。此刻，葉海特人驚慌失措，恐懼地逃向森林裡面，直喊著看到了魔鬼。

巴克也確實變成了魔鬼的化身，暴跳如雷地緊追不捨，將在林中逃竄的葉海特人撂倒，就像咬死麋鹿一般撕裂他們。那簡直是葉海特人的末日一樣，他們四處逃避，各自逃命，直到一個星期後，倖存下來的人們才又聚集在一處地勢較低的山谷裡，清查傷亡人數。巴克在厭倦追逐之後，返回了荒涼的營地。他發現，彼得才剛一驚醒就被殺死在毯子裡。松頓在地上拼命掙扎的痕跡仍然清晰可見，巴克仔細地嗅著這些痕跡的氣息，循著氣味來到一個深水的池塘邊。思姬特就躺在那裡，頭和前腿都浸在水中，池水被淘金槽流出來的泥沙弄得混濁不清，遮住了裡面的東西，也遮住了約翰‧松頓，因為巴克循著他的蹤跡而來到水邊，卻未見任何從水中離去的腳印。

整整一天，巴克不是抑鬱地坐在水池旁邊憂傷沉思，就是

心神不寧地在營地裡徘徊。死亡，就是生物行為的終結，也就是生命從生活裡消失。他知道什麼是死亡，他也知道，約翰‧松頓已經死了。他的心裡有著一種強烈的空虛感，就好像是飢餓一樣，但這種空虛感卻無法靠食物填滿，讓他的心愈來愈痛。有時，當他停下來默默地看著一具具葉海特人屍體的時候，這種傷痛會暫時消失，而且這時他會感到十分的驕傲，這種自傲感是他一生中從未有過的。他殺了人，萬物之靈的人類，而且是在面對棍棒和利齒的法則之下殺了他們的。他好奇的嗅了嗅這些屍體。他們竟然這麼輕易地就死了。連殺一隻愛斯基摩犬都還比殺他們還困難。如果沒有弓箭、長矛、和棍棒的話，他們根本就不是對手。從今以後，他再也不怕人類了，除非他們手中握有弓箭、長矛或是棍棒。

夜幕低垂，一輪滿月從樹梢上升起，當空照著大地，使得大地籠罩在一片陰森的慘白月色裡。當黑夜降臨的時候，巴克坐在池邊沉思哀悼，發現森林中有一股新的騷動，這股騷動和葉海特人所引起的大不相同。他站起身來，側耳傾聽，嗅了嗅氣味。遠處傳來一聲模糊尖銳的嗥叫，然後，一陣相似的合聲一同合唱著。隨著時間的流逝，那嗥叫越來越接近，越來越清晰。再一次地，巴克明白了這就是他記憶深處中曾經聽到的，來自另一個世界的召喚聲。他走到空地中央，凝神聆聽。這正是那種呼喚，具有多種音調的呼喚聲，比以前更有誘惑力，也更令人難以招架。同時，他也感到自己樂於服從、回應這種召喚。約翰‧松頓已經死了，他身上最後一絲的眷戀已經不存在

了。人類以及人類所宣稱的權利，再也束縛不了他了。

　　為了捕食獵物，狼群像葉海特人狩獵一樣，跟在遷徙的鹿群兩側，越過了茂密的森林和溪流縱橫的區域，到了巴克所在的山谷。他們像是一道銀色的波浪，湧進了月光流洩一地的紮營空地。巴克坐在空地的中央，等候他們的到來，像是一尊雕像一樣，動也不動。他們先是一愣，被巴克那靜止且龐大的身軀，以及毫無所動的鎮定給震懾住了。停頓了一會兒，一隻最勇敢的狼撲向巴克，巴克像是閃電般地快速反擊，咬斷了他的脖子。然後，他又站回原地，一動也不動，那隻受傷的狼，則在他的後面痛苦地打著滾。接著，有三匹狼接連向巴克撲了上來，但不是被咬傷了喉嚨，就是被撕裂了肩膀，一個個大敗而回。

　　這下所有的狼群都被惹怒了，全部一擁而上，急於撲倒獵物，結果他們自己互相妨礙，亂成一團。巴克靈敏的動作讓他佔了優勢。他用後腿支撐身體，迅速地旋轉，又咬又抓的應付著四面八方，猶如在前面築起了一道無懈可擊的防線，牢不可破。但是為了防止來自背後的偷襲，他只好邊戰邊退，經過水池旁邊，退到河床，緊緊靠著一座高聳的沙石河岸。巴克來到石岸一處因人們採礦而挖出的直角形角落，就這樣，三面都有了掩護，只需全力對付正面的敵人即可。

　　巴克做好充分的防衛，半個小時之後，狼群潰退了。每個都吐著長長的舌頭喘著氣，陰森雪白的牙齒在月光下更顯得兇殘。有些趴在地上，頭抬起來，耳朵豎著；有些站著不動，監視著他的舉動；還有些則到水池畔舔著池裡的水。這時，一隻身形瘦長的狼，以一種十分友好的態度，小心翼翼地走了過來。巴克認出來了，那就是曾經跟他奔馳了一天一夜的荒野兄弟。他輕聲地叫著，巴克也低聲呼應，彼此觸碰著鼻子。

接著，一隻瘦骨嶙峋、傷疤累累的老狼走上前來。一開始巴克齜牙咧嘴地準備咆哮出聲，但還是和他碰了碰鼻子。然後，老狼坐了下來，鼻子仰天指向月亮，發出了長長的嗥叫聲。現在，巴克聽到了那不容置疑的呼喚。他也坐了下來，一同仰天長嘯著。最後，他走出了角落，狼群一擁而上，半友善、半粗魯地對他嗅了嗅。狼群的領袖們長嗥一聲，帶頭竄入了森林之中。狼群隨即跟上，齊聲嗥叫。巴克跟著這群狼，和他那荒野的兄弟齊肩並進，邊奔跑邊叫著。

巴克的故事，基本上到這裡就結束了。幾年之後，葉海特人發現森林中的狼種起了變化，有些狼的頭部和嘴部有著棕色的斑點，胸口中央的地方有著一道白色的毛髮。更奇怪的是葉海特族中有個傳說不脛而走：有一隻魔犬領著狼群奔跑，他們十分害怕這隻魔犬，因為他甚至比他們葉海特人更加狡猾。在嚴寒的冬季裡，他會偷走他們營地的糧食，搶奪被捕獸器抓到的獵物，咬死他們的狗，還不把他們最勇敢的獵人放在眼裡。

不僅如此，傳說中的故事愈說愈玄。有些獵人出了營地後就一去不復返；有些被發現的時候，喉嚨早已被殘酷無情地撕裂，而附近的雪地上留有許多狼的腳印，比任何品種的狼都還要大。每年秋天，葉海特人追捕著遷徙的麋鹿時，有一處的山

野性的呼喚

谷永遠不敢走進去。當婦女們圍著火堆，講起這條魔犬為何偏偏選擇這座山谷作為棲息地時，不免感到哀傷。

然而，葉海特人並不知道，在每年夏天的時候，山谷裡會來一位訪客。這個訪客身型巨大，擁有一身光彩絢麗的毛皮，看起來像是狼，卻又與其他的狼不甚相像。他獨自一個穿越景色秀美的森林，走進一處樹木環繞的空地。那裡，有著一袋袋破爛的鹿皮袋子，裡頭流出了一道道黃濁的水，滲入了土裡，被長長的野草覆蓋住其金黃色的光芒。在這裡，那隻狼總是沉思良久，悲傷地長嗥一聲，轉身而去。

可是他也非孤身隻影。每當漫長冬夜來臨，狼群追逐著獵物的腳步進入較低漥的山谷。在蒼白的月光下，或是朦朧的北極光中，便可看見他奔馳在狼群的最前面，跳得比他的夥伴們更高。他放開喉嚨，唱出嘹亮的歌聲，一首在原始世界中，屬於他們的古老歌曲。

Chapter I.

Into the Primitive

"Old longings nomadic leap,
Chafing at custom's chain;
Again from its brumal sleep
Wakens the ferine strain."

Buck did not read the newspapers, or he would have known that trouble was brewing, not alone for himself, but for every tidewater dog, strong of muscle and with warm, long hair, from Puget Sound to San Diego. Because men, groping in the Arctic darkness, had found a yellow metal, and because steamship and transportation companies were booming the find, thousands of men were rushing into the

nomadic 遊牧的 *adj.*
brumal sleep 冬眠 *n.*
ferine 野性的 *adj.*
arctic 北極 *adj.*

146

Northland. These men wanted dogs, and the dogs they wanted were heavy dogs, with strong muscles by which to toil, and furry coats to protect them from the frost.

Buck lived at a big house in the sun-kissed Santa Clara Valley. Judge Miller's place, it was called. It stood back from the road, half hidden among the trees, through which glimpses could be caught of the wide cool veranda that ran around its four sides. The house was approached by gravelled driveways which wound about through wide- spreading lawns and under the interlacing boughs of tall poplars. At the rear things were on even a more spacious scale than at the front. There were great stables, where a dozen grooms and boys held forth, rows of vine-clad servants' cottages, an endless and orderly array of outhouses, long grape arbors, green pastures, orchards, and berry patches. Then there was the pumping plant for the artesian well, and the big cement tank where Judge Miller's boys took their morning plunge and kept cool in the hot afternoon.

And over this great demesne Buck ruled. Here he was born, and here he had lived the four years of his life. It was true, there were other dogs. There could not but be other dogs

gravelled 鋪有碎石的 *adj.*
interlacing 交織的 *adj.*
spacious 寬廣的 *adj.*
demesne 莊園 *n.*

on so vast a place, but they did not count. They came and went, resided in the populous kennels, or lived obscurely in the recesses of the house after the fashion of Toots, the Japanese pug, or Ysabel, the Mexican hairless- strange creatures that rarely put nose out of doors or set foot to ground. On the other hand, there were the fox terriers, a score of them at least, who yelped fearful promises at Toots and Ysabel looking out of the windows at them and protected by a legion of housemaids armed with brooms and mops.

But Buck was neither house-dog nor kennel-dog. The whole realm was his. He plunged into the swimming tank or went hunting with the Judge's sons; he escorted Mollie and Alice, the Judge's daughters, on long twilight or early morning rambles; on wintry nights he lay at the Judge's feet before the roaring library fire; he carried the Judge's grandsons on his back, or rolled them in the grass, and guarded their footsteps through wild adventures down to the fountain in the stable yard, and even beyond, where the paddocks were, and the berry patches. Among the terriers he stalked imperiously, and Toots and Ysabel he utterly ignored, for he was king-king over all creeping, crawling, flying things of Judge Miller's place,

---

kennel 狗舍 *n.*
escorted 陪伴，護送 *v.*
paddocks 馬廄 *n.*
utterly 完全地 *adv.*

humans included.

His father, Elmo, a huge St. Bernard, had been the Judge's inseparable companion, and Buck bid fair to follow in the way of his father. He was not so large-he weighed only one hundred and forty pounds-for his mother, Shep, had been a Scotch shepherd dog. Nevertheless, one hundred and forty pounds, to which was added the dignity that comes of good living and universal respect, enabled him to carry himself in right royal fashion. During the four years since his puppyhood he had lived the life of a sated aristocrat; he had a fine pride in himself, was even a trifle egotistical, as country gentlemen sometimes become because of their insular situation. But he had saved himself by not becoming a mere pampered house-dog. Hunting and kindred outdoor delights had kept down the fat and hardened his muscles; and to him, as to the cold-tubbing races, the love of water had been a tonic and a health preserver.

And this was the manner of dog Buck was in the fall of 1897, when the Klondike strike dragged men from all the world into the frozen North. But Buck did not read the newspapers, and he did not know that Manuel, one of the gardener's helpers, was an undesirable acquaintance. Manuel

---

inseparable 形影不離的 *adj.*
aristocrat 貴族 *n.*
egotistical 自我中心的 *adj.*

had one besetting sin. He loved to play Chinese lottery. Also, in his gambling, he had one besetting weakness-faith in a system; and this made his damnation certain. For to play a system requires money, while the wages of a gardener's helper do not lap over the needs of a wife and numerous progeny.

The Judge was at a meeting of the Raisin Growers' Association, and the boys were busy organizing an athletic club, on the memorable night of Manuel's treachery. No one saw him and Buck go off through the orchard on what Buck imagined was merely a stroll. And with the exception of a solitary man, no one saw them arrive at the little flag station known as College Park. This man talked with Manuel, and money chinked between them.

"You might wrap up the goods before you deliver 'm," the stranger said gruffly, and Manuel doubled a piece of stout rope around Buck's neck under the collar.

"Twist it, an' you'll choke 'm plentee," said Manuel, and the stranger grunted a ready affirmative.

Buck had accepted the rope with quiet dignity. To be sure, it was an unwonted performance: but he had learned to trust

---

besetting 困擾的，糾纏的 *adj.*
progeny 後代子孫 *n.*
treachery 背叛，欺騙 *n.*
plentee 很多，充足，**plenty** 的口語形式 *n.*
affirmative 肯定的，正面的 *adj.*

in men he knew, and to give them credit for a wisdom that outreached his own. But when the ends of the rope were placed in the stranger's hands, he growled menacingly. He had merely intimated his displeasure, in his pride believing that to intimate was to command. But to his surprise the rope tightened around his neck, shutting off his breath. In quick rage he sprang at the man, who met him halfway, grappled him close by the throat, and with a deft twist threw him over on his back. Then the rope tightened mercilessly, while Buck struggled in a fury, his tongue lolling out of his mouth and his great chest panting futilely. Never in all his life had he been so vilely treated, and never in all his life had he been so angry. But his strength ebbed, his eyes glazed, and he knew nothing when the train was flagged and the two men threw him into the baggage car.

The next he knew, he was dimly aware that his tongue was hurting and that he was being jolted along in some kind of a

---

outreached 超越，勝過 *v.*
menacingly 威脅地，恐嚇地 *adv.*
tightened 收緊 *v.*
mercilessly 無情 *adv.*
fury 憤怒，狂怒 *n.*

conveyance. The hoarse shriek of a locomotive whistling a crossing told him where he was. He had travelled too often with the Judge not to know the sensation of riding in a baggage car. He opened his eyes, and into them came the unbridled anger of a kidnapped king. The man sprang for his throat, but Buck was too quick for him. His jaws closed on the hand, nor did they relax till his senses were choked out of him once more.

"Yep, has fits," the man said, hiding his mangled hand from the baggageman, who had been attracted by the sounds of struggle. "I'm takin' 'm up for the boss to 'Frisco. A crack dog-doctor there thinks that he can cure 'm."

Concerning that night's ride, the man spoke most eloquently for himself, in a little shed back of a saloon on the San Francisco water front.

"All I get is fifty for it," he grumbled; "an' I wouldn't do it over for a thousand, cold cash."

His hand was wrapped in a bloody handkerchief, and the right trouser leg was ripped from knee to ankle.

"How much did the other mug get?" the saloon-keeper demanded.

---

conveyance 交通工具，運輸工具 *n.*
locomotive 火車頭 *n.*
handkerchief 手帕 *n.*

"A hundred," was the reply. "Wouldn't take a sou less, so help me."

"That makes a hundred and fifty," the saloon-keeper calculated; "and he's worth it, or I'm a squarehead."

The kidnapper undid the bloody wrappings and looked at his lacerated hand. "If I don't get the hydrophoby-"

"It'll be because you was born to hang," laughed the saloon-keeper. "Here, lend me a hand before you pull your freight," he added.

Dazed, suffering intolerable pain from throat and tongue, with the life half throttled out of him, Buck attempted to face his tormentors. But he was thrown down and choked repeatedly, till they succeeded in filing the heavy brass collar from off his neck. Then the rope was removed, and he was flung into a cagelike crate.

There he lay for the remainder of the weary night, nursing his wrath and wounded pride. He could not understand what it all meant. What did they want with him, these strange men? Why were they keeping him pent up in this narrow crate? He did not know why, but he felt oppressed by

squarehead 俚語，形容人愚蠢或笨拙 *n.*
hydrophoby 怕水的，在此指狂犬病 *n.*

the vague sense of impending calamity. Several times during the night he sprang to his feet when the shed door rattled open, expecting to see the Judge, or the boys at least. But each time it was the bulging face of the saloon-keeper that peered in at him by the sickly light of a tallow candle. And each time the joyful bark that trembled in Buck's throat was twisted into a savage growl.

But the saloon-keeper let him alone, and in the morning four men entered and picked up the crate. More tormentors, Buck decided, for they were evil-looking creatures, ragged and unkempt; and he stormed and raged at them through the bars. They only laughed and poked sticks at him, which he promptly assailed with his teeth till he realized that that was what they wanted. Whereupon he lay down sullenly and allowed the crate to be lifted into a wagon. Then he, and the crate in which he was imprisoned, began a passage through many hands. Clerks in the express office took charge of him; he was carted about in another wagon; a truck carried him, with an assortment of boxes and parcels, upon a ferry steamer; he was trucked off the steamer into a great railway depot, and finally he was deposited in an express car.

whereupon 於是 *conj.*
assortment 各種各樣 *n.*

Chapter I

For two days and nights this express car was dragged along at the tail of shrieking locomotives; and for two days and nights Buck neither ate nor drank. In his anger he had met the first advances of the express messengers with growls, and they had retaliated by teasing him. When he flung himself against the bars, quivering and frothing, they laughed at him and taunted him. They growled and barked like detestable dogs, mewed, and flapped their arms and crowed. It was all very silly, he knew; but therefore the more outrage to his dignity, and his anger waxed and waxed. He did not mind the hunger so much, but the lack of water caused him severe suffering and fanned his wrath to fever-pitch. For that matter, high-strung and finely sensitive, the ill treatment had flung him into a fever, which was fed by the inflammation of his parched and swollen throat and tongue.

He was glad for one thing: the rope was off his neck. That had given them an unfair advantage; but now that it was off, he would show them. They would never get another rope around his neck. Upon that he was resolved. For two days and nights he neither ate nor drank, and during those two days and nights of torment, he accumulated a fund of wrath that boded ill for whoever first fell foul of him. His eyes turned

inflammation 發炎 *n.*

bloodshot, and he was metamorphosed into a raging fiend. So changed was he that the Judge himself would not have recognized him; and the express messengers breathed with relief when they bundled him off the train at Seattle.

Four men gingerly carried the crate from the wagon into a small, high-walled back yard. A stout man, with a red sweater that sagged generously at the neck, came out and signed the book for the driver. That was the man, Buck divined, the next tormentor, and he hurled himself savagely against the bars. The man smiled grimly, and brought a hatchet and a club.

"You ain't going to take him out now?" the driver asked.

"Sure," the man replied, driving the hatchet into the crate for a pry.

There was an instantaneous scattering of the four men who had carried it in, and from safe perches on top the wall they prepared to watch the performance.

Buck rushed at the splintering wood, sinking his teeth into it, surging and wrestling with it. Wherever the hatchet fell on the outside, he was there on the inside, snarling and growling, as furiously anxious to get out as the man in the red sweater was calmly intent on getting him out.

metamorphosed 變形 *v.*
gingerly 小心翼翼地 *adv.*
instantaneous 瞬間的 *adj.*

"Now, you red-eyed devil," he said, when he had made an opening sufficient for the passage of Buck's body. At the same time he dropped the hatchet and shifted the club to his right hand.

And Buck was truly a red-eyed devil, as he drew himself together for the spring, hair bristling, mouth foaming, a mad glitter in his bloodshot eyes. Straight at the man he launched his one hundred and forty pounds of fury, surcharged with the pent passion of two days and nights. In mid air, just as his jaws were about to close on the man, he received a shock that checked his body and brought his teeth together with an agonizing clip. He whirled over, fetching the ground on his back and side. He had never been struck by a club in his life, and did not understand. With a snarl that was part bark and more scream he was again on his feet and launched into the air. And again the shock came and he was brought crushingly to the ground. This time he was aware that it was the club, but his madness knew no caution. A dozen times he charged, and as often the club broke the charge and smashed him down.

After a particularly fierce blow, he crawled to his feet, too dazed to rush. He staggered limply about, the blood flowing from nose and mouth and ears, his beautiful coat sprayed and flecked with bloody slaver. Then the man advanced and deliberately dealt him a frightful blow on the nose. All the pain he had endured was as nothing compared with the exquisite agony of this. With a roar that was almost lionlike in

surcharged 充斥，充滿 _v._

its ferocity, he again hurled himself at the man. But the man, shifting the club from right to left, coolly caught him by the under jaw, at the same time wrenching downward and backward. Buck described a complete circle in the air, and half of another, then crashed to the ground on his head and chest.

For the last time he rushed. The man struck the shrewd blow he had purposely withheld for so long, and Buck crumpled up and went down, knocked utterly senseless.

"He's no slouch at dog-breakin', that's wot I say," one of the men on the wall cried enthusiastically.

"Druther break cayuses any day, and twice on Sundays," was the reply of the driver, as he climbed on the wagon and started the horses.

Buck's senses came back to him, but not his strength. He lay where he had fallen, and from there he watched the man in the red sweater.

" 'Answers to the name of Buck,' " the man soliloquized, quoting from the saloon-keeper's letter which had announced the consignment of the crate and contents. "Well, Buck, my boy," he went on in a genial voice, "we've had our little ruction, and the best thing we can do is to let it go at that.

---

ferocity 兇猛，殘暴 *n.*
soliloquized 自言自語 *v.*

You've learned your place, and I know mine. Be a good dog and all'll go well and the goose hang high. Be a bad dog, and I'll whale the stuffin' outa you. Understand?"

As he spoke he fearlessly patted the head he had so mercilessly pounded, and though Buck's hair involuntarily bristled at touch of the hand, he endured it without protest. When the man brought him water he drank eagerly, and later bolted a generous meal of raw meat, chunk by chunk, from the man's hand.

He was beaten (he knew that); but he was not broken. He saw, once for all, that he stood no chance against a man with a club. He had learned the lesson, and in all his after life he never forgot it. That club was a revelation. It was his introduction to the reign of primitive law, and he met the introduction halfway. The facts of life took on a fiercer aspect; and while he faced that aspect uncowed, he faced it with all the latent cunning of his nature aroused. As the days went by, other dogs came, in crates and at the ends of ropes, some docilely, and some raging and roaring as he had come; and, one and all, he watched them pass under the dominion of the man in the red sweater. Again and again, as he looked at each

---

outa out of 的口語簡化形式，從 ... 之中 *adv.*

docilely 順從地 *adv.*

brutal performance, the lesson was driven home to Buck: a man with a club was a lawgiver, a master to be obeyed, though not necessarily conciliated. Of this last Buck was never guilty, though he did see beaten dogs that fawned upon the man, and wagged their tails, and licked his hand. Also he saw one dog, that would neither conciliate nor obey, finally killed in the struggle for mastery.

Now and again men came, strangers, who talked excitedly, wheedlingly, and in all kinds of fashions to the man in the red sweater. And at such times that money passed between them the strangers took one or more of the dogs away with them. Buck wondered where they went, for they never came back; but the fear of the future was strong upon him, and he was glad each time when he was not selected.

Yet his time came, in the end, in the form of a little weazened man who spat broken English and many strange and uncouth exclamations which Buck could not understand.

"Sacredam!" he cried, when his eyes lit upon Buck. "Dat one dam bully dog! Eh? How moch?"

---

conciliated 安撫，調解 *v.*
weazened 衰老的，乾枯的 *adj.*
sacredam 驚訝或感嘆的用語，無特定含義 *n.*
dat 那個，**that** 的口語縮寫 *n.*
moch 即 **much**，可能為當時作者筆誤，此處保留原文 *n.*

"Three hundred, and a present at that," was the prompt reply of the man in the red sweater. "And seein' it's government money, you ain't got no kick coming, eh, Perrault?"

Perrault grinned. Considering that the price of dogs had been boomed skyward by the unwonted demand, it was not an unfair sum for so fine an animal. The Canadian Government would be no loser, nor would its despatches travel the slower. Perrault knew dogs, and when he looked at Buck he knew that he was one in a thousand-"One in ten t'ousand," he commented mentally.

Buck saw money pass between them, and was not surprised when Curly, a good-natured Newfoundland, and he were led away by the little weazened man. That was the last he saw of the man in the red sweater, and as Curly and he looked at receding Seattle from the deck of the Narwhal, it was the last he saw of the warm Southland. Curly and he were taken below by Perrault and turned over to a black- faced giant called François. Perrault was a French-Canadian, and swarthy; but François was a French-Canadian half-breed, and twice as swarthy. They were a new kind of men to Buck (of which he was destined to see many more), and while he developed no

despatches 急件，公文 *n.*

affection for them, he none the less grew honestly to respect them. He speedily learned that Perrault and François were fair men, calm and impartial in administering justice, and too wise in the way of dogs to be fooled by dogs.

In the 'tween-decks of the Narwhal, Buck and Curly joined two other dogs. One of them was a big, snow-white fellow from Spitzbergen who had been brought away by a whaling captain, and who had later accompanied a Geological Survey into the Barrens. He was friendly, in a treacherous sort of way, smiling into one's face the while he meditated some underhand trick, as, for instance, when he stole from Buck's food at the first meal. As Buck sprang to punish him, the lash of François's whip sang through the air, reaching the culprit first; and nothing remained to Buck but to recover the bone. That was fair of François, he decided, and the half-breed began his rise in Buck's estimation.

The other dog made no advances, nor received any; also, he did not attempt to steal from the newcomers. He was a gloomy, morose fellow, and he showed Curly plainly that all he desired was to be left alone, and further, that there would be trouble if he were not left alone. "Dave" he was called, and he ate and slept, or yawned between times, and took interest in

meditated 考慮，思考 **v.**

nothing, not even when the Narwhal crossed Queen Charlotte Sound and rolled and pitched and bucked like a thing possessed. When Buck and Curly grew excited, half wild with fear, he raised his head as though annoyed, favored them with an incurious glance, yawned, and went to sleep again.

Day and night the ship throbbed to the tireless pulse of the propeller, and though one day was very like another, it was apparent to Buck that the weather was steadily growing colder. At last, one morning, the propeller was quiet, and the Narwhal was pervaded with an atmosphere of excitement. He felt it, as did the other dogs, and knew that a change was at hand. François leashed them and brought them on deck. At the first step upon the cold surface, Buck's feet sank into a white mushy something very like mud. He sprang back with a snort. More of this white stuff was falling through the air. He shook himself, but more of it fell upon him. He sniffed it curiously, then licked some up on his tongue. It bit like fire, and the next instant was gone. This puzzled him. He tried it again, with the same result. The onlookers laughed uproariously, and he felt ashamed, he knew not why, for it was his first snow.

Chapter II.

The Law of Club and Fang

Buck's first day on the Dyea beach was like a nightmare. Every hour was filled with shock and surprise. He had been suddenly jerked from the heart of civilization and flung into the heart of things primordial. No lazy, sun-kissed life was this, with nothing to do but loaf and be bored. Here was neither peace, nor rest, nor a moment's safety. All was confusion and action, and every moment life and limb were in peril. There was imperative need to be constantly alert; for these dogs and men were not town dogs and men. They were savages, all of them, who knew no law but the law of club and fang.

He had never seen dogs fight as these wolfish creatures fought, and his first experience taught him an unforgettable

civilization 文明 *n.*
primordial 原始的 *adj.*

lesson. It is true, it was a vicarious experience, else he would not have lived to profit by it. Curly was the victim. They were camped near the log store, where she, in her friendly way, made advances to a husky dog the size of a full-grown wolf, though not half so large as she. There was no warning, only a leap in like a flash, a metallic clip of teeth, a leap out equally swift, and Curly's face was ripped open from eye to jaw.

It was the wolf manner of fighting, to strike and leap away; but there was more to it than this. Thirty or forty huskies ran to the spot and surrounded the combatants in an intent and silent circle. Buck did not comprehend that silent intentness, nor the eager way with which they were licking their chops. Curly rushed her antagonist, who struck again and leaped aside. He met her next rush with his chest, in a peculiar fashion that tumbled her off her feet. She never regained them. This was what the onlooking huskies had waited for. They closed in upon her, snarling and yelping, and she was buried, screaming with agony, beneath the bristling mass of bodies.

So sudden was it, and so unexpected, that Buck was taken aback. He saw Spitz run out his scarlet tongue in a way he had

vicarious 代理的，間接的 *adj.*
comprehend 理解 *v.*
antagonist 對手、敵手 *n.*

of laughing; and he saw François, swinging an axe, spring into the mess of dogs. Three men with clubs were helping him to scatter them. It did not take long. Two minutes from the time Curly went down, the last of her assailants were clubbed off. But she lay there limp and lifeless in the bloody, trampled snow, almost literally torn to pieces, the swart half-breed standing over her and cursing horribly. The scene often came back to Buck to trouble him in his sleep. So that was the way. No fair play. Once down, that was the end of you. Well, he would see to it that he never went down. Spitz ran out his tongue and laughed again, and from that moment Buck hated him with a bitter and deathless hatred.

Before he had recovered from the shock caused by the tragic passing of Curly, he received another shock. François fastened upon him an arrangement of straps and buckles. It was a harness, such as he had seen the grooms put on the horses at home. And as he had seen horses work, so he was set to work, hauling François on a sled to the forest that fringed the valley, and returning with a load of firewood. Though his dignity was sorely hurt by thus being made a draught animal, he was too wise to rebel. He buckled down with a will and did his best, though it was all new and strange.

horribly 可怕地，恐怖地 *adv.*

François was stern, demanding instant obedience, and by virtue of his whip receiving instant obedience; while Dave, who was an experienced wheeler, nipped Buck's hind quarters whenever he was in error. Spitz was the leader, likewise experienced, and while he could not always get at Buck, he growled sharp reproof now and again, or cunningly threw his weight in the traces to jerk Buck into the way he should go.

cunningly 狡猾地 *adv.*

Buck learned easily, and under the combined tuition of his two mates and François made remarkable progress. Ere they returned to camp he knew enough to stop at "ho," to go ahead at "mush," to swing wide on the bends, and to keep clear of the wheeler when the loaded sled shot downhill at their heels.

"T'ree vair' good dogs," François told Perrault. "Dat Buck, heem pool lak hell. I tich heem queek as anyt'ing."

By afternoon, Perrault, who was in a hurry to be on the trail with his despatches, returned with two more dogs. "Billee" and "Joe" he called them, two brothers, and true huskies both. Sons of the one mother though they were, they were as different as day and night. Billee's one fault was his excessive good nature, while Joe was the very opposite, sour and introspective, with a perpetual snarl and a malignant eye. Buck received them in comradely fashion, Dave ignored them, while Spitz proceeded to thrash first one and then the other. Billee wagged his tail appeasingly, turned to run when he saw that appeasement was of no avail, and cried (still appeasingly) when Spitz's sharp teeth scored his flank. But no matter how Spitz circled, Joe whirled around on his heels to face him,

---

lak 像，如何，like 的口語拼法 **v.**
appeasingly 安撫地，撫慰地 **adv.**

mane bristling, ears laid back, lips writhing and snarling, jaws clipping together as fast as he could snap, and eyes diabolically gleaming-the incarnation of belligerent fear. So terrible was his appearance that Spitz was forced to forego disciplining him; but to cover his own discomfiture he turned upon the inoffensive and wailing Billee and drove him to the confines of the camp.

By evening Perrault secured another dog, an old husky, long and lean and gaunt, with a battle-scarred face and a single eye which flashed a warning of prowess that commanded respect. He was called "Sol-leks," which means the Angry One. Like Dave, he asked nothing, gave nothing, expected nothing; and when he marched slowly and deliberately into their midst, even Spitz left him alone. He had one peculiarity which Buck was unlucky enough to discover. He did not like to be approached on his blind side. Of this offence Buck was unwittingly guilty, and the first knowledge he had of his indiscretion was when Sol-leks whirled upon him and slashed his shoulder to the bone for three inches up and down. Forever after Buck avoided his blind side, and to the last of

---

belligerent 好戰的，挑釁的 *adj.*
forego 放棄，放過 *v.*
inoffensive 無害的，不得罪人的 *adj.*
peculiarity 特點，特性 *n.*

their comradeship had no more trouble. His only apparent ambition, like Dave's, was to be left alone; though, as Buck was afterward to learn, each of them possessed one other and even more vital ambition.

That night Buck faced the great problem of sleeping. The tent, illumined by a candle, glowed warmly in the midst of the white plain; and when he, as a matter of course, entered it, both Perrault and François bombarded him with curses and cooking utensils, till he recovered from his consternation and fled ignominiously into the outer cold. A chill wind was blowing that nipped him sharply and bit with especial venom

illumined 照亮，照明 v.

173

into his wounded shoulder. He lay down on the snow and attempted to sleep, but the frost soon drove him shivering to his feet. Miserable and disconsolate, he wandered about among the many tents, only to find that one place was as cold as another. Here and there savage dogs rushed upon him, but he bristled his neck-hair and snarled (for he was learning fast), and they let him go his way unmolested.

Finally an idea came to him. He would return and see how his own teammates were making out. To his astonishment, they had disappeared. Again he wandered about through the great camp, looking for them, and again he returned. Were they in the tent? No, that could not be, else he would not have been driven out. Then where could they possibly be? With drooping tail and shivering body, very forlorn indeed, he aimlessly circled the tent. Suddenly the snow gave way beneath his forelegs and he sank down. Something wriggled under his feet. He sprang back, bristling and snarling, fearful of the unseen and unknown. But a friendly little yelp reassured him, and he went back to

---

bristled 竦立，直立 *v.*
unmolested 未受干擾的，未受侵害的 *adj.*
astonishment 驚訝，驚奇 *n.*
forlorn 孤立的，無助的 *adj.*

investigate. A whiff of warm air ascended to his nostrils, and there, curled up under the snow in a snug ball, lay Billee. He whined placatingly, squirmed and wriggled to show his good will and intentions, and even ventured, as a bribe for peace, to lick Buck's face with his warm wet tongue.

Another lesson. So that was the way they did it, eh? Buck confidently selected a spot, and with much fuss and waste effort proceeded to dig a hole for himself. In a trice the heat from his body filled the confined space and he was asleep. The day had been long and arduous, and he slept soundly and comfortably, though he growled and barked and wrestled with bad dreams.

Nor did he open his eyes till roused by the noises of the waking camp. At first he did not know where he was. It had snowed during the night and he was completely buried. The snow walls pressed him on every side, and a great surge of fear swept through him-the fear of the wild thing for the trap. It was a token that he was harking back through his own life to the lives of his forebears; for he was a civilized dog, an unduly civilized dog, and of his own experience knew no trap and so could not of himself fear it. The muscles of his whole body contracted spasmodically and instinctively, the hair on

nostrils 鼻孔 *n.*

his neck and shoulders stood on end, and with a ferocious snarl he bounded straight up into the blinding day, the snow flying about him in a flashing cloud. Ere he landed on his feet, he saw the white camp spread out before him and knew where he was and remembered all that had passed from the time he went for a stroll with Manuel to the hole he had dug for himself the night before.

A shout from François hailed his appearance. "Wot I say?" the dog-driver cried to Perrault. "Dat Buck for sure learn queek as anyt'ing."

Perrault nodded gravely. As courier for the Canadian Government, bearing important despatches, he was anxious to secure the best dogs, and he was particularly gladdened by the possession of Buck.

Three more huskies were added to the team inside an hour, making a total of nine, and before another quarter of an hour had passed they were in harness and swinging up the trail toward the Dyea Canyon. Buck was glad to be gone, and though the work was hard he found he did not particularly despise it. He was surprised at the eagerness which animated the whole team and which was communicated to him; but still

wot what 的口語拼法 *pron.*
queek 同 quick，快速地 *adv.*
eagerness 渴望，熱切 *n.*

more surprising was the change wrought in Dave and Sol-leks. They were new dogs, utterly transformed by the harness. All passiveness and unconcern had dropped from them. They were alert and active, anxious that the work should go well, and fiercely irritable with whatever, by delay or confusion, retarded that work. The toil of the traces seemed the supreme expression of their being, and all that they lived for and the only thing in which they took delight.

Dave was wheeler or sled dog, pulling in front of him was Buck, then came Sol-leks; the rest of the team was strung out ahead, single file, to the leader, which position was filled by Spitz.

Buck had been purposely placed between Dave and Sol-leks so that he might receive instruction. Apt scholar that he was, they were equally apt teachers, never allowing him to linger long in error, and enforcing their teaching with their sharp teeth. Dave was fair and very wise. He never nipped Buck without cause, and he never failed to nip him when he stood in need of it. As François's whip backed him up, Buck found it to be cheaper to mend his ways than to retaliate. Once, during a brief halt, when he got tangled in the traces and delayed the start, both Dave and Sol-leks flew at him and administered a sound trouncing. The resulting tangle was even worse, but Buck took good care to keep the traces clear thereafter; and ere the day was done, so well had he mastered his work, his mates about ceased nagging him. François's whip

snapped less frequently, and Perrault even honored Buck by lifting up his feet and carefully examining them.

It was a hard day's run, up the Canyon, through Sheep Camp, past the Scales and the timber line, across glaciers and snowdrifts hundreds of feet deep, and over the great Chilcoot Divide, which stands between the salt water and the fresh and guards forbiddingly the sad and lonely North. They made good time down the chain of lakes which fills the craters of extinct volcanoes, and late that night pulled into the huge camp at the head of Lake Bennett, where thousands of goldseekers were building boats against the breakup of the ice in the spring. Buck made his hole in the snow and slept the sleep of the exhausted just, but all too early was routed out in the cold darkness and harnessed with his mates to the sled.

That day they made forty miles, the trail being packed; but the next day, and for many days to follow, they broke their own trail, worked harder, and made poorer time. As a rule, Perrault travelled ahead of the team, packing the snow with webbed shoes to make it easier for them. François, guiding the sled at the gee-pole, sometimes exchanged places with him, but not often. Perrault was in a hurry, and he prided himself

---

forbiddingly 嚴厲地，令人生畏地 *adv.*

gee-pole 牽引繩 *n.*

on his knowledge of ice, which knowledge was indispensable, for the fall ice was very thin, and where there was swift water, there was no ice at all.

Day after day, for days unending, Buck toiled in the traces. Always, they broke camp in the dark, and the first gray of dawn found them hitting the trail with fresh miles reeled off behind them. And always they pitched camp after dark, eating their bit of fish, and crawling to sleep into the snow. Buck was ravenous. The pound and a half of sun-dried salmon, which was his ration for each day, seemed to go nowhere. He never had enough, and suffered from perpetual hunger pangs. Yet the other dogs, because they weighed less and were born to the life, received a pound only of the fish and managed to keep in good condition.

He swiftly lost the fastidiousness which had characterized his old life. A dainty eater, he found that his mates, finishing first, robbed him of his unfinished ration. There was no defending it. While he was fighting off two or three, it was disappearing down the throats of the others. To remedy this, he ate as fast as they; and, so greatly did hunger compel him, he was not above taking what did not belong to him. He

perpetual 永恆的，不斷的 *adj.*
fastidiousness 挑剔，過分講究 *n.*

watched and learned. When he saw Pike, one of the new dogs, a clever malingerer and thief, slyly steal a slice of bacon when Perrault's back was turned, he duplicated the performance the following day, getting away with the whole chunk. A great uproar was raised, but he was unsuspected; while Dub, an awkward blunderer who was always getting caught, was punished for Buck's misdeed.

This first theft marked Buck as fit to survive in the hostile Northland environment. It marked his adaptability, his capacity to adjust himself to changing conditions, the lack of which would have meant swift and terrible death. It marked, further, the decay or going to pieces of his moral nature, a vain thing and a handicap in the ruthless struggle for existence. It was all well enough in the Southland, under the law of love and fellowship, to respect private property and personal feelings; but in the Northland, under the law of club and fang, whoso took such things into account was a fool, and in so far as he observed them he would fail to prosper.

Not that Buck reasoned it out. He was fit, that was all, and unconsciously he accommodated himself to the new mode of life. All his days, no matter what the odds, he had never run from a fight. But the club of the man in the red

misdeed 惡行，不當行為 _n._

sweater had beaten into him a more fundamental and primitive code. Civilized, he could have died for a moral consideration, say the defence of Judge Miller's riding-whip; but the completeness of his decivilization was now evidenced by his ability to flee from the defence of a moral consideration and so save his hide. He did not steal for joy of it, but because of the clamor of his stomach. He did not rob openly, but stole secretly and cunningly, out of respect for club and fang. In short, the things he did were done because it was easier to do them than not to do them.

His development (or retrogression) was rapid. His muscles became hard as iron, and he grew callous to all ordinary pain. He achieved an internal as well as external economy. He could eat anything, no matter how loathsome or indigestible; and, once eaten, the juices of his stomach extracted the last least particle of nutriment; and his blood carried it to the farthest reaches of his body, building it into the toughest and stoutest of tissues. Sight and scent became remarkably keen, while his hearing developed such acuteness that in his sleep he heard the faintest sound and knew whether

fundamental 基本的，根本的 *adj.*
decivilization 退化 *n.*
loathsome 可憎的、令人討厭的 *adj.*
nutriment 營養食品、營養 *n.*

it heralded peace or peril. He learned to bite the ice out with his teeth when it collected between his toes; and when he was thirsty and there was a thick scum of ice over the water hole, he would break it by rearing and striking it with stiff forelegs. His most conspicuous trait was an ability to scent the wind and forecast it a night in advance. No matter how breathless the air when he dug his nest by tree or bank, the wind that later blew inevitably found him to leeward, sheltered and snug.

And not only did he learn by experience, but instincts long dead became alive again. The domesticated generations

domesticated 馴化的、家養的 *adj.*

fell from him. In vague ways he remembered back to the youth of the breed, to the time the wild dogs ranged in packs through the primeval forest and killed their meat as they ran it down. It was no task for him to learn to fight with cut and slash and the quick wolf snap. In this manner had fought forgotten ancestors. They quickened the old life within him, and the old tricks which they had stamped into the heredity of the breed were his tricks. They came to him without effort or discovery, as though they had been his always. And when, on the still cold nights, he pointed his nose at a star and howled long and wolflike, it was his ancestors, dead and dust, pointing nose at star and howling down through the centuries and through him. And his cadences were their cadences, the cadences which voiced their woe and what to them was the meaning of the stiffness, and the cold, and dark.

Thus, as token of what a puppet thing life is, the ancient song surged through him and he came into his own again; and he came because men had found a yellow metal in the North, and because Manuel was a gardener's helper whose wages did not lap over the needs of his wife and diverse small copies of himself.

ancestors 祖先 *n.*

Chapter III.

The Dominant Primordial Beast

The dominant primordial beast was strong in Buck, and under the fierce conditions of trail life it grew and grew. Yet it was a secret growth. His newborn cunning gave him poise and control. He was too busy adjusting himself to the new life to feel at ease, and not only did he not pick fights, but he avoided them whenever possible. A certain deliberateness characterized his attitude. He was not prone to rashness and precipitate action; and in the bitter hatred between him and Spitz he betrayed no impatience, shunned all offensive acts.

On the other hand, possibly because he divined in Buck a dangerous rival, Spitz never lost an opportunity of showing his teeth. He even went out of his way to bully Buck, striving constantly to start the fight which could end only in the death

primordial 原始的 *adj.*
deliberateness 深思熟慮 *n.*

of one or the other. Early in the trip this might have taken place had it not been for an unwonted accident. At the end of this day they made a bleak and miserable camp on the shore of Lake Le Barge. Driving snow, a wind that cut like a white-hot knife, and darkness had forced them to grope for a camping place. They could hardly have fared worse. At their backs rose a perpendicular wall of rock, and Perrault and François were compelled to make their fire and spread their sleeping robes on the ice of the lake itself. The tent they had discarded at Dyea in order to travel light. A few sticks of driftwood furnished them with a fire that thawed down through the ice and left them to eat supper in the dark.

Close in under the sheltering rock Buck made his nest. So snug and warm was it, that he was loath to leave it when François distributed the fish which he had first thawed over the fire. But when Buck finished his ration and returned, he found his nest occupied. A warning snarl told him that the trespasser was Spitz. Till now Buck had avoided trouble with his enemy, but this was too much. The beast in him roared. He sprang upon Spitz with a fury which surprised them both, and Spitz particularly, for his whole experience with Buck had gone to teach him that his rival was an unusually timid dog,

perpendicular 垂直的 *adj.*

185

who managed to hold his own only because of his great weight and size.

François was surprised, too, when they shot out in a tangle from the disrupted nest and he divined the cause of the trouble. "A-a-ah!" he cried to Buck. "Gif it to heem, by Gar! Gif it to heem, the dirty t'eef!"

Spitz was equally willing. He was crying with sheer rage and eagerness as he circled back and forth for a chance to spring in. Buck was no less eager, and no less cautious, as he likewise circled back and forth for the advantage. But it was then that the unexpected happened, the thing which projected their struggle for supremacy far into the future, past many a weary mile of trail and toil.

An oath from Perrault, the resounding impact of a club upon a bony frame, and a shrill yelp of pain, heralded the breaking forth of pandemonium. The camp was suddenly discovered to be alive with skulking furry forms-starving huskies, four or five score of them, who had scented the camp from some Indian village. They had crept in while Buck and Spitz were fighting, and when the two men sprang among them with stout clubs they showed their teeth and fought

---

t'eef 俚語或口語用語，指小偷或賊人 *n.*

heralded 宣布，預示 *v.*

back. They were crazed by the smell of the food. Perrault found one with head buried in the grub-box. His club landed heavily on the gaunt ribs, and the grub-box was capsized on the ground. On the instant a score of the famished brutes were scrambling for the bread and bacon. The clubs fell upon them unheeded. They yelped and howled under the rain of blows, but struggled none the less madly till the last crumb had been devoured.

famished 飢餓的 *adj.*

In the meantime the astonished team-dogs had burst out of their nests only to be set upon by the fierce invaders. Never had Buck seen such dogs. It seemed as though their bones would burst through their skins. They were mere skeletons, draped loosely in draggled hides, with blazing eyes and slavered fangs. But the hunger-madness made them terrifying, irresistible. There was no opposing them. The team-dogs were swept back against the cliff at the first onset. Buck was beset by three huskies, and in a trice his head and shoulders were ripped and slashed. The din was frightful. Billee was crying as usual. Dave and Sol-leks, dripping blood from a score of wounds, were fighting bravely side by side. Joe was snapping like a demon. Once, his teeth closed on the fore leg of a husky, and he crunched down through the bone. Pike, the malingerer, leaped upon the crippled animal, breaking its neck with a quick flash of teeth and a jerk, Buck got a frothing adversary by the throat, and was sprayed with blood when his teeth sank through the jugular. The warm taste of it in his mouth goaded him to greater fierceness. He flung himself upon another, and at the same time felt teeth sink into his own throat. It was Spitz, treacherously attacking from the side.

Perrault and François, having cleaned out their part of the camp, hurried to save their sled-dogs. The wild wave of famished beasts rolled back before them, and Buck shook himself free. But it was only for a moment. The two men were compelled to run back to save the grub, upon which the huskies returned to the attack on the team. Billee, terrified into bravery, sprang through the savage circle and fled away over the ice. Pike and Dub followed on his heels, with the rest of the team behind. As Buck drew himself together to spring after them, out of the tail of his eye he saw Spitz rush upon him with the evident intention of overthrowing him. Once off his feet and under that mass of huskies, there was no hope for him. But he braced himself to the shock of Spitz's charge, then joined the flight out on the lake.

Later, the nine team-dogs gathered together and sought shelter in the forest. Though unpursued, they were in a sorry plight. There was not one who was not wounded in four or five places, while some were wounded grievously. Dub was badly injured in a hind leg; Dolly, the last husky added to the team at Dyea, had a badly torn throat; Joe had lost an eye; while Billee, the good-natured, with an ear chewed and rent to ribbons, cried and whimpered throughout the night. At daybreak they limped warily back to camp, to find the marauders gone and the two men in bad tempers. Fully half their grub supply was gone. The huskies had chewed through the sled lashings and canvas coverings. In fact, nothing, no matter how remotely eatable, had escaped them. They had eaten a pair of Perrault's moose-hide moccasins, chunks out of the leather traces, and even two feet of lash from the end of François's whip. He broke from a mournful contemplation of it to look over his wounded dogs.

"Ah, my frien's," he said softly, "mebbe it mek you mad dog, dose many bites. Mebbe all mad dog, sacredam! Wot you t'ink, eh, Perrault?"

The courier shook his head dubiously. With four hundred miles of trail still between him and Dawson, he could ill afford to have madness break out among his dogs. Two hours of cursing and exertion got the harnesses into shape, and the wound-stiffened team was under way, struggling painfully over the hardest part of the trail they had yet encountered, and for that matter, the hardest between them and Dawson.

The Thirty Mile River was wide open. Its wild water defied the frost, and it was in the eddies only and in the quiet places that the ice held at all. Six days of exhausting toil were required to cover those thirty terrible miles. And terrible they were, for every foot of them was accomplished at the risk of life to dog and man. A dozen times, Perrault, nosing the way broke through the ice bridges, being saved by the long pole he carried, which he so held that it fell each time across the hole made by his body. But a cold snap was on, the thermometer registering fifty below zero, and each time he broke through he was compelled for very life to build a fire and dry his garments.

dubiously 懷疑地 *adv.*

Nothing daunted him. It was because nothing daunted him that he had been chosen for government courier. He took all manner of risks, resolutely thrusting his little weazened face into the frost and struggling on from dim dawn to dark. He skirted the frowning shores on rim ice that bent and crackled under foot and upon which they dared not halt. Once, the sled broke through, with Dave and Buck, and they were half-frozen and all but drowned by the time they were dragged out. The usual fire was necessary to save them. They were coated solidly with ice, and the two men kept them on the run around the fire, sweating and thawing, so close that they were singed by the flames.

At another time Spitz went through, dragging the whole team after him up to Buck, who strained backward with all his strength, his fore paws on the slippery edge and the ice quivering and snapping all around. But behind him was Dave, likewise straining backward, and behind the sled was François, pulling till his tendons cracked.

Again, the rim ice broke away before and behind, and there was no escape except up the cliff. Perrault scaled it by a miracle, while François prayed for just that miracle; and with every thong and sled lashing and the last bit of harness rove into a long rope, the dogs were hoisted, one by one, to the cliff crest. François came up last, after the sled and load. Then came the search for a place to descend, which descent was ultimately made by the aid of the rope, and night found them

back on the river
with a quarter of a
mile to the day's
credit. By the time
they made the
Hootalinqua and
good ice, Buck was
played out. The rest
of the dogs were in
like condition; but
Perrault, to make up
lost time, pushed
them late and early.
The first day they
covered thirty-five
miles to the Big
Salmon; the next day
thirty-five more to
the Little Salmon;
the third day forty
miles, which brought
them well up toward
the Five Fingers.

Buck's feet were
not so compact and
hard as the feet of

the huskies. His had softened during the many generations since the day his last wild ancestor was tamed by a cave-dweller or river man. All day long he limped in agony, and camp once made, lay down like a dead dog. Hungry as he was, he would not move to receive his ration of fish, which François had to bring to him. Also, the dog-driver rubbed Buck's feet for half an hour each night after supper, and sacrificed the tops of his own moccasins to make four moccasins for Buck. This was a great relief, and Buck caused even the weazened face of Perrault to twist itself into a grin one morning, when François forgot the moccasins and Buck lay on his back, his four feet waving appealingly in the air, and refused to budge without them. Later his feet grew hard to the trail, and the worn-out footgear was thrown away.

At the Pelly one morning, as they were harnessing up, Dolly, who had never been conspicuous for anything, went suddenly mad. She announced her condition by a long, heartbreaking wolf howl that sent every dog bristling with fear, then sprang straight for Buck. He had never seen a dog go mad, nor did he have any reason to fear madness; yet he knew that here was horror, and fled away from it in a panic. Straight away he raced, with Dolly, panting and frothing, one

moccasins 莫卡辛鞋，是美洲原住民的傳統服飾，在此指鞋套。 *n.*

leap behind; nor could she gain on him, so great was his terror, nor could he leave her, so great was her madness. He plunged through the wooded breast of the island, flew down to the lower end, crossed a back channel filled with rough ice to another island, gained a third island, curved back to the main river, and in desperation started to cross it. And all the time, though he did not look, he could hear her snarling just one leap behind. François called to him a quarter of a mile away and he doubled back, still one leap ahead, gasping painfully for air and putting all his faith in that François would save him. The dog-driver held the axe poised in his hand, and as Buck shot past him the axe crashed down upon mad Dolly's head.

Buck staggered over against the sled, exhausted, sobbing for breath, helpless. This was Spitz's opportunity. He sprang upon Buck, and twice his teeth sank into his unresisting foe and ripped and tore the flesh to the bone. Then François's lash descended, and Buck had the satisfaction of watching Spitz receive the worst whipping as yet administered to any of the teams.

"One devil, dat Spitz," remarked Perrault. "Some dam day heem keel dat Buck."

"Dat Buck two devils," was François's rejoinder. "All de tam I watch dat Buck I know for sure. Lissen: some dam fine day heem get mad lak hell an' den heem chew dat Spitz all up an' spit heem out on de snow. Sure. I know."

From then on it was war between them. Spitz, as lead-dog and acknowledged master of the team, felt his supremacy threatened by this strange Southland dog. And strange Buck was to him, for of the many Southland dogs he had known, not one had shown up worthily in camp and on trail. They were all too soft, dying under the toil, the frost, and starvation. Buck was the exception. He alone endured and prospered, matching the husky in strength, savagery, and cunning. Then he was a masterful dog, and what made him dangerous was the fact that the club of the man in the red sweater had knocked all blind pluck and rashness out of his desire for mastery. He was preeminently cunning, and could bide his time with a patience that was nothing less than primitive.

It was inevitable that the clash for leadership should come. Buck wanted it. He wanted it because it was his nature, because he had been gripped tight by that nameless, incomprehensible pride of the trail and trace- that pride which holds dogs in the toil to the last gasp, which lures them to die joyfully in the harness, and breaks their hearts if they are cut out of the harness. This was the pride of Dave as wheel-dog, of Sol-leks as he pulled with all his strength; the pride that laid hold of them at break of camp, transforming them from sour

incomprehensible 難以理解的 *adj.*

and sullen brutes into straining, eager, ambitious creatures; the pride that spurred them on all day and dropped them at pitch of camp at night, letting them fall back into gloomy unrest and uncontent. This was the pride that bore up Spitz and made him thrash the sled-dogs who blundered and shirked in the traces or hid away at harness-up time in the morning. Likewise it was this pride that made him fear Buck as a possible lead-dog. And this was Buck's pride, too.

He openly threatened the other's leadership. He came between him and the shirks he should have punished. And he did it deliberately. One night there was a heavy snowfall, and in the morning Pike, the malingerer, did not appear. He was securely hidden in his nest under a foot of snow. François called him and sought him in vain. Spitz was wild with wrath. He raged through the camp, smelling and digging in every likely place, snarling so frightfully that Pike heard and shivered in his hiding-place.

But when he was at last unearthed, and Spitz flew at him to punish him, Buck flew, with equal rage, in between. So unexpected was it, and so shrewdly managed, that Spitz was hurled backward and off his feet. Pike, who had been

uncontent 不滿足的 *adj.*
deliberately 故意地 *adv.*

trembling abjectly, took heart at this open mutiny, and sprang upon his overthrown leader. Buck, to whom fair play was a forgotten code, likewise sprang upon Spitz. But François, chuckling at the incident while unswerving in the administration of justice, brought his lash down upon Buck with all his might. This failed to drive Buck from his prostrate rival, and the butt of the whip was brought into play. Half-stunned by the blow, Buck was knocked backward and the lash laid upon him again and again, while Spitz soundly punished the many times offending Pike.

In the days that followed, as Dawson grew closer and closer, Buck still continued to interfere between Spitz and the culprits; but he did it craftily, when François was not around. With the covert mutiny of Buck, a general insubordination sprang up and increased. Dave and Sol-leks were unaffected, but the rest of the team went from bad to worse. Things no longer went right. There was continual bickering and jangling. Trouble was always afoot, and at the bottom of it was Buck. He kept François busy, for the dog-driver was in constant apprehension of the life-and-death struggle between the two which he knew must take place sooner or later; and on more

culprits 罪犯 *n.*
insubordination 不順從 *n.*
apprehension 理解，憂慮 *n.*

than one night the sounds of quarrelling and strife among the other dogs turned him out of his sleeping robe, fearful that Buck and Spitz were at it.

But the opportunity did not present itself, and they pulled into Dawson one dreary afternoon with the great fight still to come. Here were many men, and countless dogs, and Buck found them all at work. It seemed the ordained order of things that dogs should work. All day they swung up and down the main street in long teams, and in the night their jingling bells still went by. They hauled cabin logs and firewood, freighted up to the mines, and did all manner of work that horses did in the Santa Clara Valley. Here and there Buck met Southland dogs, but in the main they were the wild wolf husky breed. Every night, regularly, at nine, at twelve, at three, they lifted a nocturnal song, a weird and eerie chant, in which it was Buck's delight to join.

With the aurora borealis flaming coldly overhead, or the stars leaping in the frost dance, and the land numb and frozen under its pall of snow, this song of the huskies might have been the defiance of life, only it was pitched in minor key, with long-drawn wailings and half-sobs, and was more the

---

nocturnal 夜間的 *adj.*

eerie 詭異的，怪異的 *adj.*

borealis 北極光 *n.*

pleading of life, the articulate travail of existence. It was an old song, old as the breed itself-one of the first songs of the younger world in a day when songs were sad. It was invested with the woe of unnumbered generations, this plaint by which Buck was so strangely stirred. When he moaned and sobbed, it was with the pain of living that was of old the pain of his wild fathers, and the fear and mystery of the cold and dark that was to them fear and mystery. And that he should be stirred by it marked the completeness with which he harked back through the ages of fire and roof to the raw beginnings of life in the howling ages.

Seven days from the time they pulled into Dawson, they dropped down the steep bank by the Barracks to the Yukon Trail, and pulled for Dyea and Salt Water. Perrault was carrying despatches if anything more urgent than those he had brought in; also, the travel pride had gripped him, and he purposed to make the record trip of the year. Several things favored him in this. The week's rest had recuperated the dogs and put them in thorough trim. The trail they had broken into the country was packed hard by later journeyers. And further, the police had arranged in two or three places deposits of grub for dog and man, and he was travelling light.

They made Sixty Mile, which is a fifty-mile run, on the first day; and the second day saw them booming up the Yukon well on their way to Pelly. But such splendid running was achieved not without great trouble and vexation on the part

of François. The insidious revolt led by Buck had destroyed the solidarity of the team. It no longer was as one dog leaping in the traces. The encouragement Buck gave the rebels led them into all kinds of petty misdemeanors. No more was Spitz a leader greatly to be feared. The old awe departed, and they grew equal to challenging his authority. Pike robbed him of half a fish one night, and gulped it down under the protection of Buck. Another night Dub and Joe fought Spitz and made him forego the punishment they deserved. And even Billee, the good-natured, was less good-natured, and whined not half so placatingly as in former days. Buck never came near Spitz without snarling and bristling menacingly. In fact, his conduct approached that of a bully, and he was given to swaggering up and down before Spitz's very nose.

The breaking down of discipline likewise affected the dogs in their relations with one another. They quarrelled and bickered more than ever among themselves, till at times the camp was a howling bedlam. Dave and Sol-leks alone were unaltered, though they were made irritable by the unending squabbling. François swore strange barbarous oaths, and stamped the snow in futile rage, and tore his hair. His lash was

misdemeanors 輕罪 *n.*
quarrelled 爭吵，爭執 *v.*

always singing among the dogs, but it was of small avail. Directly his back was turned they were at it again. He backed up Spitz with his whip, while Buck backed up the remainder of the team. François knew he was behind all the trouble, and Buck knew he knew; but Buck was too clever ever again to be caught red-handed. He worked faithfully in the harness, for the toil had become a delight to him; yet it was a greater delight slyly to precipitate a fight amongst his mates and tangle the traces.

At the mouth of the Tahkeena, one night after supper, Dub turned up a snowshoe rabbit, blundered it, and missed. In a second the whole team was in full cry. A hundred yards away was a camp of the Northwest Police, with fifty dogs, huskies all, who joined the chase. The rabbit sped down the river, turned off into a small creek, up the frozen bed of which it held steadily. It ran lightly on the surface of the snow, while the dogs ploughed through by main strength. Buck led the pack, sixty strong, around bend after bend, but he could not gain. He lay down low to the race, whining eagerly, his splendid body flashing forward, leap by leap, in the wan white moonlight. And leap by leap, like some pale frost wraith, the snowshoe rabbit flashed on ahead.

All that stirring of old instincts which at stated periods drives men out from the sounding cities to forest and plain to kill things by chemically propelled leaden pellets, the blood lust, the joy to kill-all this was Buck's, only it was infinitely

more intimate. He was ranging at the head of the pack, running the wild thing down, the living meat, to kill with his own teeth and wash his muzzle to the eyes in warm blood.

There is an ecstasy that marks the summit of life, and beyond which life cannot rise. And such is the paradox of living, this ecstasy comes when one is most alive, and it comes as a complete forgetfulness that one is alive. This ecstasy, this forgetfulness of living, comes to the artist, caught up and out of himself in a sheet of flame; it comes to the soldier, war-mad on a stricken field and refusing quarter; and it came to Buck, leading the pack, sounding the old wolf-cry, straining after the food that was alive and that fled swiftly before him through the moonlight. He was sounding the deeps of his nature, and of the parts of his nature that were deeper than he, going back into the womb of Time. He was mastered by the sheer surging of life, the tidal wave of being, the perfect joy of each separate muscle, joint, and sinew in that it was everything that was not death, that it was aglow and rampant, expressing itself in movement, flying exultantly under the stars and over the face of dead matter that did not move.

But Spitz, cold and calculating even in his supreme moods, left the pack and cut across a narrow neck of land

forgetfulness 遺忘，健忘 *n.*

where the creek made a long bend around. Buck did not know of this, and as he rounded the bend, the frost wraith of a rabbit still flitting before him, he saw another and larger frost wraith leap from the overhanging bank into the immediate path of the rabbit. It was Spitz. The rabbit could not turn, and as the white teeth broke its back in mid air it shrieked as loudly as a stricken man may shriek. At sound of this, the cry of Life plunging down from Life's apex in the grip of Death, the fall pack at Buck's heels raised a hell's chorus of delight.

Buck did not cry out. He did not check himself, but drove in upon Spitz, shoulder to shoulder, so hard that he missed the throat. They rolled over and over in the powdery snow. Spitz gained his feet almost as though he had not been overthrown, slashing Buck down the shoulder and leaping clear. Twice his teeth clipped together, like the steel jaws of a trap, as he backed away for better footing, with lean and lifting lips that writhed and snarled.

In a flash Buck knew it. The time had come. It was to the death. As they circled about, snarling, ears laid back, keenly watchful for the advantage, the scene came to Buck with a sense of familiarity. He seemed to remember it all-the white woods, and earth, and moonlight, and the thrill of battle. Over the whiteness and silence brooded a ghostly calm. There was not the faintest whisper of air-nothing moved, not a leaf quivered, the visible breaths of the dogs rising slowly and lingering in the frosty air. They had made short work of the

snowshoe rabbit, these dogs that were ill-tamed wolves; and they were now drawn up in an expectant circle. They, too, were silent, their eyes only gleaming and their breaths drifting slowly upward. To Buck it was nothing new or strange, this scene of old time. It was as though it had always been, the wonted way of things.

Spitz was a practised fighter. From Spitzbergen through the Arctic, and across Canada and the Barrens, he had held his own with all manner of dogs and achieved to mastery over them. Bitter rage was his, but never blind rage. In passion to rend and destroy, he never forgot that his enemy was in like passion to rend and destroy. He never rushed till he was prepared to receive a rush; never attacked till he had first defended that attack.

In vain Buck strove to sink his teeth in the neck of the big white dog. Wherever his fangs struck for the softer flesh, they were countered by the fangs of Spitz. Fang clashed fang, and lips were cut and bleeding, but Buck could not penetrate his enemy's guard. Then he warmed up and enveloped Spitz in a whirlwind of rushes. Time and time again he tried for the snow-white throat, where life bubbled near to the surface, and

practised 熟練的 *adj.*
rend 撕裂，分裂 *v.*

each time and every time Spitz slashed him and got away. Then Buck took to rushing, as though for the throat, when, suddenly drawing back his head and curving in from the side, he would drive his shoulder at the shoulder of Spitz, as a ram by which to overthrow him. But instead, Buck's shoulder was slashed down each time as Spitz leaped lightly away.

Spitz was untouched, while Buck was streaming with blood and panting hard. The fight was growing desperate. And all the while the silent and wolfish circle waited to finish off whichever dog went down. As Buck grew winded, Spitz took to rushing, and he kept him staggering for footing. Once Buck went over, and the whole circle of sixty dogs started up; but he recovered himself, almost in mid air, and the circle sank down again and waited.

But Buck possessed a quality that made for greatness- imagination. He fought by instinct, but he could fight by head as well. He rushed, as though attempting the old shoulder trick, but at the last instant swept low to the snow and in. His teeth closed on Spitz's left fore leg. There was a crunch of breaking bone, and the white dog faced him on three legs. Thrice he tried to knock him over, then repeated the trick and broke the right fore leg. Despite the pain and helplessness, Spitz struggled madly to keep up. He saw the silent circle, with gleaming eyes, lolling tongues, and silvery breaths drifting upward, closing in upon him as he had seen similar circles close in upon beaten antagonists in the past. Only this time he was the one who was beaten.

There was no hope for him. Buck was inexorable. Mercy was a thing reserved for gentler climes. He manoeuvred for the final rush. The circle had tightened till he could feel the breaths of the huskies on his flanks. He could see them, beyond Spitz and to either side, half crouching for the spring, their eyes fixed upon him. A pause seemed to fall. Every animal was motionless as though turned to stone. Only Spitz quivered and bristled as he staggered back and forth, snarling with horrible menace, as though to frighten off impending death. Then Buck sprang in and out; but while he was in, shoulder had at last squarely met shoulder. The dark circle became a dot on the moon-flooded snow as Spitz disappeared from view. Buck stood and looked on, the successful champion, the dominant primordial beast who had made his kill and found it good.

inexorable 無情的，不可動搖的 *adj.*

manoeuvred 操縱，調動 *v.*

Chapter IV.

Who Has Won to Mastership

"Eh? Wot I say? I spik true w'en I say dat Buck two devils." This was François's speech next morning when he discovered Spitz missing and Buck covered with wounds. He drew him to the fire and by its light pointed them out.

"Dat Spitz fight lak hell," said Perrault, as he surveyed the gaping rips and cuts.

"An' dat Buck fight lak two hells," was François's answer. "An' now we make good time. No more Spitz, no more trouble, sure."

While Perrault packed the camp outfit and loaded the sled, the dog-driver proceeded to harness the dogs. Buck trotted up to the place Spitz would have occupied as leader; but François, not noticing him, brought Sol-leks to the

occupied 佔據，佔有 **v.**

coveted position. In his judgment, Sol-leks was the best lead-dog left. Buck sprang upon Sol-leks in a fury, driving him back and standing in his place.

"Eh? eh?" François cried, slapping his thighs gleefully. "Look at dat Buck. Heem keel dat Spitz, heem t'ink to take de job."

"Go 'way, Chook!" he cried, but Buck refused to budge.

He took Buck by the scruff of the neck, and though the dog growled threateningly, dragged him to one side and replaced Sol-leks. The old dog did not like it, and showed plainly that he was afraid of Buck. François was obdurate, but when he turned his back Buck again displaced Sol-leks, who was not at all unwilling to go.

François was angry. "Now, by Gar, I feex you!" he cried, coming back with a heavy club in his hand.

Buck remembered the man in the red sweater, and retreated slowly; nor did he attempt to charge in when Sol-leks was once more brought forward. But he circled just beyond the range of the club, snarling with bitterness and rage; and while he circled he watched the club so as to dodge it if thrown by François, for he was become wise in the way

---

obdurate 頑固的，不願改變的 *adj.*
bitterness 苦澀，怨恨 *n.*

of clubs.

The driver went about his work, and he called to Buck when he was ready to put him in his old place in front of Dave. Buck retreated two or three steps. François followed him up, whereupon he again retreated. After some time of this, François threw down the club, thinking that Buck feared a thrashing. But Buck was in open revolt. He wanted, not to escape a clubbing, but to have the leadership. It was his by right. He had earned it, and he would not be content with less. Perrault took a hand. Between them they ran him about for the better part of an hour. They threw clubs at him. He dodged. They cursed him, and his fathers and mothers before him, and all his seed to come after him down to the remotest generation, and every hair on his body and drop of blood in his veins; and he answered curse with snarl and kept out of their reach. He did not try to run away, but retreated around and around the camp, advertising plainly that when his desire was met, he would come in and be good.

François sat down and scratched his head. Perrault looked at his watch and swore. Time was flying, and they should have been on the trail an hour gone. François scratched his head

thrashing 痛打，毆打 n.
snarl 咆哮，吠叫 v.

Chapter IV

again. He shook it and grinned sheepishly at the courier, who shrugged his shoulders in sign that they were beaten. Then François went up to where Sol-leks stood and called to Buck. Buck laughed, as dogs laugh, yet kept his distance. François unfastened Sol-leks's traces and put him back in his old place. The team stood harnessed to the sled in an unbroken line, ready for the trail. There was no place for Buck save at the front. Once more François called, and once more Buck laughed and kept away.

"T'row down de club," Perrault commanded.

François complied, whereupon Buck trotted in, laughing triumphantly, and swung around into position at the head of the team. His traces were fastened, the sled broken out, and with both men running they dashed out on to the river trail.

Highly as the dog-driver had forevalued Buck, with his two devils, he found, while the day was yet young, that he had undervalued. At a bound Buck took up the duties of leadership; and where judgment was required, and quick thinking and quick acting, he showed himself the superior even of Spitz, of whom François had never seen an equal.

But it was in giving the law and making his mates live up

forevalued 過高估價，高估 *v.*
undervalued 低估，看輕 *v.*

to it, that Buck excelled. Dave and Sol-leks did not mind the change in leadership. It was none of their business. Their business was to toil, and toil mightily, in the traces. So long as that were not interfered with, they did not care what happened. Billee, the good-natured, could lead for all they cared, so long as he kept order. The rest of the team, however, had grown unruly during the last days of Spitz, and their surprise was great now that Buck proceeded to lick them into shape.

Pike, who pulled at Buck's heels, and who never put an ounce more of his weight against the breast-band than he was compelled to do, was swiftly and repeatedly shaken for loafing; and ere the first day was done he was pulling more than ever before in his life. The first night in camp, Joe, the sour one, was punished roundly-a thing that Spitz had never succeeded in doing. Buck simply smothered him by virtue of superior weight, and cut him up till he ceased snapping and began to whine for mercy.

The general tone of the team picked up immediately. It recovered its old-time solidarity, and once more the dogs leaped as one dog in the traces. At the Rink Rapids two native

loafing 閒晃，偷懶 **v.**

huskies, Teek and Koona, were added; and the celerity with which Buck broke them in took away François's breath.

"Nevaire such a dog as dat Buck!" he cried. "No, nevaire! Heem worth one t'ousan' dollair, by Gar! Eh? Wot you say, Perrault?"

And Perrault nodded. He was ahead of the record then, and gaining day by day. The trail was in excellent condition, well packed and hard, and there was no new-fallen snow with which to contend. It was not too cold. The temperature dropped to fifty below zero and remained there the whole trip. The men rode and ran by turn, and the dogs were kept on the jump, with but infrequent stoppages.

The Thirty Mile River was comparatively coated with ice, and they covered in one day going out what had taken them ten days coming in. In one run they made a sixty-mile dash from the foot of Lake Le Barge to the White Horse Rapids. Across Marsh, Tagish, and Bennett (seventy miles of lakes), they flew so fast that the man whose turn it was to run towed behind the sled at the end of a rope. And on the last night of the second week they topped White Pass and dropped down the sea slope with the lights of Skaguay and of the shipping at

---

celerity 迅速，敏捷 **n.**
tow 拖，牽引 **v.**

their feet.

It was a record run. Each day for fourteen days they had averaged forty miles. For three days Perrault and François threw chests up and down the main street of Skaguay and were deluged with invitations to drink, while the team was the constant centre of a worshipful crowd of dog-busters and mushers. Then three or four western bad men aspired to clean out the town, were riddled like pepper-boxes for their pains, and public interest turned to other idols. Next came official orders. François called Buck to him, threw his arms around him, wept over him. And that was the last of François and Perrault. Like other men, they passed out of Buck's life for good.

A Scotch half-breed took charge of him and his mates, and in company with a dozen other dog-teams he started back over the weary trail to Dawson. It was no light running now, nor record time, but heavy toil each day, with a heavy load behind; for this was the mail train, carrying word from the world to the men who sought gold under the shadow of the Pole.

Buck did not like it, but he bore up well to the work,

deluged 淹沒，湧入 *v.*
centre 指某個事物的中心或焦點 *n.*

taking pride in it after the manner of Dave and Sol-leks, and seeing that his mates, whether they prided in it or not, did their fair share. It was a monotonous life, operating with machine-like regularity. One day was very like another. At a certain time each morning the cooks turned out, fires were built, and breakfast was eaten. Then, while some broke camp, others harnessed the dogs, and they were under way an hour or so before the darkness fell which gave warning of dawn. At night, camp was made. Some pitched the flies, others cut firewood and pine boughs for the beds, and still others carried water or ice for the cooks. Also, the dogs were fed. To them, this was the one feature of the day, though it was good to loaf around, after the fish was eaten, for an hour or so with the other dogs, of which there were fivescore and odd. There were fierce fighters among them, but three battles with the fiercest brought Buck to mastery, so that when he bristled and showed his teeth they got out of his way.

Best of all, perhaps, he loved to lie near the fire, hind legs crouched under him, forelegs stretched out in front, head raised, and eyes blinking dreamily at the flames. Sometimes he thought of Judge Miller's big house in the sun-kissed Santa

---

monotonous 單調的，乏味的 *adj.*
fivescore 代表數字「100」 *n.*

Clara Valley, and of the cement swimming-tank, and Ysabel, the Mexican hairless, and Toots, the Japanese pug; but oftener he remembered the man in the red sweater, the death of Curly, the great fight with Spitz, and the good things he had eaten or would like to eat. He was not homesick. The Sunland was very dim and distant, and such memories had no power over him. Far more potent were the memories of his heredity that gave things he had never seen before a seeming familiarity; the instincts (which were but the memories of his ancestors become habits) which had lapsed in later days, and still later, in him, quickened and become alive again.

Sometimes as he crouched there, blinking dreamily at the flames, it seemed that the flames were of another fire, and that as he crouched by this other fire he saw another and different man from the half-breed cook before him. This other man was shorter of leg and longer of arm, with muscles that were stringy and knotty rather than rounded and swelling. The hair of this man was long and matted, and his head slanted back under it from the eyes. He uttered strange sounds, and seemed very much afraid of the darkness, into which he peered continually, clutching in his hand, which hung midway between knee and foot, a stick with a heavy stone made fast to the end. He was all but naked, a ragged and fire-scorched skin hanging part way down his back, but on his body there was much hair. In some places, across the chest and shoulders and down the outside of the arms and thighs, it was matted into almost a thick fur. He did not stand erect, but with trunk inclined forward from the hips, on legs that bent at the knees. About his body there was a peculiar springiness, or resiliency, almost catlike, and a quick alertness as of one who lived in perpetual fear of things seen and unseen.

At other times this hairy man squatted by the fire with head between his legs and slept. On such occasions his elbows

resiliency 彈性 *n.*

217

were on his knees, his hands clasped above his head as though to shed rain by the hairy arms. And beyond that fire, in the circling darkness, Buck could see many gleaming coals, two by two, always two by two, which he knew to be the eyes of great beasts of prey. And he could hear the crashing of their bodies through the undergrowth, and the noises they made in the night. And dreaming there by the Yukon bank, with lazy eyes blinking at the fire, these sounds and sights of another world would make the hair to rise along his back and stand on end across his shoulders and up his neck, till he whimpered low and suppressedly, or growled softly, and the half-breed cook shouted at him, "Hey, you Buck, wake up!" Whereupon the other world would vanish and the real world come into his eyes, and he would get up and yawn and stretch as though he had been asleep.

It was a hard trip, with the mail behind them, and the heavy work wore them down. They were short of weight and in poor condition when they made Dawson, and should have had a ten days' or a week's rest at least. But in two days' time they dropped down the Yukon bank from the Barracks, loaded with letters for the outside. The dogs were tired, the drivers grumbling, and to make matters worse, it snowed every day.

suppressedly 壓抑地 *adv.*

This meant a soft trail, greater friction on the runners, and heavier pulling for the dogs; yet the drivers were fair through it all, and did their best for the animals.

Each night the dogs were attended to first. They ate before the drivers ate, and no man sought his sleeping-robe till he had seen to the feet of the dogs he drove. Still, their strength went down. Since the beginning of the winter they had travelled eighteen hundred miles, dragging sleds the whole weary distance; and eighteen hundred miles will tell upon life of the toughest. Buck stood it, keeping his mates up to their work and maintaining discipline, though he, too, was very tired. Billee cried and whimpered regularly in his sleep each night. Joe was sourer than ever, and Sol-leks was unapproachable, blind side or other side.

But it was Dave who suffered most of all. Something had gone wrong with him. He became more morose and irritable, and when camp was pitched at once made his nest, where his driver fed him. Once out of the harness and down, he did not get on his feet again till harness-up time in the morning. Sometimes, in the traces, when jerked by a sudden stoppage of the sled, or by straining to start it, he would cry out with pain. The driver examined him, but could find nothing. All the

morose 陰鬱的 *adj.*

drivers became interested in his case. They talked it over at mealtime, and over their last pipes before going to bed, and one night they held a consultation. He was brought from his nest to the fire and was pressed and prodded till he cried out many times. Something was wrong inside, but they could locate no broken bones, could not make it out.

By the time Cassiar Bar was reached, he was so weak that he was falling repeatedly in the traces. The Scotch half-breed called a halt and took him out of the team, making the next dog, Sol-leks, fast to the sled. His intention was to rest Dave, letting him run free behind the sled. Sick as he was, Dave resented being taken out, grunting and growling while the traces were unfastened, and whimpering brokenheartedly when he saw Sol-leks in the position he had held and served so long. For the pride of trace and trail was his, and, sick unto death, he could not bear that another dog should do his work.

When the sled started, he floundered in the soft snow alongside the beaten trail, attacking Sol-leks with his teeth, rushing against him and trying to thrust him off into the soft snow on the other side, striving to leap inside his traces and get between him and the sled, and all the while whining and

prodded 戳、刺 v.
resented 憤怒、怨恨 v.
floundered 掙扎、蹣跚 v.

yelping and crying with grief and pain. The half-breed tried to drive him away with the whip; but he paid no heed to the stinging lash, and the man had not the heart to strike harder. Dave refused to run quietly on the trail behind the sled, where the going was easy, but continued to flounder alongside in the soft snow, where the going was most difficult, till exhausted. Then he fell, and lay where he fell, howling lugubriously as the long train of sleds churned by.

With the last remnant of his strength he managed to stagger along behind till the train made another stop, when he floundered past the sleds to his own, where he stood alongside Sol-leks. His driver lingered a moment to get a light for his pipe from the man behind. Then he returned and started his dogs. They swung out on the trail with remarkable lack of exertion, turned their heads uneasily, and stopped in surprise. The driver was surprised, too; the sled had not moved. He called his comrades to witness the sight. Dave had bitten through both of Sol-leks's traces, and was standing directly in front of the sled in his proper place.

He pleaded with his eyes to remain there. The driver was

lugubriously 悲傷地、哀傷地 *adv.*
remnant 剩餘部分、殘餘 *n.*
exertion 努力、費力 *n.*

perplexed. His comrades talked of how a dog could break its heart through being denied the work that killed it, and recalled instances they had known, where dogs, too old for the toil, or injured, had died because they were cut out of the traces. Also, they held it a mercy, since Dave was to die anyway, that he should die in the traces, heart-easy and content. So he was harnessed in again, and proudly he pulled as of old, though more than once he cried out involuntarily from the bite of his inward hurt. Several times he fell down and was dragged in the traces, and once the sled ran upon him so that he limped thereafter in one of his hind legs.

But he held out till camp was reached, when his driver made a place for him by the fire. Morning found him too weak to travel. At harness-up time he tried to crawl to his driver. By convulsive efforts he got on his feet, staggered, and fell. Then he wormed his way forward slowly toward where the harnesses were being put on his mates. He would advance his forelegs and drag up his body with a sort of hitching movement, when he would advance his forelegs and hitch ahead again for a few more inches. His strength left him, and the last his mates saw of him he lay gasping in the snow and

perplexed 困惑的、迷惑的 *adj.*
convulsive 抽搐的、痙攣的 *adj.*
hitching 顛簸、拖 *v.*

223

yearning toward them. But they could hear him mournfully howling till they passed out of sight behind a belt of river timber.Here the train was halted. The Scotch half-breed slowly retraced his steps to the camp they had left. The men ceased talking. A revolver-shot rang out. The man came back hurriedly. The whips snapped, the bells tinkled merrily, the sleds churned along the trail; but Buck knew, and every dog knew, what had taken place behind the belt of river trees.

Chapter V.

The Toil of Trace and Trail

Thirty days from the time it left Dawson, the Salt Water Mail, with Buck and his mates at the fore, arrived at Skaguay. They were in a wretched state, worn out and worn down. Buck's one hundred and forty pounds had dwindled to one hundred and fifteen. The rest of his mates, though lighter dogs, had relatively lost more weight than he. Pike, the malingerer, who, in his lifetime of deceit, had often successfully feigned a hurt leg, was now limping in earnest. Sol-leks was limping, and Dub was suffering from a wrenched shoulder-blade.

They were all terribly footsore. No spring or rebound was left in them. Their feet fell heavily on the trail, jarring their bodies and doubling the fatigue of a day's travel. There was

malingerer 裝病者 *n.*
wrenched 扭傷 *v.*

226

nothing the matter with them except that they were dead tired. It was not the dead-tiredness that comes through brief and excessive effort, from which recovery is a matter of hours; but it was the dead-tiredness that comes through the slow and prolonged strength drainage of months of toil. There was no power of recuperation left, no reserve strength to call upon. It had been all used, the last least bit of it. Every muscle, every fibre, every cell, was tired, dead tired. And there was reason for it. In less than five months they had travelled twenty-five hundred miles, during the last eighteen hundred of which they had had but five days' rest. When they arrived at Skaguay they were apparently on their last legs. They could barely keep the traces taut, and on the down grades just managed to keep out of the way of the sled.

"Mush on, poor sore feets," the driver encouraged them as they tottered down the main street of Skaguay. "Dis is de las'. Den we get one long res'. Eh? For sure. One bully long res'."

The drivers confidently expected a long stopover. Themselves, they had covered twelve hundred miles with two days' rest, and in the nature of reason and common justice

---

fibre 細胞組織或肌肉組織中的纖維 **n.**

tottered 蹣跚的 **v.**

they deserved an interval of loafing. But so many were the men who had rushed into the Klondike, and so many were the sweethearts, wives, and kin that had not rushed in, that the congested mail was taking on Alpine proportions; also, there were official orders. Fresh batches of Hudson Bay dogs were to take the places of those worthless for the trail. The worthless ones were to be got rid of, and, since dogs count for little against dollars, they were to be sold.

Three days passed, by which time Buck and his mates found how really tired and weak they were. Then, on the morning of the fourth day, two men from the States came along and bought them, harness and all, for a song. The men addressed each other as "Hal" and "Charles." Charles was a middle-aged, lightish-colored man, with weak and watery eyes and a mustache that twisted fiercely and vigorously up, giving the lie to the limply drooping lip it concealed. Hal was a youngster of nineteen or twenty, with a big Colt's revolver and a hunting-knife strapped about him on a belt that fairly bristled with cartridges. This belt was the most salient thing about him. It advertised his callowness-a callowness sheer and

congested 擁擠的 *adj.*
lightish-colored 淺色的 *adj.*
callowness 幼稚、未成熟 *n.*

unutterable. Both men were manifestly out of place, and why such as they should adventure the North is part of the mystery of things that passes understanding.

Buck heard the chaffering, saw the money pass between the man and the Government agent, and knew that the Scotch half-breed and the mail-train drivers were passing out of his life on the heels of Perrault and François and the others who had gone before. When driven with his mates to the new owners' camp, Buck saw a slipshod and slovenly affair, tent half stretched, dishes unwashed, everything in disorder; also, he saw a woman. "Mercedes" the men called her. She was Charles's wife and Hal's sister-a nice family party.

Buck watched them apprehensively as they proceeded to take down the tent and load the sled. There was a great deal of effort about their manner, but no businesslike method. The tent was rolled into an awkward bundle three times as large as it should have been. The tin dishes were packed away unwashed. Mercedes continually fluttered in the way of her men and kept up an unbroken chattering of remonstrance and advice. When they put a clothes-sack on the front of the sled, she suggested it should go on the back; and when they had

---

unutterable 難以言喻的、無法形容的 *adj.*
chaffering 喧譁、爭論 *v.*
remonstrance 抗議、反對 *n.*

put it on the back, and covered it over with a couple of other bundles, she discovered overlooked articles which could abide nowhere else but in that very sack, and they unloaded again.

Three men from a neighboring tent came out and looked on, grinning and winking at one another.

"You've got a right smart load as it is," said one of them; "and it's not me should tell you your business, but I wouldn't tote that tent along if I was you."

"Undreamed of!" cried Mercedes, throwing up her hands in dainty dismay. "However in the world could I manage without a tent?"

"It's springtime, and you won't get any more cold weather," the man replied.

She shook her head decidedly, and Charles and Hal put the last odds and ends on top the mountainous load.

"Think it'll ride?" one of the men asked.

"Why shouldn't it?" Charles demanded rather shortly. "Oh, that's all right, that's all right," the man hastened

meekly to say. "I was just a-wonderin', that is all. It seemed a mite top-heavy."

Charles turned his back and drew the lashings down as well as he could, which was not in the least well.

"An' of course the dogs can hike along all day with that contraption behind them," affirmed a second of the men.

contraption 設備、裝置 *n.*

231

"Certainly," said Hal, with freezing politeness, taking hold of the gee-pole with one hand and swinging his whip from the other. "Mush!" he shouted. "Mush on there!"

The dogs sprang against the breast-bands, strained hard for a few moments, then relaxed. They were unable to move the sled.

"The lazy brutes, I'll show them," he cried, preparing to lash out at them with the whip.

But Mercedes interfered, crying, "Oh, Hal, you mustn't," as she caught hold of the whip and wrenched it from him. "The poor dears! Now you must promise you won't be harsh with them for the rest of the trip, or I won't go a step."

"Precious lot you know about dogs," her brother sneered; "and I wish you'd leave me alone. They're lazy, I tell you, and you've got to whip them to get anything out of them. That's their way. You ask anyone. Ask one of those men."

Mercedes looked at them imploringly, untold repugnance at sight of pain written in her pretty face.

"They're weak as water, if you want to know," came the reply from one of the men. "Plum tuckered out, that's what's the matter. They need a rest."

repugnance 厭惡、反感 *n.*
tuckered out 精疲力竭 *adj.*

"Rest be blanked," said Hal, with his beardless lips; and Mercedes said, "Oh!" in pain and sorrow at the oath.

But she was a clannish creature, and rushed at once to the defence of her brother. "Never mind that man," she said pointedly. "You're driving our dogs, and you do what you think best with them."

Again Hal's whip fell upon the dogs. They threw themselves against the breast-bands, dug their feet into the packed snow, got down low to it, and put forth all their strength. The sled held as though it were an anchor. After two efforts, they stood still, panting. The whip was whistling savagely, when once more Mercedes interfered. She dropped on her knees before Buck, with tears in her eyes, and put her arms around his neck.

"You poor, poor dears," she cried sympathetically, "why don't you pull hard?-then you wouldn't be whipped." Buck did not like her, but he was feeling too miserable to resist her, taking it as part of the day's miserable work.

One of the onlookers, who had been clenching his teeth to suppress hot speech, now spoke up:-

"It's not that I care a whoop what becomes of you, but

beardless 未長鬍鬚的 *adj.*
clannish 具部落意識的、排他的 *adj.*
clenching 緊咬、緊握 *v.*

for the dogs' sakes I just want to tell you, you can help them a mighty lot by breaking out that sled. The runners are froze fast. Throw your weight against the gee-pole, right and left, and break it out."

A third time the attempt was made, but this time, following the advice, Hal broke out the runners which had been frozen to the snow. The overloaded and unwieldy sled forged ahead, Buck and his mates struggling frantically under the rain of blows. A hundred yards ahead the path turned and sloped steeply into the main street. It would have required an experienced man to keep the top-heavy sled upright, and Hal was not such a man. As they swung on the turn the sled went over, spilling half its load through the loose lashings. The dogs never stopped. The lightened sled bounded on its side behind them. They were angry because of the ill treatment they had received and the unjust load. Buck was raging. He broke into a run, the team following his lead. Hal cried "Whoa! whoa!" but they gave no heed. He tripped and was pulled off his feet. The capsized sled ground over him, and the dogs dashed on up the street, adding to the gayety of Skaguay as they scattered the remainder of the outfit along its

---

unwieldy 不受控制的 *adj.*

gayety 歡樂 *n.*

chief thoroughfare.

Kindhearted citizens caught the dogs and gathered up the scattered belongings. Also, they gave advice. Half the load and twice the dogs, if they ever expected to reach Dawson, was what was said. Hal and his sister and brother-in-law listened unwillingly, pitched tent, and overhauled the outfit. Canned goods were turned out that made men laugh, for canned goods on the Long Trail is a thing to dream about. "Blankets for a hotel," quoth one of the men who laughed and helped. "Half as many is too much; get rid of them. Throw away that tent, and all those dishes-who's going to wash them, anyway? Good Lord, do you think you're travelling on a Pullman?"

And so it went, the inexorable elimination of the superfluous. Mercedes cried when her clothes-bags were dumped on the ground and article after article was thrown out. She cried in general, and she cried in particular over each discarded thing. She clasped hands about knees, rocking back and forth brokenheartedly. She averred she would not go an inch, not for a dozen Charleses. She appealed to everybody and to everything, finally wiping her eyes and proceeding to cast out even articles of apparel that were imperative

---

quoth 表示某人說了某些話 *v.*

superfluous 多餘的 *adj.*

necessaries. And in her zeal, when she had finished with her own, she attacked the belongings of her men and went through them like a tornado.

This accomplished, the outfit, though cut in half, was still a formidable bulk. Charles and Hal went out in the evening and bought six Outside dogs. These, added to the six of the original team, and Teek and Koona, the huskies obtained at the Rink Rapids on the record trip, brought the team up to fourteen. But the Outside dogs, though practically broken in since their landing, did not amount to much. Three were short-haired pointers, one was a Newfoundland, and the other two were mongrels of indeterminate breed. They did not seem to know anything, these newcomers. Buck and his comrades looked upon them with disgust, and though he speedily taught them their places and what not to do, he could not teach them what to do. They did not take kindly to trace and trail. With the exception of the two mongrels, they were bewildered and spirit-broken by the strange savage environment in which they found themselves and by the ill treatment they had received. The two mongrels were without spirit at all; bones were the only things breakable about them.

❀　❀　❀　❀　❀　❀　❀　❀　❀　❀　❀　❀　❀

mongrels 混種狗 *n.*
indeterminate 不確定的 *adj.*
ill treatment 虐待 *n.*

❀　❀　❀　❀　❀　❀　❀　❀　❀　❀　❀　❀　❀

Chapter V.

With the newcomers hopeless and forlorn, and the old team worn out by twenty-five hundred miles of continuous trail, the outlook was anything but bright. The two men, however, were quite cheerful. And they were proud, too. They were doing the thing in style, with fourteen dogs. They had seen other sleds depart over the Pass for Dawson, or come in from Dawson, but never had they seen a sled with so many as fourteen dogs. In the nature of Arctic travel there was a reason why fourteen dogs should not drag one sled, and that was that one sled could not carry the food for fourteen dogs. But Charles and Hal did not know this. They had worked the trip out with a pencil, so much to a dog, so many dogs, so many days, Q.E.D. Mercedes looked over their shoulders and nodded comprehensively, it was all so very simple.

Late next morning Buck led the long team up the street. There was nothing lively about it, no snap or go in him and his fellows. They were starting dead weary. Four times he had covered the distance between Salt Water and Dawson, and the knowledge that, jaded and tired, he was facing the same trail once more, made him bitter. His heart was not in the work, nor was the heart of any dog. The Outsides were timid and

---

Q.E.D. 此事已證明（拉丁文 **"quod erat demonstrandum"** 的縮寫）

timid 膽怯的，害羞的 *adj.*

frightened, the Insides without confidence in their masters.

Buck felt vaguely that there was no depending upon these two men and the woman. They did not know how to do anything, and as the days went by it became apparent that they could not learn. They were slack in all things, without order or discipline. It took them half the night to pitch a slovenly camp, and half the morning to break that camp and get the sled loaded in fashion so slovenly that for the rest of the day they were occupied in stopping and rearranging the load. Some days they did not make ten miles. On other days they were unable to get started at all. And on no day did they succeed in making more than half the distance used by the men as a basis in their dog-food computation.

It was inevitable that they should go short on dog-food. But they hastened it by overfeeding, bringing the day nearer when underfeeding would commence. The Outside dogs, whose digestions had not been trained by chronic famine to make the most of little, had voracious appetites. And when, in addition to this, the worn-out huskies pulled weakly, Hal decided that the orthodox ration was too small. He doubled it. And to cap it all, when Mercedes, with tears in her pretty eyes

---

slack 懈怠的，鬆弛的 *adj.*
rearranging 重新整理，重新排列 *v.*
orthodox 傳統的，正統的 *adj.*

and a quaver in her throat, could not cajole him into giving the dogs still more, she stole from the fish- sacks and fed them slyly. But it was not food that Buck and the huskies needed, but rest. And though they were making poor time, the heavy load they dragged sapped their strength severely.

Then came the underfeeding. Hal awoke one day to the fact that his dog-food was half gone and the distance only quarter covered; further, that for love or money no additional dog-food was to be obtained. So he cut down even the orthodox ration and tried to increase the day's travel. His sister and brother-in-law seconded him; but they were frustrated by their heavy outfit and their own incompetence. It was a simple matter to give the dogs less food; but it was impossible to make the dogs travel faster, while their own inability to get under way earlier in the morning prevented them from travelling longer hours. Not only did they not know how to work dogs, but they did not know how to work themselves.

The first to go was Dub. Poor blundering thief that he was, always getting caught and punished, he had none the less been a faithful worker. His wrenched shoulder-blade, untreated and unrested, went from bad to worse, till finally

---

slyly 暗中地，偷偷地 *adv.*
underfeeding 營養不良，飲食不足 *n.*
blundering 粗心的，笨拙的 *v.*

Hal shot him with the big Colt's revolver. It is a saying of the country that an Outside dog starves to death on the ration of the husky, so the six Outside dogs under Buck could do no less than die on half the ration of the husky. The Newfoundland went first, followed by the three short-haired pointers, the two mongrels hanging more grittily on to life, but going in the end.

By this time all the amenities and gentlenesses of the Southland had fallen away from the three people. Shorn of its glamour and romance, Arctic travel became to them a reality too harsh for their manhood and womanhood. Mercedes ceased weeping over the dogs, being too occupied with weeping over herself and with quarrelling with her husband and brother. To quarrel was the one thing they were never too weary to do. Their irritability arose out of their misery, increased with it, doubled upon it, outdistanced it. The wonderful patience of the trail which comes to men who toil hard and suffer sore, and remain sweet of speech and kindly, did not come to these two men and the woman. They had no inkling of such a patience. They were stiff and in pain; their muscles ached, their bones ached, their very hearts ached; and because of this they became sharp of speech, and hard words

grittily 堅韌地，毫不屈服地 *adv.*

were first on their lips in the morning and last at night.

Charles and Hal wrangled whenever Mercedes gave them a chance. It was the cherished belief of each that he did more than his share of the work, and neither forbore to speak this belief at every opportunity. Sometimes Mercedes sided with her husband, sometimes with her brother. The result was a beautiful and unending family quarrel. Starting from a dispute as to which should chop a few sticks for the fire (a dispute which concerned only Charles and Hal), presently would be lugged in the rest of the family, fathers, mothers, uncles, cousins, people thousands of miles away, and some of them dead. That Hal's views on art, or the sort of society plays his mother's brother wrote, should have anything to do with the chopping of a few sticks of firewood, passes comprehension; nevertheless the quarrel was as likely to tend in that direction as in the direction of Charles's political prejudices. And that Charles's sister's talebearing tongue should be relevant to the building of a Yukon fire, was apparent only to Mercedes, who disburdened herself of copious opinions upon that topic, and incidentally upon a few other traits unpleasantly peculiar to her husband's family. In the meantime the fire remained

❖ ❖ ❖ ❖ ❖ ❖ ❖ ❖ ❖ ❖ ❖ ❖ ❖

wrangled 爭吵，爭執 *v.*

disburdened 卸下，解除 *v.*

❖ ❖ ❖ ❖ ❖ ❖ ❖ ❖ ❖ ❖ ❖ ❖ ❖

unbuilt, the camp half pitched, and the dogs unfed.

Mercedes nursed a special grievance-the grievance of sex. She was pretty and soft, and had been chivalrously treated all her days. But the present treatment by her husband and brother was everything save chivalrous. It was her custom to be helpless. They complained. Upon which impeachment of what to her was her most essential sex-prerogative, she made their lives unendurable. She no longer considered the dogs, and because she was sore and tired, she persisted in riding on the sled. She was pretty and soft, but she weighed one hundred and twenty pounds-a lusty last straw to the load dragged by the weak and starving animals. She rode for days, till they fell in the traces and the sled stood still. Charles and Hal begged her to get off and walk, pleaded with her, entreated, the while she wept and importuned Heaven with a recital of their brutality.

On one occasion they took her off the sled by main strength. They never did it again. She let her legs go limp like a spoiled child, and sat down on the trail. They went on their way, but she did not move. After they had travelled three miles they unloaded the sled, came back for her, and by main

---

chivalrously 騎士般地，彬彬有禮地 *adv.*
essential sex-prerogative 性別特權 *n.*
recital 敘述，描述 *n.*

strength put her on the sled again.

In the excess of their own misery they were callous to the suffering of their animals. Hal's theory, which he practised on others, was that one must get hardened. He had started out preaching it to his sister and brother-in-law. Failing there, he hammered it into the dogs with a club. At the Five Fingers the dog-food gave out, and a toothless old squaw offered to trade them a few pounds of frozen horsehide for the Colt's revolver that kept the big hunting-knife company at Hal's hip. A poor substitute for food was this hide, just as it had been stripped from the starved horses of the cattlemen six months back. In its frozen state it was more like strips of galvanized iron, and when a dog wrestled it into his stomach it thawed into thin and innutritious leathery strings and into a mass of short hair, irritating and indigestible.

And through it all Buck staggered along at the head of the team as in a nightmare. He pulled when he could; when he could no longer pull, he fell down and remained down till blows from whip or club drove him to his feet again. All the stiffness and gloss had gone out of his beautiful furry coat. The hair hung down, limp and draggled, or matted with dried

callous 冷漠的，無情的 *adj.*
innutritious 營養不良的 *adv.*

blood where Hal's club had bruised him. His muscles had wasted away to knotty strings, and the flesh pads had disappeared, so that each rib and every bone in his frame were outlined cleanly through the loose hide that was wrinkled in folds of emptiness. It was heartbreaking, only Buck's heart was unbreakable. The man in the red sweater had proved that.

As it was with Buck, so was it with his mates. They were perambulating skeletons. There were seven all together, including him. In their very great misery they had become insensible to the bite of the lash or the bruise of the club. The pain of the beating was dull and distant, just as the things their eyes saw and their ears heard seemed dull and distant. They were not half living, or quarter living. They were simply so many bags of bones in which sparks of life fluttered faintly. When a halt was made, they dropped down in the traces like dead dogs, and the spark dimmed and paled and seemed to go out. And when the club or whip fell upon them, the spark fluttered feebly up, and they tottered to their feet and staggered on.

There came a day when Billee, the good-natured, fell and could not rise. Hal had traded off his revolver, so he took the

---

knotty 多節的，多結的 *adj.*
perambulating 徘徊的，漫遊的 *adj.*

axe and knocked Billee on the head as he lay in the traces, then cut the carcass out of the harness and dragged it to one side. Buck saw, and his mates saw, and they knew that this thing was very close to them. On the next day Koona went, and but five of them remained: Joe, too far gone to be malignant; Pike, crippled and limping, only half conscious and not conscious enough longer to malinger; Sol-leks, the one-eyed, still faithful to the toil of trace and trail, and mournful in that he had so little strength with which to pull; Teek, who had not travelled so far that winter and who was now beaten more than the others because he was fresher; and Buck, still at the head of the team, but no longer enforcing discipline or striving to enforce it, blind with weakness half the time and keeping the trail by the loom of it and by the dim feel of his feet.

It was beautiful spring weather, but neither dogs nor humans were aware of it. Each day the sun rose earlier and set later. It was dawn by three in the morning, and twilight lingered till nine at night. The whole long day was a blaze of sunshine. The ghostly winter silence had given way to the great spring murmur of awakening life. This murmur arose from all the land, fraught with the joy of living. It came from

loom 隱約出現，逼近 v.

the things that lived and moved again, things which had been as dead and which had not moved during the long months of frost. The sap was rising in the pines. The willows and aspens were bursting out in young buds. Shrubs and vines were putting on fresh garbs of green. Crickets sang in the nights, and in the days all manner of creeping, crawling things rustled forth into the sun. Partridges and woodpeckers were booming and knocking in the forest. Squirrels were chattering, birds singing, and overhead honked the wildfowl driving up from the south in cunning wedges that split the air.

From every hill slope came the trickle of running water, the music of unseen fountains. All things were thawing, bending, snapping. The Yukon was straining to break loose the ice that bound it down. It ate away from beneath; the sun ate from above. Air-holes formed, fissures sprang and spread apart, while thin sections of ice fell through bodily into the river. And amid all this bursting, rending, throbbing of awakening life, under the blazing sun and through the soft-sighing breezes, like wayfarers to death, staggered the two men, the woman, and the huskies.

With the dogs falling, Mercedes weeping and riding, Hal

cunning 狡猾的，巧妙的 *n.*

swearing innocuously, and Charles's eyes wistfully watering, they staggered into John Thornton's camp at the mouth of White River. When they halted, the dogs dropped down as though they had all been struck dead. Mercedes dried her eyes and looked at John Thornton. Charles sat down on a log to rest. He sat down very slowly and painstakingly what of his great stiffness. Hal did the talking. John Thornton was whittling the last touches on an axe-handle he had made from a stick of birch. He whittled and listened, gave monosyllabic replies, and, when it was asked, terse advice. He knew the breed, and he gave his advice in the certainty that it would not be followed.

"They told us up above that the bottom was dropping out of the trail and that the best thing for us to do was to lay over," Hal said in response to Thornton's warning to take no more chances on the rotten ice. "They told us we couldn't make White River, and here we are." This last with a sneering ring of triumph in it.

"And they told you true," John Thornton answered. "The bottom's likely to drop out at any moment. Only fools, with

---

innocuously 無害地，無傷大雅地 *adj.*
monosyllabic 簡短的 *v.*
terse 簡明的，簡潔的 *n.*
sneering 嘲笑，輕蔑 *n.*

the blind luck of fools, could have made it. I tell you straight, I wouldn't risk my carcass on that ice for all the gold in Alaska."

"That's because you're not a fool, I suppose," said Hal. "All the same, we'll go on to Dawson." He uncoiled his whip. "Get up there, Buck! Hi! Get up there! Mush on!"

Thornton went on whittling. It was idle, he knew, to get between a fool and his folly; while two or three fools more or less would not alter the scheme of things.

But the team did not get up at the command. It had long since passed into the stage where blows were required to rouse it. The whip flashed out, here and there, on its merciless errands. John Thornton compressed his lips. Sol- leks was the first to crawl to his feet. Teek followed. Joe came next, yelping with pain. Pike made painful efforts. Twice he fell over, when half up, and on the third attempt managed to rise. Buck made no effort. He lay quietly where he had fallen. The lash bit into him again and again, but he neither whined nor struggled. Several times Thornton started, as though to speak, but changed his mind. A moisture came into his eyes, and, as the whipping continued, he arose and walked irresolutely up and down.

carcass 屍體，死屍 *adj.*
irresolutely 猶豫不決地 *adv.*

This was the first time Buck had failed, in itself a sufficient reason to drive Hal into a rage. He exchanged the whip for the customary club. Buck refused to move under the rain of heavier blows which now fell upon him. Like his mates, he was barely able to get up, but, unlike them, he had made up his mind not to get up. He had a vague feeling of impending doom. This had been strong upon him when he pulled in to the bank, and it had not departed from him. What of the thin and rotten ice he had felt under his feet all day, it seemed that he sensed disaster close at hand, out there ahead on the ice where his master was trying to drive him. He refused to stir. So greatly had he suffered, and so far gone was he, that the blows did not hurt much. And as they continued to fall upon him, the spark of life within flickered and went down. It was nearly out. He felt strangely numb. As though from a great distance, he was aware that he was being beaten. The last sensations of pain left him. He no longer felt anything, though very faintly he could hear the impact of the club upon his body. But it was no longer his body, it seemed so far away.

And then, suddenly, without warning, uttering a cry that was inarticulate and more like the cry of an animal, John Thornton sprang upon the man who wielded the club. Hal

inarticulate 言語不清的，不善言辭的 *adj.*

was hurled backward, as though struck by a falling tree. Mercedes screamed. Charles looked on wistfully, wiped his watery eyes, but did not get up because of his stiffness.

John Thornton stood over Buck, struggling to control himself, too convulsed with rage to speak.

"If you strike that dog again, I'll kill you," he at last managed to say in a choking voice.

"It's my dog," Hal replied, wiping the blood from his mouth as he came back. "Get out of my way, or I'll fix you. I'm going to Dawson."

Thornton stood between him and Buck, and evinced no intention of getting out of the way. Hal drew his long hunting-knife. Mercedes screamed, cried, laughed, and manifested the chaotic abandonment of hysteria. Thornton rapped Hal's knuckles with the axe-handle, knocking the knife to the ground. He rapped his knuckles again as he tried to pick it up. Then he stooped, picked it up himself, and with two strokes cut Buck's traces.

Hal had no fight left in him. Besides, his hands were full with his sister, or his arms, rather; while Buck was too near dead to be of further use in hauling the sled. A few minutes

evinced 表現，表達 *n.*
hysteria 歇斯底里，情緒失控 *v.*

later they pulled out from the bank and down the river. Buck heard them go and raised his head to see, Pike was leading, Sol-leks was at the wheel, and between were Joe and Teek. They were limping and staggering. Mercedes was riding the loaded sled. Hal guided at the gee-pole, and Charles stumbled along in the rear.

As Buck watched them, Thornton knelt beside him and with rough, kindly hands searched for broken bones. By the time his search had disclosed nothing more than many bruises and a state of terrible starvation, the sled was a quarter of a mile away. Dog and man watched it crawling along over the ice. Suddenly, they saw its back end drop down, as into a rut, and the gee-pole, with Hal clinging to it, jerk into the air. Mercedes's scream came to their ears. They saw Charles turn and make one step to run back, and then a whole section of ice give way and dogs and humans disappear. A yawning hole was all that was to be seen. The bottom had dropped out of the trail.

John Thornton and Buck looked at each other.

"You poor devil," said John Thornton, and Buck licked his hand.

rut 凹陷 *n.*
yawning 張大口的，巨大的 *adj.*

Chapter VI.

For the Love of a Man

When John Thornton froze his feet in the previous December his partners had made him comfortable and left him to get well, going on themselves up the river to get out a raft of saw-logs for Dawson. He was still limping slightly at the time he rescued Buck, but with the continued warm weather even the slight limp left him. And here, lying by the river bank through the long spring days, watching the running water, listening lazily to the songs of birds and the hum of nature, Buck slowly won back his strength.

A rest comes very good after one has travelled three thousand miles, and it must be confessed that Buck waxed lazy as his wounds healed, his muscles swelled out, and the flesh came back to cover his bones. For that matter, they were all

limping 跛行 *n.*

loafing-Buck, John Thornton, and Skeet and Nig- waiting for
the raft to come that was to carry them down to Dawson.
Skeet was a little Irish setter who early made friends with
Buck, who, in a dying condition, was unable to resent her first
advances. She had the doctor trait which some dogs possess;
and as a mother cat washes her kittens, so she washed and
cleansed Buck's wounds. Regularly, each morning after he had
finished his breakfast, she performed her self-appointed task,
till he came to look for her ministrations as much as he did for
Thornton's. Nig, equally friendly, though less demonstrative,
was a huge black dog, half bloodhound and half deerhound,
with eyes that laughed and a boundless good nature.

To Buck's surprise these dogs manifested no jealousy
toward him. They seemed to share the kindliness and
largeness of John Thornton. As Buck grew stronger they
enticed him into all sorts of ridiculous games, in which
Thornton himself could not forbear to join; and in this
fashion Buck romped through his convalescence and into a
new existence. Love, genuine passionate love, was his for the
first time. This he had never experienced at Judge Miller's
down in the sun-kissed Santa Clara Valley. With the Judge's

ministrations 服務，照料 *n.*
forbear 忍受，克制 *adj.*
convalescence 康復期，復原期 *adj.*

sons, hunting and tramping, it had been a working partnership; with the Judge's grandsons, a sort of pompous guardianship; and with the Judge himself, a stately and dignified friendship. But love that was feverish and burning, that was adoration, that was madness, it had taken John Thornton to arouse.

This man had saved his life, which was something; but, further, he was the ideal master. Other men saw to the welfare of their dogs from a sense of duty and business expediency; he saw to the welfare of his as if they were his own children, because he could not help it. And he saw further. He never forgot a kindly greeting or a cheering word, and to sit down for a long talk with them ("gas" he called it) was as much his delight as theirs. He had a way of taking Buck's head roughly between his hands, and resting his own head upon Buck's, of shaking him back and forth, the while calling him ill names that to Buck were love names. Buck knew no greater joy than that rough embrace and the sound of murmured oaths, and at each jerk back and forth it seemed that his heart would be shaken out of his body so great was its ecstasy. And when, released, he sprang to his feet, his mouth laughing, his eyes

pompous 自大的，浮誇的 *adj.*
adoration 崇拜，愛慕 *n.*
expediency 適宜，方便 *v.*

eloquent, his throat vibrant with unuttered sound, and in that fashion remained without movement, John Thornton would reverently exclaim, "God! you can all but speak!"

Buck had a trick of love expression that was akin to hurt. He would often seize Thornton's hand in his mouth and close so fiercely that the flesh bore the impress of his teeth for some time afterward. And as Buck understood the oaths to be love words, so the man understood this feigned bite for a caress.

For the most part, however, Buck's love was expressed in adoration. While he went wild with happiness when Thornton touched him or spoke to him, he did not seek these tokens. Unlike Skeet, who was wont to shove her nose under Thornton's hand and nudge and nudge till petted, or Nig, who would stalk up and rest his great head on Thornton's knee, Buck was content to adore at a distance. He would lie by the hour, eager, alert, at Thornton's feet, looking up into his face, dwelling upon it, studying it, following with keenest interest each fleeting expression, every movement or change of feature. Or, as chance might have it, he would lie farther away, to the side or rear, watching the outlines of the man and the

---

eloquent 雄辯的，有說服力的 *n.*
vibrant 振動的，充滿活力的 *v.*
feigned 假的，虛偽的 *n.*

occasional movements of his body. And often, such was the
communion in which they lived, the strength of Buck's gaze
would draw John Thornton's head around, and he would
return the gaze, without speech, his heart shining out of his
eyes as Buck's heart shone out.

For a long time after his rescue, Buck did not like
Thornton to get out of his sight. From the moment he left
the tent to when he entered it again, Buck would follow at his
heels. His transient masters since he had come into the
Northland had bred in him a fear that no master could be
permanent. He was afraid that Thornton would pass out of
his life as Perrault and François and the Scotch half-breed had
passed out. Even in the night, in his dreams, he was haunted
by this fear. At such times he would shake off sleep and creep
through the chill to the flap of the tent, where he would stand
and listen to the sound of his master's breathing.

But in spite of this great love he bore John Thornton,
which seemed to bespeak the soft civilizing influence, the
strain of the primitive, which the Northland had aroused in
him, remained alive and active. Faithfulness and devotion,
things born of fire and roof, were his; yet he retained his

---

communion 共融，共感 *v.*
bespeak 預示，顯示 *adv.*

wildness and wiliness. He was a thing of the wild, come in from the wild to sit by John Thornton's fire, rather than a dog of the soft Southland stamped with the marks of generations of civilization. Because of his very great love, he could not steal from this man, but from any other man, in any other camp, he did not hesitate an instant; while the cunning with which he stole enabled him to escape detection.

His face and body were scored by the teeth of many dogs, and he fought as fiercely as ever and more shrewdly. Skeet and Nig were too good-natured for quarrelling-besides, they belonged to John Thornton; but the strange dog, no matter what the breed or valor, swiftly acknowledged Buck's supremacy or found himself struggling for life with a terrible antagonist. And Buck was merciless. He had learned well the law of club and fang, and he never forewent an advantage or drew back from a foe he had started on the way to Death. He had lessoned from Spitz, and from the chief fighting dogs of the police and mail, and knew there was no middle course. He must master or be mastered; while to show mercy was a weakness. Mercy did not exist in the primordial life. It was misunderstood for fear, and such misunderstandings made for

---

supremacy 至高無上，優越 **n.**

forewent 放棄 **v.**

death. Kill or be killed, eat or be eaten, was the law; and this mandate, down out of the depths of Time, he obeyed.

He was older than the days he had seen and the breaths he had drawn. He linked the past with the present, and the eternity behind him throbbed through him in a mighty rhythm to which he swayed as the tides and seasons swayed. He sat by John Thornton's fire, a broad-breasted dog, white-fanged and long-furred; but behind him were the shades of all manner of dogs, half-wolves and wild wolves, urgent and prompting, tasting the savor of the meat he ate, thirsting for the water he drank, scenting the wind with him, listening with him and telling him the sounds made by the wild life in the forest, dictating his moods, directing his actions, lying down to sleep with him when he lay down, and dreaming with him and beyond him and becoming themselves the stuff of his dreams.

So peremptorily did these shades beckon him, that each day mankind and the claims of mankind slipped farther from him. Deep in the forest a call was sounding, and as often as he heard this call, mysteriously thrilling and luring, he felt compelled to turn his back upon the fire and the beaten earth

---

mandate 命令，指令 *n.*
throbbed 脈動，悸動 *adv.*
peremptorily 斷然地，嚴厲地 *n.*
beckon 引導，招手示意 *v.*

around it, and to plunge into the forest, and on and on, he knew not where or why; nor did he wonder where or why, the call sounding imperiously, deep in the forest. But as often as he gained the soft unbroken earth and the green shade, the love for John Thornton drew him back to the fire again.

Thornton alone held him. The rest of mankind was as nothing. Chance travellers might praise or pet him; but he was cold under it all, and from a too demonstrative man he would get up and walk away. When Thornton's partners, Hans and Pete, arrived on the long-expected raft, Buck refused to notice them till he learned they were close to Thornton; after that he tolerated them in a passive sort of way, accepting favors from them as though he favored them by accepting. They were of the same large type as Thornton, living close to the earth, thinking simply and seeing clearly; and ere they swung the raft into the big eddy by the sawmill at Dawson, they understood Buck and his ways, and did not insist upon an intimacy such as obtained with Skeet and Nig.

For Thornton, however, his love seemed to grow and grow. He, alone among men, could put a pack upon Buck's back in the summer travelling. Nothing was too great for Buck

---

tolerated 忍受，容忍 *v.*
intimacy 關係，親密 *n.*

to do, when Thornton commanded. One day (they had grub-staked themselves from the proceeds of the raft and left Dawson for the headwaters of the Tanana) the men and dogs were sitting on the crest of a cliff which fell away, straight down, to naked bedrock three hundred feet below. John Thornton was sitting near the edge, Buck at his shoulder. A thoughtless whim seized Thornton, and he drew the attention of Hans and Pete to the experiment he had in mind. "Jump, Buck!" he commanded, sweeping his arm out and over the chasm. The next instant he was grappling with Buck on the extreme edge, while Hans and Pete were dragging them back into safety.

"It's uncanny," Pete said, after it was over and they had caught their speech.

Thornton shook his head. "No, it is splendid, and it is terrible, too. Do you know, it sometimes makes me afraid." "I'm not hankering to be the man that lays hands on you while he's around," Pete announced conclusively, nodding

his head toward Buck.

"Py Jingo!" was Hans's contribution. "Not mineself either." It was at Circle City, ere the year was out, that Pete's

grub-staked 資助 *v.*
whim 一時興起的念頭 *n.*
uncanny 奇異的，神秘的 *adj.*

apprehensions were realized. "Black" Burton, a man evil-tempered and malicious, had been picking a quarrel with a tenderfoot at the bar, when Thornton stepped good- naturedly between. Buck, as was his custom, was lying in a corner, head on paws, watching his master's every action. Burton struck out, without warning, straight from the shoulder. Thornton was sent spinning, and saved himself from falling only by clutching the rail of the bar.

Those who were looking on heard what was neither bark nor yelp, but a something which is best described as a roar, and they saw Buck's body rise up in the air as he left the floor for Burton's throat. The man saved his life by instinctively throwing out his arm, but was hurled backward to the floor with Buck on top of him. Buck loosed his teeth from the flesh of the arm and drove in again for the throat. This time the man succeeded only in partly blocking, and his throat was torn open. Then the crowd was upon Buck, and he was driven off; but while a surgeon checked the bleeding, he prowled up and down, growling furiously, attempting to rush in, and being forced back by an array of hostile clubs. A "miners' meeting," called on the spot, decided that the dog had sufficient

apprehensions 擔憂 *n.*
instinctively 本能地 *adv.*

provocation, and Buck was discharged. But his reputation was made, and from that day his name spread through every camp in Alaska.

Later on, in the fall of the year, he saved John Thornton's life in quite another fashion. The three partners were lining a long and narrow poling-boat down a bad stretch of rapids on the Forty-Mile Creek. Hans and Pete moved along the bank, snubbing with a thin Manila rope from tree to tree, while Thornton remained in the boat, helping its descent by means of a pole, and shouting directions to the shore. Buck, on the bank, worried and anxious, kept abreast of the boat, his eyes never off his master.

At a particularly bad spot, where a ledge of barely submerged rocks jutted out into the river, Hans cast off the rope, and, while Thornton poled the boat out into the stream, ran down the bank with the end in his hand to snub the boat when it had cleared the ledge. This it did, and was flying downstream in a current as swift as a millrace, when Hans checked it with the rope and checked too suddenly. The boat flirted over and snubbed in to the bank bottom up, while Thornton, flung sheer out of it, was carried downstream toward the worst part of the rapids, a stretch of wild water in

discharged 解雇 **v.**

which no swimmer could live.

Buck had sprung in on the instant; and at the end of three hundred yards, amid a mad swirl of water, he overhauled Thornton. When he felt him grasp his tail, Buck headed for the bank, swimming with all his splendid strength. But the progress shoreward was slow; the progress downstream amazingly rapid. From below came the fatal roaring where the wild current went wilder and was rent in shreds and spray by the rocks which thrust through like the teeth of an enormous comb. The suck of the water as it took the beginning of the last steep pitch was frightful, and Thornton knew that the shore was impossible. He scraped furiously over a rock, bruised across a second, and struck a third with crushing force. He clutched its slippery top with both hands, releasing Buck, and above the roar of the churning water shouted: "Go, Buck! Go!"

Buck could not hold his own, and swept on downstream, struggling desperately, but unable to win back. When he heard Thornton's command repeated, he partly reared out of the water, throwing his head high, as though for a last look, then

bruised 擦傷 v.

clutched 抓住，緊握 v.

turned obediently toward the bank. He swam powerfully and was dragged ashore by Pete and Hans at the very point where swimming ceased to be possible and destruction began.

They knew that the time a man could cling to a slippery rock in the face of that driving current was a matter of minutes, and they ran as fast as they could up the bank to a point far above where Thornton was hanging on. They attached the line with which they had been snubbing the boat to Buck's neck and shoulders, being careful that it should neither strangle him nor impede his swimming, and launched him into the stream. He struck out boldly, but not straight enough into the stream. He discovered the mistake too late, when Thornton was abreast of him and a bare half- dozen strokes away while he was being carried helplessly past.

Hans promptly snubbed with the rope, as though Buck were a boat. The rope thus tightening on him in the sweep of the current, he was jerked under the surface, and under the surface he remained till his body struck against the bank and he was hauled out. He was half drowned, and Hans and Pete threw themselves upon him, pounding the breath into him

obediently 順從地 _adv._
cling 抓住，緊貼 _v._
impede 阻礙，妨礙 _v._
abreast 並排，一致 _adv._

and the water out of him. He staggered to his feet and fell down. The faint sound of Thornton's voice came to them, and though they could not make out the words of it, they knew that he was in his extremity. His master's voice acted on Buck like an electric shock, He sprang to his feet and ran up the bank ahead of the men to the point of his previous departure.

Again the rope was attached and he was launched, and again he struck out, but this time straight into the stream. He had miscalculated once, but he would not be guilty of it a second time. Hans paid out the rope, permitting no slack, while Pete kept it clear of coils. Buck held on till he was on a line straight above Thornton; then he turned, and with the speed of an express train headed down upon him. Thornton saw him coming, and, as Buck struck him like a battering ram, with the whole force of the current behind him, he reached up and closed with both arms around the shaggy neck. Hans snubbed the rope around the tree, and Buck and Thornton were jerked under the water. Strangling, suffocating, sometimes one uppermost and sometimes the other, dragging over the jagged bottom, smashing against rocks and snags,

---

miscalculated 估錯，誤算 v.

battering ram 衝擊器，攻城槌 n.

they veered in to the bank.

Thornton came to, belly downward and being violently propelled back and forth across a drift log by Hans and Pete. His first glance was for Buck, over whose limp and apparently lifeless body Nig was setting up a howl, while Skeet was licking the wet face and closed eyes. Thornton was himself bruised and battered, and he went carefully over Buck's body, when he had been brought around, finding three broken ribs.

"That settles it," he announced. "We camp right here." And camp they did, till Buck's ribs knitted and he was able to travel.

That winter, at Dawson, Buck performed another exploit, not so heroic, perhaps, but one that put his name many notches higher on the totem-pole of Alaskan fame. This exploit was particularly gratifying to the three men; for they stood in need of the outfit which it furnished, and were enabled to make a long-desired trip into the virgin East, where miners had not yet appeared. It was brought about by a conversation in the Eldorado Saloon, in which men waxed boastful of their favorite dogs. Buck, because of his record, was the target for these men, and Thornton was driven stoutly

❖ ❖ ❖ ❖ ❖ ❖ ❖ ❖ ❖ ❖ ❖ ❖ ❖

veered 轉向，改變方向 *v.*
drift log 漂流木 *n.*
totem-pole 圖騰柱 *n.*

❖ ❖ ❖ ❖ ❖ ❖ ❖ ❖ ❖ ❖ ❖ ❖ ❖

to defend him. At the end of half an hour one man stated that his dog could start a sled with five hundred pounds and walk off with it; a second bragged six hundred for his dog; and a third, seven hundred.

"Pooh! pooh!" said John Thornton; "Buck can start a thousand pounds."

"And break it out? and walk off with it for a hundred yards?" demanded Matthewson, a Bonanza King, he of the seven hundred vaunt.

"And break it out, and walk off with it for a hundred yards," John Thornton said coolly.

"Well," Matthewson said, slowly and deliberately, so that all could hear, "I've got a thousand dollars that says he can't. And there it is." So saying, he slammed a sack of gold dust of the size of a bologna sausage down upon the bar.

Nobody spoke. Thornton's bluff, if bluff it was, had been called. He could feel a flush of warm blood creeping up his face. His tongue had tricked him. He did not know whether Buck could start a thousand pounds. Half a ton! The enormousness of it appalled him. He had great faith in Buck's strength and had often thought him capable of starting such a

---

vaunt 吹噓，自吹自擂 v.

bluff 虛張聲勢，吹牛 v.

appalled 震驚，驚恐 v.

load; but never, as now, had he faced the possibility of it, the eyes of a dozen men fixed upon him, silent and waiting. Further, he had no thousand dollars; nor had Hans or Pete.

"I've got a sled standing outside now, with twenty fifty-pound sacks of flour on it," Matthewson went on with brutal directness; "so don't let that hinder you."

Thornton did not reply. He did not know what to say. He glanced from face to face in the absent way of a man who has lost the power of thought and is seeking somewhere to find the thing that will start it going again. The face of Jim O'Brien, a Mastodon King and old-time comrade, caught his eyes. It was as a cue to him, seeming to rouse him to do what he would never have dreamed of doing.

"Can you lend me a thousand?" he asked, almost in a whisper.

"Sure," answered O'Brien, thumping down a plethoric sack by the side of Matthewson's. "Though it's little faith I'm having, John, that the beast can do the trick."

The Eldorado emptied its occupants into the street to see the test. The tables were deserted, and the dealers and gamekeepers came forth to see the outcome of the wager and

comrade 夥伴 *n.*
plethoric 過多的，過剩的 *adj.*

to lay odds. Several hundred men, furred and mittened, banked around the sled within easy distance. Matthewson's sled, loaded with a thousand pounds of flour, had been standing for a couple of hours, and in the intense cold (it was sixty below zero) the runners had frozen fast to the hard-packed snow. Men offered odds of two to one that Buck could not budge the sled. A quibble arose concerning the phrase "break out." O'Brien contended it was Thornton's privilege to knock the runners loose, leaving Buck to "break it out" from a dead standstill. Matthewson insisted that the phrase included breaking the runners from the frozen grip of the snow. A majority of the men who had witnessed the making of the bet decided in his favor, whereat the odds went up to three to one against Buck.

There were no takers. Not a man believed him capable of the feat. Thornton had been hurried into the wager, heavy with doubt; and now that he looked at the sled itself, the concrete fact, with the regular team of ten dogs curled up in the snow before it, the more impossible the task appeared.

---

mittened 戴手套的 *adj.*
banked 圍繞，圍住 *v.*
quibble 吹毛求疵，瑣事 *n.*
concrete 具體的，實際的 *adj.*

Matthewson waxed jubilant.

"Three to one!" he proclaimed. "I'll lay you another thousand at that figure, Thornton. What d'ye say?"

Thornton's doubt was strong in his face, but his fighting spirit was aroused-the fighting spirit that soars above odds, fails to recognize the impossible, and is deaf to all save the clamor for battle. He called Hans and Pete to him. Their sacks were slim, and with his own the three partners could rake together only two hundred dollars. In the ebb of their fortunes, this sum was their total capital; yet they laid it unhesitatingly against Matthewson's six hundred.

The team of ten dogs was unhitched, and Buck, with his own harness, was put into the sled. He had caught the contagion of the excitement, and he felt that in some way he must do a great thing for John Thornton. Murmurs of admiration at his splendid appearance went up. He was in perfect condition, without an ounce of superfluous flesh, and the one hundred and fifty pounds that he weighed were so many pounds of grit and virility. His furry coat shone with the sheen of silk. Down the neck and across the shoulders, his mane, in repose as it was, half bristled and seemed to lift with

jubilant 歡欣鼓舞的，高興的 *adj.*
virility 男子氣概，生命力 *n.*

every movement, as though excess of vigor made each particular hair alive and active. The great breast and heavy forelegs were no more than in proportion with the rest of the body, where the muscles showed in tight rolls underneath the skin. Men felt these muscles and proclaimed them hard as iron, and the odds went down to two to one.

"Gad, sir! Gad, sir!" stuttered a member of the latest dynasty, a king of the Skookum Benches. "I offer you eight hundred for him, sir, before the test, sir; eight hundred just as he stands."

Thornton shook his head and stepped to Buck's side.

"You must stand off from him," Matthewson protested. "Free play and plenty of room."

The crowd fell silent; only could be heard the voices of the gamblers vainly offering two to one. Everybody acknowledged Buck a magnificent animal, but twenty fifty-pound sacks of flour bulked too large in their eyes for them to loosen their pouch-strings.

Thornton knelt down by Buck's side. He took his head in his two hands and rested cheek on cheek. He did not playfully shake him, as was his wont, or murmur soft love curses; but he

stuttered 口吃，結巴地 *v.*
pouch-strings 錢袋 *n.*

whispered in his ear. "As you love me, Buck. As you love me," was what he whispered. Buck whined with suppressed eagerness.

The crowd was watching curiously. The affair was growing mysterious. It seemed like a conjuration. As Thornton got to his feet, Buck seized his mittened hand between his jaws, pressing in with his teeth and releasing slowly, half-reluctantly. It was the answer, in terms, not of speech, but of love. Thornton stepped well back.

"Now, Buck," he said.

Buck tightened the traces, then slacked them for a matter of several inches. It was the way he had learned.

"Gee!" Thornton's voice rang out, sharp in the tense silence.

Buck swung to the right, ending the movement in a plunge that took up the slack and with a sudden jerk arrested his one hundred and fifty pounds. The load quivered, and from under the runners arose a crisp crackling.

"Haw!" Thornton commanded.

Buck duplicated the manoeuvre, this time to the left. The crackling turned into a snapping, the sled pivoting and the

conjuration 巫術，魔法 *n.*
manoeuvre 動作 *n.*

runners slipping and grating several inches to the side. The sled was broken out. Men were holding their breaths, intensely unconscious of the fact.

"Now, mush!"

Thornton's command cracked out like a pistol-shot. Buck threw himself forward, tightening the traces with a jarring lunge. His whole body was gathered compactly together in the tremendous effort, the muscles writhing and knotting like live things under the silky fur. His great chest was low to the ground, his head forward and down, while his feet were flying like mad, the claws scarring the hard-packed snow in parallel grooves. The sled swayed and trembled, half-started forward. One of his feet slipped, and one man groaned aloud. Then the sled lurched ahead in what appeared a rapid succession of jerks, though it never really came to a dead stop again ... half an inch ... an inch ... two inches ... The jerks perceptibly diminished; as the sled gained momentum, he caught them up, till it was moving steadily along.

Men gasped and began to breathe again, unaware that for a moment they had ceased to breathe. Thornton was running behind, encouraging Buck with short, cheery words. The distance had been measured off, and as he neared the pile of

perceptibly 可察覺地 *adv.*

firewood which marked the end of the hundred yards, a cheer began to grow and grow, which burst into a roar as he passed the firewood and halted at command. Every man was tearing himself loose, even Matthewson. Hats and mittens were flying in the air. Men were shaking hands, it did not matter with whom, and bubbling over in a general incoherent babel.

But Thornton fell on his knees beside Buck. Head was against head, and he was shaking him back and forth. Those who hurried up heard him cursing Buck, and he cursed him long and fervently, and softly and lovingly.

"Gad, sir! Gad, sir!" spluttered the Skookum Bench king. "I'll give you a thousand for him, sir, a thousand, sir-twelve hundred, sir."

Thornton rose to his feet. His eyes were wet. The tears were streaming frankly down his cheeks. "Sir," he said to the Skookum Bench king, "no, sir. You can go to hell, sir. It's the best I can do for you, sir."

Buck seized Thornton's hand in his teeth. Thornton shook him back and forth. As though animated by a common impulse, the onlookers drew back to a respectful distance; nor were they again indiscreet enough to interrupt.

❀ ❀ ❀ ❀ ❀ ❀ ❀ ❀ ❀ ❀ ❀ ❀ ❀
incoherent 不連貫的，語無倫次的 *adj.*
spluttered 噴濺 *v.*
indiscreet 不謹慎的 *adj.*
❀ ❀ ❀ ❀ ❀ ❀ ❀ ❀ ❀ ❀ ❀ ❀ ❀

Chapter VII.

The Sounding of the Call

When Buck earned sixteen hundred dollars in five minutes for John Thornton, he made it possible for his master to pay off certain debts and to journey with his partners into the East after a fabled lost mine, the history of which was as old as the history of the country. Many men had sought it; few had found it; and more than a few there were who had never returned from the quest. This lost mine was steeped in tragedy and shrouded in mystery. No one knew of the first man. The oldest tradition stopped before it got back to him. From the beginning there had been an ancient and ramshackle cabin. Dying men had sworn to it, and to the mine the site of which it marked, clinching their testimony with nuggets that were unlike any known grade of gold in the Northland.

But no living man had looted this treasure house, and the dead were dead; wherefore John Thornton and Pete and Hans, with Buck and half a dozen other dogs, faced into the East on an unknown trail to achieve where men and dogs as good as themselves had failed. They sledded seventy miles up the Yukon, swung to the left into the Stewart River, passed the Mayo and the McQuestion, and held on until the Stewart itself became a streamlet, threading the upstanding peaks which marked the backbone of the continent.

John Thornton asked little of man or nature. He was unafraid of the wild. With a handful of salt and a rifle he could plunge into the wilderness and fare wherever he pleased and as long as he pleased. Being in no haste, Indian fashion, he hunted his dinner in the course of the day's travel; and if he failed to find it, like the Indian, he kept on travelling, secure in the knowledge that sooner or later he would come to it. So, on this great journey into the East, straight meat was the bill of fare, ammunition and tools principally made up the load on the sled, and the timecard was drawn upon the

clinching 確保，證實 ⓥ

looted 掠奪，搶奪 ⓥ

limitless future.

To Buck it was boundless delight, this hunting, fishing, and indefinite wandering through strange places. For weeks at a time they would hold on steadily, day after day; and for weeks upon end they would camp, here and there, the dogs loafing and the men burning holes through frozen muck and gravel and washing countless pans of dirt by the heat of the fire. Sometimes they went hungry, sometimes they feasted riotously, all according to the abundance of game and the fortune of hunting. Summer arrived, and dogs and men packed on their backs, rafted across blue mountain lakes, and descended or ascended unknown rivers in slender boats whipsawed from the standing forest.

The months came and went, and back and forth they twisted through the uncharted vastness, where no men were and yet where men had been if the Lost Cabin were true. They went across divides in summer blizzards, shivered under the midnight sun on naked mountains between the timber line and the eternal snows, dropped into summer valleys amid swarming gnats and flies, and in the shadows of glaciers picked strawberries and flowers as ripe and fair as any the Southland could boast. In the fall of the year they penetrated

whipsawed 交叉鋸 **v.**

Chapter VII

a weird lake country, sad and silent, where wildfowl had been, but where then there was no life nor sign of life-only the blowing of chill winds, the forming of ice in sheltered places, and the melancholy rippling of waves on lonely beaches.

And through another winter they wandered on the obliterated trails of men who had gone before. Once, they came upon a path blazed through the forest, an ancient path, and the Lost Cabin seemed very near. But the path began nowhere and ended nowhere, and it remained mystery, as the man who made it and the reason he made it remained mystery. Another time they chanced upon the time-graven wreckage of a hunting lodge, and amid the shreds of rotted blankets John Thornton found a long-barrelled flintlock. He knew it for a Hudson Bay Company gun of the young days in the Northwest, when such a gun was worth its height in beaver skins packed flat. And that was all-no hint as to the man who in an early day had reared the lodge and left the gun among the blankets.

Spring came on once more, and at the end of all their

---

melancholy 憂鬱，沮喪 *adj.*
obliterated 抹去，消除 *v.*
blazed 在樹上劃記 *v.*
time-graven 受到時間侵蝕的 *adj.*
flintlock 火石擊發槍 *n.*

wandering they found, not the Lost Cabin, but a shallow placer in a broad valley where the gold showed like yellow butter across the bottom of the washing-pan. They sought no farther. Each day they worked earned them thousands of dollars in clean dust and nuggets, and they worked every day. The gold was sacked in moose-hide bags, fifty pounds to the bag, and piled like so much firewood outside the spruce-bough lodge. Like giants they toiled, days flashing on the heels of days like dreams as they heaped the treasure up.

There was nothing for the dogs to do, save the hauling in of meat now and again that Thornton killed, and Buck spent long hours musing by the fire. The vision of the short-legged hairy man came to him more frequently, now that there was little work to be done; and often, blinking by the fire, Buck wandered with him in that other world which he remembered.

The salient thing of this other world seemed fear. When he watched the hairy man sleeping by the fire, head between his knees and hands clasped above, Buck saw that he slept restlessly, with many starts and awakenings, at which times he would peer fearfully into the darkness and fling more wood upon the fire. Did they walk by the beach of a sea, where the

---

placer 沖積層金礦 *n.*
salient 顯著的，突出的 *adj.*

hairy man gathered shellfish and ate them as he gathered, it was with eyes that roved everywhere for hidden danger and with legs prepared to run like the wind at its first appearance. Through the forest they crept noiselessly, Buck at the hairy man's heels; and they were alert and vigilant, the pair of them, ears twitching and moving and nostrils quivering, for the man heard and smelled as keenly as Buck. The hairy man could spring up into the trees and travel ahead as fast as on the ground, swinging by the arms from limb to limb, sometimes a dozen feet apart, letting go and catching, never falling, never missing his grip. In fact, he seemed as much at home among the trees as on the ground; and Buck had memories of nights of vigil spent beneath trees wherein the hairy man roosted, holding on tightly as he slept.

And closely akin to the visions of the hairy man was the call still sounding in the depths of the forest. It filled him with a great unrest and strange desires. It caused him to feel a vague, sweet gladness, and he was aware of wild yearnings and stirrings for he knew not what. Sometimes he pursued the call into the forest, looking for it as though it were a tangible thing, barking softly or defiantly, as the mood might dictate. He would thrust his nose into the cool wood moss, or into the

vigilant 警惕的，警覺的 *adj.*

black soil where long grasses grew, and snort with joy at the fat earth smells; or he would crouch for hours, as if in concealment, behind fungus-covered trunks of fallen trees, wide-eyed and wide-eared to all that moved and sounded about him. It might be, lying thus, that he hoped to surprise this call he could not understand. But he did not know why he did these various things. He was impelled to do them, and did not reason about them at all.

Irresistible impulses seized him. He would be lying in camp, dozing lazily in the heat of the day, when suddenly his head would lift and his ears cock up, intent and listening, and he would spring to his feet and dash away, and on and on, for hours, through the forest aisles and across the open spaces where the niggerheads bunched. He loved to run down dry watercourses, and to creep and spy upon the bird life in the woods. For a day at a time he would lie in the underbrush where he could watch the partridges drumming and strutting up and down. But especially he loved to run in the dim twilight of the summer midnights, listening to the subdued and sleepy murmurs of the forest, reading signs and sounds as man may read a book, and seeking for the mysterious

---

fungus 菌類，黴菌 *n.*
partridges 山鷓鴣 *n.*

something that called-called, waking or sleeping, at all times, for him to come.

One night he sprang from sleep with a start, eager-eyed, nostrils quivering and scenting, his mane bristling in recurrent waves. From the forest came the call (or one note of it, for the call was many noted), distinct and definite as never before-a long-drawn howl, like, yet unlike, any noise made by husky dog. And he knew it, in the old familiar way, as a sound heard before. He sprang through the sleeping camp and in swift silence dashed through the woods. As he drew closer to the cry he went more slowly, with caution in every movement, till he came to an open place among the trees, and looking out saw, erect on haunches, with nose pointed to the sky, a long, lean, timber wolf.

He had made no noise, yet it ceased from its howling and tried to sense his presence. Buck stalked into the open, half crouching, body gathered compactly together, tail straight and stiff, feet falling with unwonted care. Every movement advertised commingled threatening and overture of friendliness. It was the menacing truce that marks the meeting of wild beasts that prey. But the wolf fled at sight of him. He followed, with

commingled 混合、交融 *v.*
overture 試探 *n.*

wild leapings, in a frenzy to overtake. He ran him into a blind channel, in the bed of the creek where a timber jam barred the way. The wolf whirled about, pivoting on his hind legs after the fashion of Joe and of all cornered husky dogs, snarling and bristling, clipping his teeth together in a continuous and rapid succession of snaps.

Buck did not attack, but circled him about and hedged him in with friendly advances. The wolf was suspicious and afraid; for Buck made three of him in weight, while his head barely reached Buck's shoulder. Watching his chance, he darted away, and the chase was resumed. Time and again he was cornered, and the thing repeated, though he was in poor condition, or Buck could not so easily have overtaken him. He would run till Buck's head was even with his flank, when he would whirl around at bay, only to dash away again at the first opportunity.

But in the end Buck's pertinacity was rewarded; for the wolf, finding that no harm was intended, finally sniffed noses with him. Then they became friendly, and played about in the nervous, half-coy way with which fierce beasts belie their

---

pivoting 擺動、轉動 *v.*
hedged 圍困 *v.*
whirl 旋轉 *v.*
pertinacity 固執 *n.*

288

fierceness. After some time of this the wolf started off at an easy lope in a manner that plainly showed he was going somewhere. He made it clear to Buck that he was to come, and they ran side by side through the sombre twilight, straight up the creek bed, into the gorge from which it issued, and across the bleak divide where it took its rise.

On the opposite slope of the watershed they came down into a level country where were great stretches of forest and many streams, and through these great stretches they ran steadily, hour after hour, the sun rising higher and the day growing warmer. Buck was wildly glad. He knew he was at last answering the call, running by the side of his wood brother toward the place from where the call surely came. Old memories were coming upon him fast, and he was stirring to them as of old he stirred to the realities of which they were the shadows. He had done this thing before, somewhere in that other and dimly remembered world, and he was doing it again, now, running free in the open, the unpacked earth underfoot, the wide sky overhead.

They stopped by a running stream to drink, and, stopping, Buck remembered John Thornton. He sat down.

sombre 寂靜、陰沉、昏暗 *adj.*
watershed 分水嶺 *n.*

The wolf started on toward the place from where the call surely came, then returned to him, sniffing noses and making actions as though to encourage him. But Buck turned about and started slowly on the back track. For the better part of an hour the wild brother ran by his side, whining softly. Then he sat down, pointed his nose upward, and howled. It was a mournful howl, and as Buck held steadily on his way he heard it grow faint and fainter until it was lost in the distance.

John Thornton was eating dinner when Buck dashed into camp and sprang upon him in a frenzy of affection, overturning him, scrambling upon him, licking his face, biting his hand-"playing the general tomfool," as John Thornton characterized it, the while he shook Buck back and forth and cursed him lovingly.

For two days and nights Buck never left camp, never let Thornton out of his sight. He followed him about at his work, watched him while he ate, saw him into his blankets at night and out of them in the morning. But after two days the call in the forest began to sound more imperiously than ever. Buck's restlessness came back on him, and he was haunted by recollections of the wild brother, and of the smiling land beyond the divide and the run side by side through the wide

mournful 憂鬱的 *adj.*

forest stretches. Once again he took to wandering in the woods, but the wild brother came no more; and though he listened through long vigils, the mournful howl was never raised.

He began to sleep out at night, staying away from camp for days at a time; and once he crossed the divide at the head of the creek and went down into the land of timber and streams. There he wandered for a week, seeking vainly for fresh sign of the wild brother, killing his meat as he travelled and travelling with the long, easy lope that seems never to tire. He fished for salmon in a broad stream that emptied somewhere into the sea, and by this stream he killed a large black bear, blinded by the mosquitoes while likewise fishing, and raging through the forest helpless and terrible. Even so, it was a hard fight, and it aroused the last latent remnants of Buck's ferocity. And two days later, when he returned to his kill and found a dozen wolverenes quarrelling over the spoil, he scattered them like chaff; and those that fled left two behind who would quarrel no more.

The blood-longing became stronger than ever before. He was a killer, a thing that preyed, living on the things that lived,

vigils 守夜 *n.*
wolverenes 美洲獾 *n.*

unaided, alone, by virtue of his own strength and prowess, surviving triumphantly in a hostile environment where only the strong survived. Because of all this he became possessed of a great pride in himself, which communicated itself like a contagion to his physical being. It advertised itself in all his movements, was apparent in the play of every muscle, spoke plainly as speech in the way he carried himself, and made his glorious furry coat if anything more glorious. But for the stray brown on his muzzle and above his eyes, and for the splash of white hair that ran midmost down his chest, he might well have been mistaken for a gigantic wolf, larger than the largest of the breed. From his St. Bernard father he had inherited size and weight, but it was his shepherd mother who had given shape to that size and weight. His muzzle was the long wolf muzzle, save that it was larger than the muzzle of any wolf; and his head, somewhat broader, was the wolf head on a massive scale.

His cunning was wolf cunning, and wild cunning; his intelligence, shepherd intelligence and St. Bernard intelligence; and all this, plus an experience gained in the fiercest of

---

prowess 傑出的能力、高超的技能 *n.*
contagion 傳染 *n.*
breed 品種、種類 *n.*
massive 龐大的、巨大的 *adj.*

schools, made him as formidable a creature as any that roamed
the wild. A carnivorous animal living on a straight meat diet,
he was in full flower, at the high tide of his life, overspilling
with vigor and virility. When Thornton passed a caressing
hand along his back, a snapping and crackling followed the
hand, each hair discharging its pent magnetism at the contact.
Every part, brain and body, nerve tissue and fibre, was keyed
to the most exquisite pitch; and between all the parts there
was a perfect equilibrium or adjustment. To sights and sounds
and events which required action, he responded with
lightning-like rapidity. Quickly as a husky dog could leap to
defend from attack or to attack, he could leap twice as quickly.
He saw the movement, or heard sound, and responded in less
time than another dog required to compass the mere seeing or
hearing. He perceived and determined and responded in the
same instant. In point of fact the three actions of perceiving,
determining, and responding were sequential; but so
infinitesimal were the intervals of time between them that they
appeared simultaneous. His muscles were surcharged with
vitality, and snapped into play sharply, like steel springs. Life

---

vigor 活力、精力 *n.*
equilibrium 平衡、均衡 *n.*
infinitesimal 極微小的、極微不足道的 *adj.*

The Call of the Wild

streamed through him in splendid flood, glad and rampant, until it seemed that it would burst him asunder in sheer ecstasy and pour forth generously over the world.

"Never was there such a dog," said John Thornton one day, as the partners watched Buck marching out of camp.

"When he was made, the mould was broke," said Pete. "Py jingo! I t'ink so mineself," Hans affirmed.

They saw him marching out of camp, but they did not see the instant and terrible transformation which took place as soon as he was within the secrecy of the forest. He no longer marched. At once he became a thing of the wild, stealing along softly, cat-footed, a passing shadow that appeared and disappeared among the shadows. He knew how to take advantage of every cover, to crawl on his belly like a snake, and like a snake to leap and strike. He could take a ptarmigan from its nest, kill a rabbit as it slept, and snap in mid air the little chipmunks fleeing a second too late for the trees. Fish, in open pools, were not too quick for him; nor were beaver, mending their dams, too wary. He killed to eat, not from wantonness; but he preferred to eat what he killed himself. So a lurking humor ran through his deeds, and it was his delight

---

rampant 猖獗的、不受約束的 *adj.*

mould 模具、模型 *n.*

wantonness 肆意、任性 *n.*

to steal upon the squirrels, and, when he all but had them, to let them go, chattering in mortal fear to the treetops.

As the fall of the year came on, the moose appeared in greater abundance, moving slowly down to meet the winter in the lower and less rigorous valleys. Buck had already dragged down a stray part-grown calf; but he wished strongly for larger and more formidable quarry, and he came upon it one day on the divide at the head of the creek. A band of twenty moose had crossed over from the land of streams and timber, and chief among them was a great bull. He was in a savage temper, and, standing over six feet from the ground, was as formidable an antagonist as even Buck could desire. Back and forth the bull tossed his great palmated antlers, branching to fourteen points and embracing seven feet within the tips. His small eyes burned with a vicious and bitter light, while he roared with fury at sight of Buck.

From the bull's side, just forward of the flank, protruded a feathered arrow-end, which accounted for his savageness. Guided by that instinct which came from the old hunting days of the primordial world, Buck proceeded to cut the bull out

abundance 豐富、充裕 *n.*
quarry 獵物、獵捕目標 *n.*
palmated 呈掌狀的 *adj.*

from the herd. It was no slight task. He would bark and dance about in front of the bull, just out of reach of the great antlers and of the terrible splay hoofs which could have stamped his life out with a single blow. Unable to turn his back on the fanged danger and go on, the bull would be driven into paroxysms of rage. At such moments he charged Buck, who retreated craftily, luring him on by a simulated inability to escape. But when he was thus separated from his fellows, two or three of the younger bulls would charge back upon Buck and enable the wounded bull to rejoin the herd.

There is a patience of the wild-dogged, tireless, persistent as life itself-that holds motionless for endless hours the spider in its web, the snake in its coils, the panther in its ambuscade; this patience belongs peculiarly to life when it hunts its living food; and it belonged to Buck as he clung to the flank of the herd, retarding its march, irritating the young bulls, worrying the cows with their half-grown calves, and driving the wounded bull mad with helpless rage. For half a day this continued. Buck multiplied himself, attacking from all sides, enveloping the herd in a whirlwind of menace, cutting out his victim as fast as it could rejoin its mates, wearing out the

paroxysms 突發的發作、痙攣 *n.*
ambuscade 埋伏、伏擊 *n.*

patience of creatures preyed upon, which is a lesser patience than that of creatures preying.

As the day wore along and the sun dropped to its bed in the northwest (the darkness had come back and the fall nights were six hours long), the young bulls retraced their steps more and more reluctantly to the aid of their beset leader. The down-coming winter was harrying them on to the lower levels, and it seemed they could never shake off this tireless creature that held them back. Besides, it was not the life of the herd, or of the young bulls, that was threatened. The life of only one member was demanded, which was a remoter interest than their lives, and in the end they were content to pay the toll.

As twilight fell the old bull stood with lowered head, watching his mates-the cows he had known, the calves he had fathered, the bulls he had mastered-as they shambled on at a rapid pace through the fading light. He could not follow, for before his nose leaped the merciless fanged terror that would not let him go. Three hundredweight more than half a ton he weighed; he had lived a long, strong life, full of fight and struggle, and at the end he faced death at the teeth of a creature whose head did not reach beyond his great knuckled knees.

toll 代價、損失 *n.*

From then on, night and day, Buck never left his prey, never gave it a moment's rest, never permitted it to browse the leaves of trees or the shoots of young birch and willow. Nor did he give the wounded bull opportunity to slake his burning thirst in the slender trickling streams they crossed. Often, in desperation, he burst into long stretches of flight. At such times Buck did not attempt to stay him, but loped easily at his heels, satisfied with the way the game was played, lying down when the moose stood still, attacking him fiercely when he strove to eat or drink.

The great head drooped more and more under its tree of horns, and the shambling trot grew weak and weaker. He took to standing for long periods, with nose to the ground and dejected ears dropped limply; and Buck found more time in which to get water for himself and in which to rest. At such moments, panting with red lolling tongue and with eyes fixed upon the big bull, it appeared to Buck that a change was coming over the face of things. He could feel a new stir in the land. As the moose were coming into the land, other kinds of life were coming in. Forest and stream and air seemed

❖ ❖ ❖ ❖ ❖ ❖ ❖ ❖ ❖ ❖ ❖ ❖ ❖
prey 獵物 *n.*
browse 吃草、吃樹葉 *v.*
lolling 伸出 *v.*
❖ ❖ ❖ ❖ ❖ ❖ ❖ ❖ ❖ ❖ ❖ ❖ ❖

palpitant with their presence. The news of it was borne in upon him, not by sight, or sound, or smell, but by some other and subtler sense. He heard nothing, saw nothing, yet knew that the land was somehow different; that through it strange things were afoot and ranging; and he resolved to investigate after he had finished the business in hand.

At last, at the end of the fourth day, he pulled the great moose down. For a day and a night he remained by the kill, eating and sleeping, turn and turn about. Then, rested, refreshed and strong, he turned his face toward camp and John Thornton. He broke into the long easy lope, and went on, hour after hour, never at loss for the tangled way, heading straight home through strange country with a certitude of direction that put man and his magnetic needle to shame.

As he held on he became more and more conscious of the new stir in the land. There was life abroad in it different from the life which had been there throughout the summer. No longer was this fact borne in upon him in some subtle, mysterious way. The birds talked of it, the squirrels chattered about it, the very breeze whispered of it. Several times he

palpitant 顫動的、跳動的 *adj.*
subtler 更細微的、更隱約的 *adj.*
afoot 在進行中、發生中 *adj.*
certitude 確定、確實性 *n.*

stopped and drew in the fresh morning air in great sniffs, reading a message which made him leap on with greater speed. He was oppressed with a sense of calamity happening, if it were not calamity already happened; and as he crossed the last watershed and dropped down into the valley toward camp, he proceeded with greater caution.

Three miles away he came upon a fresh trail that sent his neck hair rippling and bristling, It led straight toward camp and John Thornton. Buck hurried on, swiftly and stealthily, every nerve straining and tense, alert to the multitudinous details which told a story-all but the end. His nose gave him a varying description of the passage of the life on the heels of which he was travelling. He remarked the pregnant silence of the forest. The bird life had flitted. The squirrels were in hiding. One only he saw-a sleek gray fellow, flattened against a gray dead limb so that he seemed a part of it, a woody excrescence upon the wood itself.

As Buck slid along with the obscureness of a gliding shadow, his nose was jerked suddenly to the side as though a positive force had gripped and pulled it. He followed the new scent into a thicket and found Nig. He was lying on his side,

excrescence 生長、突起 *n.*
obscureness 黯淡、不明朗 *n.*

dead where he had dragged himself, an arrow protruding, head and feathers, from either side of his body.

A hundred yards farther on, Buck came upon one of the sled-dogs Thornton had bought in Dawson. This dog was thrashing about in a death-struggle, directly on the trail, and Buck passed around him without stopping. From the camp came the faint sound of many voices, rising and falling in a singsong chant. Bellying forward to the edge of the clearing, he found Hans, lying on his face, feathered with arrows like a porcupine. At the same instant Buck peered out where the spruce-bough lodge had been and saw what made his hair leap straight up on his neck and shoulders. A gust of overpowering rage swept over him. He did not know that he growled, but he growled aloud with a terrible ferocity. For the last time in his life he allowed passion to usurp cunning and reason, and it was because of his great love for John Thornton that he lost his head.

The Yeehats were dancing about the wreckage of the spruce-bough lodge when they heard a fearful roaring and saw rushing upon them an animal the like of which they had never seen before. It was Buck, a live hurricane of fury, hurling

protruding 突出的 _adj._
porcupine 豪豬 _n._
usurp 篡奪、奪取 _v._

himself upon them in a frenzy to destroy. He sprang at the foremost man (it was the chief of the Yeehats), ripping the throat wide open till the rent jugular spouted a fountain of blood. He did not pause to worry the victim, but ripped in passing, with the next bound tearing wide the throat of a second man. There was no withstanding him. He plunged about in their very midst, tearing, rending, destroying, in constant and terrific motion which defied the arrows they discharged at him. In fact, so inconceivably rapid were his movements, and so closely were the Indians tangled together, that they shot one another with the arrows; and one young hunter, hurling a spear at Buck in mid air, drove it through the chest of another hunter with such force that the point broke through the skin of the back and stood out beyond. Then a panic seized the Yeehats, and they fled in terror to the woods, proclaiming as they fled the advent of the Evil Spirit.

And truly Buck was the fiend incarnate, raging at their heels and dragging them down like deer as they raced through the trees. It was a fateful day for the Yeehats. They scattered far and wide over the country, and it was not till a week later

---

jugular 頸動脈 *n.*
inconceivably 難以置信地 *adv.*
advent 出現、到來 *n.*
fiend 惡魔、凶猛的生物 *n.*

that the last of the survivors gathered together in a lower valley and counted their losses. As for Buck, wearying of the pursuit, he returned to the desolated camp. He found Pete where he had been killed in his blankets in the first moment of surprise. Thornton's desperate struggle was fresh-written on the earth, and Buck scented every detail of it down to the edge of a deep pool. By the edge, head and fore feet in the water, lay Skeet, faithful to the last. The pool itself, muddy and discolored from the sluice boxes, effectually hid what it contained, and it contained John Thornton; for Buck followed his trace into the water, from which no trace led away.

All day Buck brooded by the pool or roamed restlessly about the camp. Death, as a cessation of movement, as a passing out and away from the lives of the living, he knew, and he knew John Thornton was dead. It left a great void in him, somewhat akin to hunger, but a void which ached and ached, and which food could not fill. At times, when he paused to contemplate the carcasses of the Yeehats, he forgot the pain of it; and at such times he was aware of a great pride in himself-a pride greater than any he had yet experienced. He

---

desolated 荒涼的、被摧毀的 *adj.*

brooded 沉思、凝視 *v.*

void 空虛、缺乏 *n.*

contemplate 沉思、思考 *adv.*

had killed man, the noblest game of all, and he had killed in the face of the law of club and fang. He sniffed the bodies curiously. They had died so easily. It was harder to kill a husky dog than them. They were no match at all, were it not for their arrows and spears and clubs. Thenceforward he would be unafraid of them except when they bore in their hands their arrows, spears, and clubs.

Night came on, and a full moon rose high over the trees into the sky, lighting the land till it lay bathed in ghostly day. And with the coming of the night, brooding and mourning by the pool, Buck became alive to a stirring of the new life in the forest other than that which the Yeehats had made. He stood up, listening and scenting. From far away drifted a faint, sharp yelp, followed by a chorus of similar sharp yelps. As the moments passed the yelps grew closer and louder. Again Buck knew them as things heard in that other world which persisted in his memory. He walked to the centre of the open space and listened. It was the call, the many-noted call, sounding more luringly and compellingly than ever before. And as never before, he was ready to obey. John Thornton was dead. The last tie was broken. Man and the claims of man no longer

noblest 最高貴的、崇高的 *adj.*
luringly 誘人地、引人入勝地 *v.*

bound him.

Hunting their living meat, as the Yeehats were hunting it, on the flanks of the migrating moose, the wolf pack had at last crossed over from the land of streams and timber and invaded Buck's valley. Into the clearing where the moonlight streamed, they poured in a silvery flood; and in the centre of the clearing stood Buck, motionless as a statue, waiting their coming. They were awed, so still and large he stood, and a moment's pause fell, till the boldest one leaped straight for him. Like a flash Buck struck, breaking the neck. Then he stood, without movement, as before, the stricken wolf rolling in agony behind him. Three others tried it in sharp succession; and one after the other they drew back, streaming blood from slashed throats or shoulders.

This was sufficient to fling the whole pack forward, pell-mell, crowded together, blocked and confused by its eagerness to pull down the prey. Buck's marvellous quickness and agility stood him in good stead. Pivoting on his hind legs, and snapping and gashing, he was everywhere at once, presenting a front which was apparently unbroken so swiftly did he whirl and guard from side to side. But to prevent them from getting

---

pell-mell 混亂地、一窩蜂地 *adv.*
marvellous 令人驚奇的 *adj.*

behind him, he was forced back, down past the pool and into the creek bed, till he brought up against a high gravel bank. He worked along to a right angle in the bank which the men had made in the course of mining, and in this angle he came to bay, protected on three sides and with nothing to do but face the front.

And so well did he face it, that at the end of half an hour the wolves drew back discomfited. The tongues of all were out and lolling, the white fangs showing cruelly white in the moonlight. Some were lying down with heads raised and ears pricked forward; others stood on their feet, watching him; and still others were lapping water from the pool. One wolf, long and lean and gray, advanced cautiously, in a friendly manner, and Buck recognized the wild brother with whom he had run for a night and a day. He was whining softly, and, as Buck whined, they touched noses.

Then an old wolf, gaunt and battle-scarred, came forward. Buck writhed his lips into the preliminary of a snarl, but sniffed noses with him. Whereupon the old wolf sat down, pointed nose at the moon, and broke out the long wolf howl. The others sat down and howled. And now the call came to

bay 逼到絕境、無路可逃 *n.*
discomfited 打擊、挫敗 *v.*
preliminary 初步的、開始的 *adj.*

Buck in unmistakable accents. He, too, sat down and howled. This over, he came out of his angle and the pack crowded around him, sniffing in half-friendly, half-savage manner. The leaders lifted the yelp of the pack and sprang away into the woods. The wolves swung in behind, yelping in chorus. And Buck ran with them, side by side with the wild brother, yelping as he ran.

And here may well end the story of Buck. The years were not many when the Yeehats noted a change in the breed of timber wolves; for some were seen with splashes of brown on head and muzzle, and with a rift of white centring down the chest. But more remarkable than this, the Yeehats tell of a Ghost Dog that runs at the head of the pack. They are afraid of this Ghost Dog, for it has cunning greater than they, stealing from their camps in fierce winters, robbing their traps, slaying their dogs, and defying their bravest hunters.

Nay, the tale grows worse. Hunters there are who fail to return to the camp, and hunters there have been whom their tribesmen found with throats slashed cruelly open and with wolf prints about them in the snow greater than the prints of any wolf. Each fall, when the Yeehats follow the movement of

rift 裂縫、分歧 *n.*

308

the moose, there is a certain valley which they never enter. And women there are who become sad when the word goes over the fire of how the Evil Spirit came to select that valley for an abiding-place.

In the summers there is one visitor, however, to that valley, of which the Yeehats do not know. It is a great, gloriously coated wolf, like, and yet unlike, all other wolves. He crosses alone from the smiling timber land and comes down into an open space among the trees. Here a yellow stream flows from rotted moose-hide sacks and sinks into the ground, with long grasses growing through it and vegetable mould overrunning it and hiding its yellow from the sun; and here he muses for a time, howling once, long and mournfully, ere he departs.

But he is not always alone. When the long winter nights come on and the wolves follow their meat into the lower valleys, he may be seen running at the head of the pack through the pale moonlight or glimmering borealis, leaping gigantic above his fellows, his great throat a-bellow as he sings a song of the younger world, which is the song of the pack.

abiding 不變的 *adj.*

國家圖書館出版品預行編目 (CIP) 資料

野性的呼喚 / 傑克‧倫敦（Jack London）著；楊宛靜繪；吳
凱雯譯 .-- 初版 .-- 臺中市：晨星出版有限公司 , 2024.02
　　面；　　公分 .--（愛藏本；121）
中英雙語典藏版
譯自：The call of the wild
ISBN 978-626-320-766-0（精裝）

874.59　　　　　　　　　　　　　　　　　　　113000086

愛藏本；121

野性的呼喚（中英雙語典藏版）
The Call of the Wild

作　　者｜傑克‧倫敦（Jack London）
繪　　者｜楊宛靜
譯　　者｜吳凱雯

執行編輯｜李迎華
文字校潤｜李迎華
封面設計｜張蘊方
美術編輯｜張蘊方

創 辦 人｜陳銘民
發 行 所｜晨星出版有限公司
　　　　　台中市 407 工業區 30 路 1 號 1 樓
　　　　　TEL:(04)23595820　FAX:(04)23550581
　　　　　http://star.morningstar.com.tw
　　　　　行政院新聞局局版台業字第 2500 號
法律顧問｜陳思成律師
初版日期｜2024 年 02 月 15 日
　ISBN　｜978-626-320-766-0
　定價　｜新台幣 350 元

讀者服務專線｜TEL：（02）23672044 /（04）23595819#212
讀者傳真專線｜FAX：（02）23635741 /（04）23595493
讀者專用信箱｜service@morningstar.com.tw
　　網路書店｜http://www.morningstar.com.tw
　　郵政劃撥｜15060393（知己圖書股份有限公司）

印　　刷｜上好印刷股份有限公司

填寫線上回函，立即
獲得 50 元購書金。